Praise for *Angel with a Bullet:*

"Lots of action, colorful characters, and a surprising plot twist…
Will have readers eager for more."

—*Booklist Online*

"The book is a fun murder-mystery filled with action, humor and
intrigue—written in first-person-female perspective, which is
something unexpected from a male author."

—*Victoria News* (Canada)

"*Angel with a Bullet* is part gritty detective novel, part chick lit,
with a fast pace and a wise-cracking reporter."

—*The Mystery Reader*

"If you have a taste for vintage crime fiction, screwball comedies,
and the lighter side of noir, *Angel with a Bullet* might be right up
your alley."

—Victoria Janssen, writing for *Criminal Element*

DEVIL WITH
A GUN

m. c. grant

A Dixie Flynn Mystery

DEVIL WITH A GUN

MIDNIGHT INK
WOODBURY, MINNESOTA

FIRST EDITION
First Printing, 2013

Book format by Bob Gaul
Cover design by Ellen Lawson
Cover image: Fernando Fernández/age fotostock/SuperStock
Editing by Nicole Nugent

Midnight Ink, an imprint of Llewellyn Worldwide Ltd.

This is a work of fiction. Names, characters, places, and incidents are either the product of the author's imagination or are used fictitiously, and any resemblance to actual persons living or dead, business establishments, events, or locales is entirely coincidental.

Library of Congress Cataloging-in-Publication Data
Grant, M. C., 1963–
  Devil with a gun/by M. C. Grant.—First Edition.
     pages cm.—(A Dixie Flynn Mystery; #2)
  ISBN 978-0-7387-3499-6
Summary: "Assigned to write a soft piece for Father's Day, journalist Dixie Flynn investigates a missing father story pulled from her weekly paper's classified pages. The story turns deadly serious when it takes Dixie into the realm of a Russian mobster." (Provided by publisher)
1. Women journalists—Fiction. 2. Organized crime—Fiction. 3. San Francisco (Calif.)—Fiction. I. Title.
  PS3607.R362953D48 2013
  813'.6—dc23
                              2013018767

Midnight Ink
Llewellyn Worldwide Ltd.
2143 Wooddale Drive
Woodbury, MN 55125-2989
www.midnightinkbooks.com

Printed in the United States of America

PROLOGUE

BAILEY'S EYELIDS FLUTTERED IN the thin veil between sleep and awake. The room was purple from her Snoopy nightlight, and shadows played across the walls where no shadows were supposed to be.

A voice inside her head whispered to her—her secret voice. The one she never told anyone about except for Teddy, her stuffed protector who sat on the corner of her bed, one arm on her pillow, keeping watch for monsters and bad dreams.

Her secret voice whispered, *Don't wake up. Keep your eyes closed. Be very still and quiet.*

Bailey listened to the voice. It was clever. It understood things before she did. And though she knew it was really her voice, her thoughts, she had come to trust it.

When the voice told her to curl into a ball, she curled and absorbed the blows on her back and head. When it said to cry, she spilled tears. When it said not to cry, she didn't make a sound. And when it told her to hide, she disappeared like a ghost.

Tonight it said, *Don't open your eyes.* And she wouldn't. But closing her eyes made her nose and ears open up.

There was a stranger in her room: a man with a strong, doggy smell that wasn't covered up by his man-scented cologne and deodorant. She smelled cigarettes, but not regular cigarettes; it was too sweet. The alcohol on his breath and in his sweat wasn't whiskey, beer, or wine—she knew those scents by heart. Like the tobacco, it had an unfamiliar sweetness, and for a reason she couldn't explain, she thought it was expensive.

There was another smell, too. One that always scared her, because it meant her mom and dad would argue before he stormed off into the night. When he returned—sometimes within hours, more often after several days—his mood could never be predicted. Bailey had seen him arrive with flowers and sweet bubbly stuff in bottles for her mom, and they would dance and kiss and drink the bubbly stuff and everyone would be smiling. Other times the voice would tell her to hide when her dad came home. If she didn't hide fast enough, the voice would tell her to curl into a ball and protect her head.

That smell, she had learned, was gun oil.

"I don't want you in here." It was her father's voice.

The stranger answered, "If I was you, I wouldn't want it either."

The floor creaked as the stranger moved closer to her bed. Bailey wanted to squeeze her eyes tighter, but the secret voice whispered again, *Don't move. Pretend you're dead. A mummy wrapped in bandages. Safe.*

"How old is she now?" asked the stranger.

He had an accent, but Bailey didn't know much about other countries. She had met a brown-skinned boy who once lived in a warm place called "chilly," which sounded backward to her. And her best friend, Shreya, said her family was from India, where they had a farm with goats and grew mangos. Shreya's parents had musical voices, almost like they were singing rather than talking.

This man was from neither of those places.

"She's five," answered her father.

He didn't mention the half! Bailey really liked the half because it meant she was closer to six than five, and that was better because it meant later bedtimes and full days at school. A six-year-old was practically a grown-up.

"A valuable age," said the stranger.

"She's not for sale."

Bailey didn't understand. How could the stranger think she was for sale? That didn't make sense. She wasn't milk or eggs or a doll in the store. You can't buy a person.

"Everything's for sale."

"No."

The smelly stranger moved so close to the bed that he was leaning over her. Bailey could feel his eyes on her face and blanketed body. There was heat coming from him and everywhere his gaze touched, her skin tingled. She kept breathing and remained still, but it was so hard not to scream and run and hide. She didn't like this man being in her room, or the way she knew he was looking at her.

"You have another on the way," said the stranger.

"I said no."

Another on the way, thought Bailey. *What does that mean?*

"You make it sound like you have an option."

"But you said—"

The stranger laughed softly. "Yes, Joseph, I did. I just want to make sure you understand the consequences if you let me down."

Joseph? The only time she heard her father called anything but Joe was when her mother was either really angry or really happy. If she was angry, the words that came with her father's full name were the ugly ones. Bailey didn't like those words.

"I understand," said her father, but his voice sounded small. It was the same voice he had when he was drinking, before he had too much—before he changed into the man she hated. "Can we leave now?"

"Aren't you going to kiss your daughter goodbye?"

"No."

The stranger laughed, but it wasn't a nice sound; it was sharp, like a knife. "Then allow me."

Bailey tensed but tried not to let it show as the stranger bent down and kissed her forehead. His lips were soft, but instead of heat there was coldness. It seeped through her skin and bones and deep into her brain, like when she drank lemonade too fast.

The stranger whispered, "Obedient child. I have plans for you."

Bailey might have screamed if her secret voice hadn't shown her a picture of Teddy clad in shining armor, stabbing a sword into the stranger's eye so that it stuck into *his* brain.

Bailey lay still, pretending to be asleep as the stranger and her father left the room and closed the door behind them.

ONE

I DO LOVE A handsome, younger man, especially one with ginger hair and a kissable face. But when his sandpaper tongue scrapes the length of my nose at six in the morning, it takes a moment for me to find it endearing.

I groan and roll over, but the silly boy believes I'm being playful and that my earlobe needs a none-too-gentle nibble.

"Hey!"

I swat him away, but this only serves to inspire rather than deter. With a purr that shakes the walls, Prince Marmalade sprints to the foot of the bed, pivots one hundred and eighty degrees and leaps. All four paws crash onto my chest and the top of his furry head collides with my chin in an ebullient love tap.

I can't help but laugh until his tiny claws suddenly spring from their sheaths to knead my tender breast.

"Ouch, ouch. Enough. I'm awake."

I pull the ginger kitten into my arms and allow his purring to bring me fully awake. He rolls onto his back and stretches to his full length—reaching from my chin to navel—so that I can stroke the length of his exposed belly and chest. He's vulnerable, tender, and madly in love with me.

Who can blame him? I'm a great catch.

Well, for twenty-two days of every month at least.

——————

After feeding Prince and preparing the coffeemaker, I head to the front door of my apartment, wait two seconds, and open it.

Standing in the hallway with her balled fist mere inches from striking the door, Kristy screams in surprise. Behind her, Sam chuckles.

"Dixie! Stop doing that," says Kristy. "Scares me to death. I think you must be psychic."

"Or you're predictable," I say.

Kristy gasps. "Bite your tongue! I'm never predictable."

"Especially in bed," Sam adds quietly with a cockeyed grin.

Kristy's mouth gapes open in disbelief at her lover's inappropriate comment before she covers it with her hand and giggles. "Well, that's true," she admits.

I open the door wider. "Really, girls, it's far too early in the morning to be going into your bedroom activities. Especially when one of us is straight and pathetically single."

Kristy is about to say something more until she spots Prince Marmalade slinking across the floor to greet them. "Princely!" Kristy squeals with delight and rushes in to sweep the kitten into her arms.

Prince puts up a good show of being uninterested by immediately increasing the volume of his purr and licking the bottom of his newfound friend's chin. Kristy giggles again and carries him to the couch where, in typical male fashion, he splays himself between her breasts.

"Coffee?" I ask Sam as she enters the apartment.

She nods and produces a plate of baked goods from behind her back. "We brought pastries."

I look at the plate and frown. Each item is in the shape of an intimate body part.

"We saved you the penis," says Sam.

"Really?" I ask sarcastically. "How kind."

"A new bakery opened around the corner," adds Kristy. "It's run by this lovely lesbo couple, Miriam and Sindra. They're trying something new with erotic, exotic, healthy baking."

"Because everybody wants to eat a penis in the morning," I say, sarcasm still dripping since I haven't had my morning coffee yet—and because I have a tendency to be sarcastic even when caffeinated.

"It's a good shape for dipping into your coffee," says Kristy. "Although I prefer the assorted boobs. They have ones with a cherry on top, others with chocolate drops—milk or dark—and they're open to special orders if you'd like the nipples pierced."

"Good to know," I say. "And, ouch! Coffee?"

"Please," says Kristy. "And I'll have a chocolate boob."

"Cherry boob for me," says Sam.

I roll my eyes as the two women look at each other and giggle again.

Kristy and Sam live directly across the hall from me in the six-apartment Painted Lady we call home in the heart of San Francisco.

The building is owned by Mrs. Pennell, who lives directly below me with her bobcat-sized feline, King William. King William also happens to be Prince Marmalade's sire.

The lovely Mr. French and his parakeet, Baccarat, have the misfortune to live beneath Kristy and Sam, but I've yet to hear him complain. Then again, I don't follow him on Twitter.

On the top floor, Derek and Shahnaz are young and beautiful but seem too busy working to really appreciate it. Across from them, the apartment is currently empty. The previous tenants, Ben and Saffron, had an ugly breakup that became so intense the rest of us didn't realize we were holding our collective breath until after they moved out.

Ben, especially, is missed; along with being a sweet and gentle man, he was our resident technology geek. Once I discovered his weakness for Australian soft licorice, he was only ever a door-knock away from solving any computer problems I had. Saffron was lovely, too, but the extent of his betrayal soured him for us.

I pour three coffees, add a splash of cream to each, and take them over to the cozy little nook I created by the main windows. I've never owned much furniture, but the unexpected gift of a large painting from the family of a deceased ex-boyfriend has inspired me to purchase a couple of items.

The painting is an unfinished collage that I feel is one of Diego Chino's strongest works. It shows just how much true greatness he had within—if his driven ego had allowed him to savor his accomplishments rather than dwell on his perceived failures. And because of his premature death, the unfinished quality of the piece speaks volumes to me.

I hung it in a place of prominence on my otherwise bare walls, moved my couch nearby to admire the work, and added a chrome-legged coffee table that offers the pretense of single-woman maturity—until you actually look at it. A local artist covered the top of the rectangular table in bright Lego bricks and sealed them beneath a layer of clear resin. Closer inspection reveals a maze-like pattern, four different-colored ghosts, and a hungry yellow ball with a red bow on her head. It is childish, colorful, and fun. I absolutely love it.

To complete the space, I purchased a comfortable wingback reading chair in soft blue velvet and mahogany nailhead trim, and an antique floor lamp that had actually been designed with an ornate porcelain ashtray on its stem. I found both items for a bargain price at a nearby estate sale Mrs. Pennell tipped me off to. And while the entire building had original hardwood flooring, Ben had given me a gorgeous Persian rug that he bought for Saffron before the breakup. The rug completed my homey little island of serenity.

On the other side of the room, closer to the door, I have a small writing desk where I keep my laptop and notebooks for whatever stories I am working on for the weekly *San Francisco NOW*, the job that keeps me in a lifestyle that could easily be improved, but in this economy, could also be worse. I am thankful for what I have—especially when it comes to friends.

I lift the pastry penis off the plate to examine it. It's heavier than I expect, solid and substantial. It's also coated in a thin layer of white and pink icing.

"Are you supposed to lick it or bite?" I ask.

"Lick," says Kristy.

"Bite," argues Sam.

I take a small bite and am rewarded by a delicious tingle of apple, cinnamon, brown sugar, and raisin.

"Oh, boy," I say. "This is delicious."

Kristy beams with delight. "I told Sam all you needed was a tasty cock in the morning to put a smile back on your face."

My mouth falls open in shock before the three of us erupt into a fit of giggles that lasts so long I am nearly late catching the cable car to work.

TWO

THE SAN FRANCISCO NOW offices are located above a Greek restaurant, one block west of Alta Plaza. If you arrive at work hungry, it's impossible to make it up the stairs. This is especially true when the owner, Dmitri, has been playing around with new recipes.

One morning I arrived to find he had whipped up a batch of deep-fried mango spring rolls with a coconut-lime dipping sauce that he was eager to share with a fellow foodie. There's nothing a cook likes better than an appreciative audience, and there are few things I appreciate more than good food made by someone else.

Halfway though the platter, I asked Dmitri if he was planning to add it to the menu. His answer was a laugh and a shake of his large, pear-shaped head.

"It's no Greek," he said in broken English. "I may sell recipe to Cuban place in exchange for rum and cigars. The owner like my recipes; I like his rum and cigars. Win, win."

I couldn't fault that logic.

After climbing the stairs to the third floor, I enter the newsroom. Once upon a time that phrase would have sent a spark of electricity through me, but time and economics has drained most of the color from the place. The characters—those messed-up human beings whose only saving grace was the effortless flow of their words—have been replaced by clean-cut, social media–savvy youngsters who are far too easy to drink under the table.

Back in my nearly innocent youth, when I got my start at what has now become my competition, the *San Francisco Chronicle*, the silver age of journalism was coming to its inevitably tarnished end. On my first day as a reporter—bright-eyed, bushy tailed, and arriving far too early—I found the managing editor snoring loudly at his desk. His suit jacket was torn down one arm, exposing scraped and bloody flesh; his hair was in rebellion as every strand attempted to go in a different direction; and he had the stench of having broken into a local brewery and gone swimming in one of its hop-heavy fermenting vats.

When he awoke, I asked him what happened. Naturally, I was hoping for some great story involving undercover cops, biker gangs, and a stakeout gone wrong. Instead, it turned out he had been drinking with the assistant managing editor and their heart-to-heart, clear-the-air discussion turned violent in an alley when they each had to relieve their bladders and their frustrations.

Blood was spilled, the cops arrived, and, thinking they were Butch Cassidy and the Sundance Kid, the two aging men decided to run. The ME eluded the cops by slipping into the *Chronicle* building, but he had no clue where the AME ended up.

My assignment for the rest of the day turned out to be getting the AME out of jail and using my natural charm and wit to have all charges dropped. The upside was that I was able to convince the guy to put me on the police beat, which is where I wanted to be.

One of the last characters left in the business is Edward Stoogan, my editor at *NOW*. On first meeting him, people often make the mistake of thinking he's of low intelligence and slow wit because of his sluggish physicality. He's a large, overtly pale man who's lost his grip on the slippery edge of obesity, with a pug nose, pink eyes, and shock-white hair.

His eyesight is so bad that he actually uses a small telescope to read the words on screen, but his mind is that of a poet wrapped in a journalist's gift for compelling storytelling. And although his communication style is more along the line of grunts and chirps, put his chubby fingers on a keyboard and he turns jingles into sonatas.

No sooner have I checked my mailbox for angry letters (fans never write as often as critics) than Stoogan's rabbitlike senses catch the overhead fluorescents bouncing off my frenetic copper locks.

"Dixie!" he calls across the newsroom. "My office." If his voice wasn't closer to squeak than growl, he may have almost sounded authoritative.

"Be right with you, boss," I call back. "Just want to check my voicemail." I was expecting good news. Before leaving work last night, I placed a $50 bet on a local greyhound race and my long shot had paid off at ten-to-one odds.

Dixie's Tips #13: *Any good journalist who may later have to claim that getting to know the local, underground gambling scene was research for a story should always give the bookies their work number.*

"Check it later," Stoogan fires back. "I want you now."

Not one to let a Freudian slip pass without comment, I pounce. "Geez, boss. I didn't know your feelings ran that deep. The wife been making you sleep on the sofa again?"

Stoogan stops in his tracks and turns, his cheeks turning a flushed shade of boiled beet. The other reporters in the room lower their heads like frightened ostriches, which is something that never would have happened when dinosaurs wrote the news. In the waning pre-computer days, when one reporter cracked a joke or fired an insult, the other jackals climbed over top of each other to best it—until someone inevitably went too far and we all gave up in disgust.

Sarcasm and cheekiness, it seems, have sadly become politically incorrect. Fortunately, Stoogan is still old-school.

"If I have any feelings for you, Dixie, they lean more toward pity than lust."

"Pity?" I fire back as I close the gap between us. "Care to elaborate?"

Stoogan shows his teeth, fully aware of the silence that is filling the room but knowing, like me, that a good reporter needs a bit of iron in his or her balls to get to the heart of a story. And the best iron is forged in the company of bastards who have lived through wars—not spent the time sitting behind a computer.

"A picture tells a thousand words," he says with a grin. "You're wound so tight, I'm surprised you don't bounce on your tail like Tigger. When's the last time you enjoyed some male company"— he pauses for effect—"that, you know, didn't try to sue us after?"

"I had cock for breakfast."

The newsroom erupts in startled gasps as Stoogan's face collapses in on itself and he erupts with laughter. When I reach his side, he has tears in his eyes and is wheezing from the exertion.

"Your office?" I say as I take hold of his arm.

He nods, still chuckling. "Remind me never to play chess with you. You probably arm the knights with grenades."

"I'm more of a dominoes gal," I say. "I like the dots."

Stoogan starts laughing again and once I get him to his office, I immediately have to fetch him a glass of water.

"I'm glad you spend most of your time outside the office," Stoogan says after his breathing is back to normal. "You'd kill me otherwise."

"But you miss me all the same," I say.

He hesitates.

"Right?" I insist.

He grins and shrugs his massive shoulders beneath a baby-blue shirt and coffee-brown tie, the tip of which appears to have recently been dunked in a cup of actual coffee. Along with being legally blind, Stoogan also has the worst fashion sense of any human being on the planet.

"So, what's up?" I ask.

"First the good news."

"My favorite kind, especially if it involves the words, 'Dixie, you deserve a big fat raise.'"

Stoogan ignores me. "I just received word from the lawyers this morning that all lawsuits against us pertaining to your stories have either been dropped or settled. For the first time this year, you're officially lawsuit free."

"I don't like the term *settled*," I say. "It implies I did something wrong. People sue because they don't like what I write, but I only report the truth, which is still the ultimate defense. There should be no settling."

"Calm down," says Stoogan. "I know you're a good reporter and I stand behind you a hundred percent, otherwise I'd fire your ass, but—"

I interrupt. "You keep mentioning my ass, boss. That's sexual harassment."

"One look at your boyish frame and they'd dismiss the charges."

I grin, pleased with the speed of his retort. "OK. Go on."

"*Settled* simply means the top brass chose the cheapest way out."

I grunt. "Hmmm, so long as we're not saying that I was in the wrong. That would bug me."

"Got it. Now you ready for the bad news?"

"Nope. Let's just end the conversation here. This feels right." I stand up to leave.

"Sit down."

I puff out my lower lip in a pout, but it has no effect. Must be my boyish frame.

"Nobody's telling me what to print, but—"

"That's a bad start," I interrupt.

"But," Stoogan continues, "the publisher would like to see us do a few more softer and advertiser-friendly cover features."

"I just vomited in my mouth."

Stoogan tries to hide his smirk by taking another drink of water. "The first one he wants is something dealing with Father's Day."

"Seriously?" I ask.

"Seriously."

"A FOK note?" FOK (long *o*) stands for Friend of Kenji—Kenji Kobayashi being our publisher—and usually refers to a story that Ken wants written about one of the advertisers that he's golf buddies

16

with. It's every reporter's nightmare, unless you're a total suck-up. "And you're not assigning this to Mary Jane?"

"She would sexualize it, and she already does enough of that on her celebrity beat."

"What about one of the junior—"

"This is yours," Stoogan interrupts. "The publisher likes your writing. He just wants to see you expand a bit out of the crime scene."

"So I'm being punished for being good?"

"That's one way to look at it."

I take a deep breath and grit my teeth. "Any particular angle to this bullshit consumerism event he would like to see illuminated?"

"You've got free reign to find the story, but it should probably have something to do with fathers. HR tells me that even you have one."

"Funny."

"That's me," agrees Stoogan. "A million laughs."

"Only when you look in the mirror," I answer before standing up and walking out.

———

My voicemail contains the good news I was hoping for. Eddie the Wolf says he'll have my $500 waiting for me at Mario's Deli anytime after 10 a.m. I can tell from the tone of his voice that the recent NHL playoff upset means my winnings don't compare to his.

Pleased with myself, I head across the floor to the newspaper morgue where Lulu "formerly known as Bruce" Lovejoy puts Google to shame with her ability to search through the *NOW* archives. A computer is only as intelligent as its user, which is why I rely on Lulu. She finds me the answers that I don't even know I'm looking for.

When I enter, Lulu is down on her knees with her butt in the air, exposing a purple thong and too much skin due to the shortness of her skirt.

I clear my throat loudly. "Lulu, are you trying to give Stoogan a heart attack?"

She looks over her shoulder. "Damn Ethernet cable came loose and it's an orgy of freaking snakes down here."

"Yeah, but unless you're making an amateur porno, short skirts and under-the-desk IT don't mix."

Lulu laughs. "Got it."

Getting back to her feet, Lulu brushes her hand across her skirt to smooth out any wrinkles and remove particles of fluff. Standing six feet four, Lulu is a big girl in every way. Broad shoulders, thick legs, biceps that make buying off-the-rack a difficult chore. Fortunately, we live in San Francisco where there are designers and boutique shops for every size and taste. If you can't find what you need here, you must be visiting from another galaxy.

"How's my hair?" she asks.

"Like you've just finished making IT porn."

She gasps. "Really?"

I laugh. "No, it's fine."

She runs manicured fingers through her locks. "I don't want just fine, dahling." She winks at me. "I want magnificent."

"Then magnificent it is."

"And how is my ass?"

"I tried not to stare."

"But you couldn't help yourself?"

"True. It's magnificent, too. But whose name is tattooed on the left—"

"What?" she screeches and lifts her skirt to look before catching my smirk. She drops the hem and wags her finger. "That's not nice."

"What I love is you thought it could be a possibility!"

"Well," she sighs. "I do have some incredibly adventurous evenings."

"Where waking up with a tattooed butt cheek is not unreasonable?" I ask.

"Oh, honey," Lulu beams. "You have no idea. So, what can I do for my favorite reporter today?"

I try not to grimace as I tell her about my fluff-piece assignment.

"Father's Day." Lulu rolls the words around her mouth in contemplation. "You could bang out a quick piece on what the mayor's kids have planned for him, but I don't think they like him much."

"Plus the mayor hates me," I add.

"Oh, don't put those parameters on me," Lulu says with a chuckle. "If we eliminate every authority figure in town who doesn't like you—"

"Yeah, yeah," I interrupt. "Moving on."

Lulu grins and then snaps her fingers and points down to a copy of the latest edition of *NOW* laying on top of the counter.

"Do you read our Classifieds section?"

"Occasionally," I admit.

"Check this out."

Lulu opens the paper to the Classifieds and points down to a column where people post public messages to each other. Mostly it's people who passed in the night and forgot to get a name or phone number; some were even too shy to approach each other but are now positive they may have missed meeting their soul mate. These messages tend to go along the lines of: *You, stunning in a white jumpsuit and hoop earrings; Me in the Spider-Man costume with a broken zipper. Our eyes met as I zip-lined away.*

Others are letters from rageaholics who need to tell the world who pissed them off by humming too loud on the bus or picking their nose in public.

Lulu points to one with a bold header that reads: **Father In Name.**

"This one caught my eye," says Lulu, "and I wanted to know more. Could make for an interesting piece."

The notice is only five lines. It reads:

> Twenty years, you disappeared.
> No word, no sign. Alive or dead?
> Did you ever think of us? Even love us?
> Mother tried, but the mess …
> I can never forgive.

"What do you think?" asks Lulu.

"Can you find out who submitted it?"

"Can a badger brush its teeth?"

"I have no idea," I admit.

Lulu laughs. "I'll get the name."

THREE

MARIO'S DELI IS A hole in the wall that native San Franciscans don't like to tell tourists about. But if you walk down the right street, your nose will lead you directly to it.

The owner kneads and boils his own bagels before baking them in a wood-fired brick oven. He also smokes his own meat and ships in giant jars of the tastiest dill pickles from New York. His cream cheese comes from a local farm where no calories are left behind, and he blends it by hand with such wonderful ingredients as fresh scallions, local steamed crab, roasted elephant garlic, heirloom tomatoes, and a variety of Napa Valley wines.

Mario's food is an enemy to every woman's hips and the greatest lover to her lips. His business partner, Eddie the Wolf, occupies the red vinyl booth farthest from the front door, where he sips coffee and practices frowning beneath an abused plaid woolen cap.

It would be easy to dismiss Eddie as a cranky old-timer until you notice the way his fingers dance across the keyboard of a modern aluminum laptop and the smooth juggle he does between four constantly vibrating cellphones. The man's a maestro in a wolf's jacket.

He frowns when I approach, but it's not full on, so I know he's actually pleased to see me.

"Come to rob an old man?" he asks.

I slide into the booth across from him and flash one of my golden smiles.

Behind Eddie is a door that leads to a back room. I've heard stories about what goes on behind that door, but so far I've never been invited through. One of the stories says that Eddie doesn't travel anywhere without his minder—a bull-headed guard who is so loyal he wouldn't hesitate to take a bullet, spit it out, and then break your neck if you dared attack his boss.

The story continues that the minder is always just behind the door, watching on a monitor, ready to react at the first sign of trouble. If true, it's no wonder Eddie always seems at ease.

"How old are you anyway?" I ask.

"Twenty-six."

I laugh. "Is that in dog years?"

"Live fast, die young."

"You never leave this booth."

"Give me a reason."

"There's a big, beautiful world out there," I say.

"You can keep it. I got everything I need right here. You want a sandwich? Onion bagel with lox is today's special. Not sure what Mario did to the onion, but man it's spectacular."

I look to my right and see Mario beaming at me with delight.

"It's true." Mario kisses the tips of his fingers. "Spectacular."

My mouth is watering so much I have to swallow the drool. "I'll take one to go."

Mario winks at me. "*Eccellente.*"

When I turn back to Eddie, he's holding an envelope out to me. I reach to take it, but he continues to hold one end.

"Double or nothing?" he asks.

"On what?"

"Name it."

I grin. "You just can't help yourself can you?"

"I'm a generous man. What can I say?"

I shake my head. "Generous men don't play on people's weakness."

"Of course we do. The only difference between rich and poor is that rich people don't rely on luck. We seize opportunity. I offer people the opportunity to be lucky."

I tug the envelope out of his hand and slide it into my pocket.

"If I start placing five-hundred-dollar bets, I hope you'll have the decency to tell me I've lost my goddamn mind."

Eddie shrugs. "Who am I to tell you not to take a flutter? But tell you what, I'll take fifty that you make such a bet before the end of the year."

"And if I don't?"

"You make another five bills."

I hesitate for just a moment—10:1 odds are a beautiful and rare thing—before pulling the envelope back out of my pocket and removing a $50. I slide it across the table and watch it vanish with barely a flicker of his hand, like a magic trick.

"Anything else I can do for you today? Horses, dogs, baseball, soccer, boxing, reality shows—"

"Reality shows?" I ask.

"Sure. People place bets on who'll be voted off *American Idol* or *Survivor*, even the number of times Sheldon will say 'Bazinga' on *The Big Bang Theory*."

"Do you even know what those shows are?" I ask.

Eddie shrugs. "I have people who do. Odds are odds."

"And poor people want to be lucky," I add.

He nods. "The great American dream: get famous, sue somebody, or win the lottery."

"I don't think that's quite what the Founding Fathers had in mind."

He shrugs. "They owned mansions and slaves—what the hell do they know about microwave dinners for one or selling your ass to pay the rent?"

My eyes grow wide. "Jeez, Eddie. You sound like you're about to rush out and join the Occupy Wall Street movement."

"Me?" Eddie nearly grins. "Nah. I may not like people who run a rigged game, but you gotta admire the gumption."

"I'll take your word for it."

I slide out of the booth and cross to the counter to pick up my bagel. Warmth oozes from within its waxed-paper wrapper.

When I turn back to say bye to Eddie, he's busy chatting on one of his cellphones. His frown has deepened and his voice is gruff, which makes me think the schmuck on the other end of the line has bet too big and come up short.

I hit the street, unwrapping the bagel as I go. Eddie's right; whatever Mario did to the onion, it's spectacular.

———

Finding a pay phone in San Francisco can be tricky, but I've been resisting the cellphone trend for so long that I have the inside track on most of them.

Stoogan has warned me the company is planning to make it mandatory that all reporters carry a cell—especially since the cameras have improved so much that they now shoot print-quality stills and web-ready video—so I told him to let me know when they have an app that tells me where all the pay phones are, then I might consider it.

I wipe my greasy hands on a napkin and dial the *NOW* morgue.

Lulu answers with, "What you eating, Dix?"

"What makes you think I'm eating something?"

"You're not in the office."

"Yeah."

"So you're eating. You're always eating."

"I am not."

"What was it?"

I sigh and tell her about the bagel.

"That's my girl, one nostril for news and another for grub. I just don't know where you put it all. If I ate like you, I'd be the size of a horse."

"They're vegetarians," I say. "That's why I'm not."

Lulu laughs. "Good point. Who knew hay and apples could be so bad for you?"

"Don't tell Kellogg's." After she finishes snickering, I ask, "Did you get a name and number on that ad?"

"Yep, no sweat. She paid by credit card. Name is Bailey Brown. I called the number on file and her roommate told me she works days at Scissors & Sizzle on California Street, you know it?"

"I'll find it. Thanks."

"Anytime, sweets."

My next call is to Mo, who runs my favorite independent cab company. We chat about the rigors of the chemo he's undergoing for throat cancer, while he dispatches a cab. As someone who's never known how to relax, Mo hates how tired the treatment leaves him, but he's also discovered some interesting people.

"We talk to pass the time, you know," he says in a guttural Bronx accent that's been sandblasted into a perverse whisper. "And some of these guys have *done* things with their lives. This one, I swear to God, he's Indiana Jones. He's discovered mummies and real buried treasure. Imagine? The only mummy I ever seen was in an old Abbott and Costello movie. But this guy—Wilfred is his name—this guy dug one up. Crazy."

"Sounds cool," I say.

"Yeah, you should talk to him. He donated a bunch of archeological stuff to the museums here. Interesting guy."

"I'll keep it in mind."

I can hear phones ringing mercilessly in the background.

"Gotta go. You keep safe, Dix."

"Always."

Mo snickers. "Yeah."

When the cab arrives, the driver already knows where to drop me.

FOUR

Scissors & Sizzle is a small and cozy salon with sun-bleached posters in the front window that have been ripped out of fashion magazines. Each page shows a sensual woman with cold eyes and perfect hair that, in reality, only looks good if you spend all day avoiding the weather—preferably without moving your head.

I keep my natural copper curls in a don't-give-a-damn cut that some say reflects the chaos of my life and others say makes it look like I simply don't give a damn. I like to tell the curious that it goes with my tattoo, which makes them curious (since it's not visible) about just exactly where and what it is.

I enter the salon and ask for Bailey Brown.

"Do you have an appointment?" asks the young receptionist. Her eye shadow is the color of a day-old bruise, and I wonder what she's trying to hide.

I shake my head. "Sorry, no, but I was hoping—"

"That's OK," she interrupts. "We're not busy today." She pauses and wrinkles her nose as she points at my hair. "She didn't do that to you, did she?"

"No," I say curtly, suddenly understanding why bruise-colored eye shadow may be an appropriate choice.

"Oh, good, I was worried." She exhales. "Take a seat and I'll get Bails to fix you up."

I take a seat by the window and study the room. There's not much to it: four cutting stations with thin partitions offering a modicum of privacy, a bank of three sinks, a lone nail technician, and four padded chairs with chrome-accented, helmet-style hairdryers. It's the type of place that depends on local repeat business rather than flashy advertising and designer prices.

My mother ran a similar salon in the town where I grew up, and I remember an argument she had when I was about twelve and working summers sweeping hair. A strong-willed feminist, who was visiting our town to promote her self-help book and generally cause a ruckus, accused her of being a traitor to womankind by glamorizing beauty over substance.

No wilting daisy, my mother unleashed a tirade on how beauty salons were the original foundation stones feminism was built upon. Her argument was based on her own mother's story—one I hadn't heard until that day.

At a time when women were second-class citizens to their hardworking husbands, my grandmother had grown bored of being a housewife and mother. Starting small, she opened a home business for the neighbors, offering cuts and perms and colors at a very reasonable cost.

After paying for her supplies, she saved every cent, until one day she had enough to lease a small storefront on Main Street. Her salon was the very first business in town not owned and operated by a man. By the time the Sixties rolled around and feminists began burning their bras and shouting louder about equality, my grandma had already proven that women were more than a man's equal when it came to business. And although time and gravity had made it too uncomfortable to burn her own bra, my grandma saw nothing wrong with looking one's best while rattling cages.

"You're smiling," says a woman's voice. "Happy memory?"

I look up into a face that's lean, taut, and overly angular. Her cheekbones are sharp with deep-set eyes more almond-shaped than round. Thin-lipped and blunt-chinned, the young woman has the face of someone who finds her calories in cigarettes, cocaine, or vodka rather than onion bagels.

With a shorter haircut, she would be fierce, almost scary, but her hair is the tri-tone color of honey and falls in soft curls to her shoulders. And yet, there's something off. But I can't put my finger on it, so I dismiss the thought.

"I was thinking of my grandma," I say. "Are you Bailey?"

The woman nods and holds out her hand. It's an unusual gesture and slightly awkward, more something one expects of men when they're trying hard to be grown-ups. I put her in her mid-twenties. I stand and shake. Her skin is rougher than it should be and on the colder side of room temperature. I can feel small bones move beneath my thumb.

"Do you want to follow me to the sink?" she asks.

"Actually, I'm not looking for a haircut. I was hoping we could talk."

I dig in my pocket for a business card and hand it over.

Her forehead wrinkles as she reads the card.

"I recognize your name from the paper." Her gaze lifts to study my face, comparing it to the grinning picture on my card. "I liked that piece you did awhile back on the dead artist. Tragic."

"Thanks."

"It read like you really knew him."

"I did. Kind of. Part of him anyway."

Her lips tighten into a thin line. "Yeah, guys can be like that. What do you want to talk to me about?"

"You placed a Classified ad in our paper recently. It intrigued me."

"Really? You read it?"

"This morning."

"Huh. Well, I don't know what else to say about it."

"It was written for your father?"

"Yeah."

"Are you hoping he'll read it?" I ask.

She looks away and reaches up to touch her eye. I can't tell if she's attempting to stop a tear or just flicking away a loose eyelash.

"I never really thought that far," she says. "I just had to let it out, you know?"

I nod. "I find writing cathartic, too."

"And you want to talk to me?"

"If you'll let me. Maybe we can go somewhere, grab a coffee, see where it takes us."

She looks away again in contemplation before bringing her eyes back to mine. Her gaze is deep as if she wants to pull back the curtains of my mind to see what's going on inside. I worry she'll frighten the imaginary clockmaker—who, oddly enough, looks a lot like Geppetto from the Disney version of *Pinocchio*—who keeps all my gears oiled and rolling.

"Give me a minute," she says and heads to the back room.

I sit down again and shuffle through the magazines to see which Hollywood stars have lost too much weight and which have ballooned to the size of a normal person. Pity the poor starlet who's feeling bloated and gets snapped by the paparazzi as she's dashing into the drug store to buy tampons. The damning photographic evidence will obviously appear in one tabloid as a pregnancy scare, while another will quote an unnamed "close friend" as saying she's now addicted to OxyContin or Percocet.

I worked with an old-timer once who had spent a few years with the *National Enquirer* in Florida at the same time Hunter S. Thompson was causing havoc over at *Rolling Stone*. His name was Ray—a very short, very stout, flush-faced man who reminded me of a whiskery weasel from *Wind in the Willows*: cunning, smart, and better to have on your side than your opponent's. Once Ray started drinking, the stories he told of journalism on the tabloid beat kept me in stitches for hours.

"You're smiling again," Bailey says.

I look up to see that she's wearing her coat.

"Bad habit," I say as I rise to my feet.

"There's a new bakery up the block that I've heard good things about if you'd like to go there."

"They don't sell penises, do they?"

Bailey blinks rapidly, not sure how to respond.

———

The bakery doesn't sell penises (or any other body parts), but it does make a fabulous dark roast, which looks lonely and sad until I add a saucer-sized oatmeal cookie half dunked in milk chocolate and sprinkled with toasted coconut.

Bailey doesn't mind that her coffee is lonesome, but I restrain myself from calling her selfish.

We find a quiet table and sit.

"Your father's been missing for twenty years?" I begin.

Bailey sips her coffee and nods.

"What's the last thing you remember about him?"

Bailey tells me about a night when she was five years old. Her father and a stranger stood in her room, believing that she was asleep. She still recalls the scent of gun oil and the strange conversation where her father said she wasn't for sale.

"I haven't seen him since," she says. "Leslie—that's my mom—and I were left to fend for ourselves, which was like expecting a toaster to make omelets. She was barely out of her teens, no skills or education, pregnant with my sister, Roxanne. Dad always told her he would take care of us, and the stupid bitch believed him."

"You're not close with your mom, then?" I ask in reaction to her harsh tone.

Bailey takes another sip of coffee, and I watch her fingers quiver as though desperate to hold a cigarette.

"She's dead. Five years now."

"Sorry."

"No need. She dived head first down a path that sliced and diced her from head to toe. The only miracle is that I'm not lying beside her."

She scratches nervously at her shoulder. Beneath the fabric of her top, I notice the outline of a nicotine patch.

"And your sister?" I ask.

"She's around, but she's walking the same damn path. You'd think with what we saw—" She breaks off and stares into her coffee cup. From this angle, the overhead fluorescents dig beneath the carefully applied makeup, picking up pocks and scars that she's worked hard to hide.

When she looks up again, her face has re-formed into a mask of resolve: the hairdresser who has to work at being pleasant and normal because the anger and betrayal she feels inside never stops gnawing.

"Sorry," she says and attempts a smile. "I don't usually share that much with perfect strangers. Did you spike my coffee or something?"

"No," I answer with a chuckle, "but great idea. I'll keep that in mind for next time I'm interviewing the mayor. Get the real scoop on where the bodies are buried at city hall."

This time her smile has a touch of genuineness to it.

"Do you have any idea who this stranger in your bedroom was?" I ask.

Surprisingly, she answers, "Yeah."

Bailey lifts her purse off the floor and digs around inside. Removing a fake crocodile-leather wallet, she opens the compartment designed to hold family photos. There's only one: a young girl with blond hair and an untamed fringe that nearly covers her large blue eyes. She can't be more than five, but her face is softer and more oval than Bailey's.

"That Roxanne?" I ask.

"Yeah," Bailey says dismissively.

From one of the plastic sleeves, she slides out a decade-old newspaper clipping, unfolds it, and hands it over.

The newsprint is yellowed with age, but it's still clear enough to read the article. Printed beneath a one-column, head-and-shoulders mugshot of a dapper-looking gentleman with an Errol Flynn moustache and distinguished gray temples, the headline reads: **Crime Boss Cleared of All Charges.**

I point at the mugshot. "This is him? You're sure?"

Bailey nods.

"Did you ever talk to him?"

"I tried once, after Leslie died, but I couldn't get close. From what I was told, he isn't interested in girls after they hit puberty."

"Charming," I say.

"That's not the word I'd use."

At another time, I would have high-fived her in agreement, but I can tell she isn't receptive to female bonding. I lean back and scan the story. The facts are bare, but between the lines is everything I need to know.

I exhale quietly and lean forward. "Would you mind if I looked into what happened to your dad?"

Bailey's eyes lock onto mine; she's probing again, digging deep. "Why?" she asks.

"The honest answer is I'm looking for a Father's Day story to appease my publisher, but that's only part of it. The other part is I'm curious, and I believe that finding out what happened will help bring you some closure. We don't know each other, but I'd like to do this."

I gauge her response and continue. "I don't know where I would be today without the love and support of my own father. He isn't perfect, but I've never felt safer or more secure in my life than when I'm in his arms."

I reach down my leg and pull a small, pearl-handled switchblade out of my boot. I show it to Bailey.

"Her name's Lily. This may seem odd," I say. "But when I'm feeling scared or lonely or just in a damn foul mood, I like to hold this knife. Smell the oil he used to lubricate its hinge and know that part of my dad is in here and that he gave me this not just because he loves me and worries about me, but because he wants to be close to me at all times." I smile. "Silly thing to say about a knife, huh?"

Bailey's eyes are moist as she shakes her head. "I don't even know if he's alive or dead."

"Let me find out."

"How?"

I place my finger on the newspaper clipping. "With the person who walked him out of your life. Krasnyi Lebed," I read.

"He won't talk to you. I've tried."

My smile is thin and sharp. "You might be surprised."

FIVE

I FIND A PAY phone on the corner and let Stoogan know that I'm following a few leads on a Father's Day piece that will make for a nice cover.

"Why am I suddenly worried," he deadpans.

"Because I'm not breaking your balls about it?"

"Yeah, why aren't you?"

"Because I always do what—"

"You never do what I ask," he interrupts.

"First time for everything."

"Now I'm not just worried, I'm petrified."

I laugh. "Trust me."

"Yeah, I can see that engraved on my tombstone: *He trusted Dixie.*"

I laugh louder. "I like it. Catchy yet poignant."

"Just don't put me in the ground too soon, Dix."

"Wouldn't dream of it, boss."

My next call is to Detective Sergeant Fury, an imposing homicide detective with the San Francisco Police Department who took me under his wing after a feature I wrote about the murder of his wife at the hands of a thief, and the subsequent "death by misadventure" of her killer.

The thief's death proved controversial, as he was shot while climbing out the window of an apartment he had just robbed. The cop who shot him was Frank Fury.

"You have time for a chat?" I ask when Frank answers the phone.

"I was thinking of being totally unpredictable and dropping into the Dog House tonight," he says.

I laugh. The Dog House is a dungeon of a pub two blocks from the Hall of Justice on Bryant Street that is a local drinking hole for the sad sacks of the night crew, who often prefer to drink alone: cops, journalists, musicians, and a few curious writers and misfits who've heard about the bar's resident ghost, Al Capone.

Frank and I are regulars.

"I was hoping to see you sooner than that," I say. "Want to pick your brain about something."

"You in trouble?" he asks.

"Not yet."

I can almost hear his lips bending into a thin smile, but he's not going to give me the satisfaction of a chuckle.

"I have a proficiency test coming up and need to get in some practice."

"Perfect," I say. "Meet you there."

———

I own a gun license but not a gun. However, I've been toying with the idea ever since a scary encounter in my apartment with someone who seemed intent on throwing me out of my second-story window.

An ugly scar that puckers the center of my left palm aches when the weather gets cold, but that's nothing compared to how the attack damaged my confidence. I never actually believed I was invincible, but I certainly lacked a proper respect for how unprepared I was for direct violence.

And although I don't like to admit weakness, neither do I ever want to be considered a victim. Since that event, Sam has introduced me to her Mixed Martial Arts class, and Frank's been teaching me how to shoot.

Off the books, I also called in a favor from a former mob enforcer named Pinch. Our paths crossed on a feature I was writing for *NOW*, when he took a chance on trusting me and I earned his respect by staying true to my word.

Pinch—who, at five-foot-four and more stout than wiry, looks nothing like my preconceptions of a trained killer—has been teaching me the proper way to use my switchblade and unladylike ways in which my feet, thighs, teeth, and nails can become lethal weapons.

Every bruise on my body since that day has been a medal, earned through sweat and determination. They are marks I wear proudly— like my silly, hidden tattoo.

The indoor shooting range that Frank uses is called Duck! It's a private members' club in an unremarkable corrugated steel Quonset hut located on the edge of an industrial park near the docks. Catering mostly to the law enforcement and private security crowd, its name comes from the front entrance: a black steel door that, for a reason nobody's yet been able to explain to me, is only five feet six inches tall. Unless you're Pinch, to gain entrance you need to, quite literally, duck.

The interior of the club looks nothing like its exterior. Sound-proofing foam, still visible on the high, curved ceiling, is sprayed thickly over the ribbed steel skin. The front area is finished in oak, chrome, and glass for a boys' clubhouse feel: chairs designed for comfort, plasma TVs on the wall, and a small bar.

The much larger rear area—separated from the front by a steel-core wall and safety prep area that still allowed for a few bullet-proof acrylic windows—is kept clean, sparse, and professional to accommodate twelve shooting lanes. Electric target retrievers allow the shooter to pick any distance he or she desires.

"Hey, Dix," calls Benny as I make my way to the gun bar. "Frank's inside, lane 6. I booked you on 5."

Benny, a pug-nosed veteran who likes to wear crisp military green T-shirts even though the color doesn't suit his complexion, is the owner. If he listened to me he'd switch to navy blue to highlight his eyes, but he doesn't, so green it stays.

Reaching the glass display case, I'm surprised he hasn't already pulled out the Glock 19 and smaller Glock 26 that I've been renting.

Benny reads my face. "I know you're enjoying the Glocks," he says. "But I'm thinking there's something missing."

I smile. "And what's that?"

"They're too plain. Lacking that bit of pizazz to get your teeth watering, am I right?"

I shrug. "It's a gun, Benny. Not a fashion accessory."

"You kiddin' me?" His cheeks balloon in mirth. "You think these guys don't brag on their hardware? I don't know about fashion, but the kinda gun you shoot is definitely a statement."

"OK, what you got?"

"You've tried the automatics," he begins. "And you made a nice, safe choice with the Glocks, but I'm still a fan of a good six-shot revolver. Easy to clean and maintain, always reliable, and there's more of a connection between you and the gun. In my humble opinion, it just feels better in the hand. And for personal defense, who needs seventeen bullets? Keep a level head and one does the trick."

My lips twitch in amusement. "You're kinda sexy when you go all gun geek, Benny."

He flushes. "Don't fool with an old man," he warns. "Our hearts can't take it."

"So what do you recommend?" I ask.

From under the counter, he produces a matte-black revolver that's about eight and a half inches from tip to tail and lays it on the glass.

"I'm liking this Smith & Wesson Governor that you can load with .45 ACP or Long Colt, plus .410 shotgun shells. This gives you great stopping power with the buckshot loads for close-quarter confrontations, and the .45s for a longer, cleaner shot. It's a few ounces heavier than what you're used to with the Glock, but I got a feeling you'll actually like the added heft."

I pick up the revolver and move into a two-handed stance. It is slightly heavier, but Benny's right, it feels good.

I smile again. "I'm liking it."

Benny nods. "Thought you might."

"Can I take it for a spin?"

He slides the blue plastic gun case over, plus a box of .45 ACP ammo and a handful of two-and-a-half-inch .410 shells.

"Lane 5 is waiting."

You don't get much talking done on the actual range unless you're looking for monosyllabic grunts and head shakes. So while I gain an intimate knowledge of the Governor, Frank is showing what a few decades of practice can do to a paper silhouette that done did him wrong.

Frank doesn't shoot fancy or try any tricks. He's strictly a heart and lungs kind of guy, with every shot finding its mark. As he lectured when I first asked for his help: "Remember, TV is bullshit. You never shoot to injure, always to kill. Aim for a leg or an arm and you'll put a ricochet through some unlucky civilian before the perp puts you down. Always aim for the chest, center mass. If the first bullet doesn't stop him, it'll at least slow him down. Keep hitting that mark and he'll eventually stop moving and lay down to die."

I load two shotgun shells and fill the remaining four chambers with .45s. Shooting is like yoga, except noisier. I control my breath, balance my stance, aim, and fire.

The silhouette doesn't stand a chance as the first shell unleashes fifteen projectiles: three .10-caliber discs alongside twelve pellets of plated BB. The spread hits center mass to punch a hole in the target as wide as my hand.

If that doesn't knock an intruder on his ass and have his lowlife friends calling an undertaker rather than an ambulance, I don't know what will.

With a devilish grin, I fire the second shotgun round and follow up in rapid succession with the four .45s.

As I reload, Frank moves around behind me and taps my shoulder. I lower my protective ear guards and turn to face him.

"What in hell are you shooting?" he asks.

I show him the gun and point to the black-jacketed shotgun shells.

"Not exactly a purse gun," he says.

"No," I agree, "but I kinda like it. Wanna try?"

I don't need to ask twice. Frank grasps the loaded gun and a fresh silhouette has its chest turned to confetti before joining its siblings in the range's recycle bin.

When he hands the gun back, Frank says, "Should have called it the Don't Fuck With Me instead of Governor."

I laugh. "So which gun is your favorite?"

"Whichever one I have with me when I need to use it," he quips.

Frank turns to reload the magazine of his department issue Sig Sauer with .40-caliber brass, while I put in some more one-on-one time with the Governor.

———

Once our skills are sharpened, I offer to buy Frank a coffee and we grab a couple of comfortable chairs in a quiet corner of the clubhouse.

"So, what's up?" Frank asks.

I tell him about my idea for the Father's Day piece before asking, "How well do you know a Krasnyi Lebed?"

"The Red Swan?" Frank exhales through his nose. "Seriously?"

"Yeah. He's connected to the story."

"He's connected to a lot of things, Dix. The man traffics in drugs, women, organs, you name it. He's bad news."

"You ever nailed him?"

"Once, but we lost in court."

"Was this about ten years back?"

"Twelve. Why?"

I tell him about the newspaper clipping that Bailey had shown me: **Crime Boss Cleared of All Charges.**

Frank nods. "That's the case. He might be called a swan, but Krasnyi's also slippery as a damn eel."

"How did he get the nickname?" I picture a swan swimming through a lake of blood, its snowy feathers changing color as the death toll mounts.

"It's the literal translation of his name from Russian," says Frank. "Maybe his parents hoped he'd be a redhead like you."

"Have you ever met him?" I ask.

"Sure."

"What's he like?"

"Charming and slick," says Frank. "Reminded me of the first time I read Bram Stoker's *Dracula*. If the novel had been set in Russia, it could have been called *Red Swan*."

I raise my eyebrows. "I doubt he drinks blood."

"No, but he spills enough of it and is very good at hiding the evidence."

"Would he meet with me?"

Frank sips his coffee before answering. "I wouldn't advise it."

"I get that, but would he?"

"You're not his type."

"So I've heard." I notice Frank's avoiding my gaze. "But what, Frank? You're hiding something."

Frank sighs. "He's a news junkie."

"So he'll have heard of me?"

"Without a doubt."

"And that'll get me in to see him?"

"Possibly, but if you get in trouble, there are some places even I can't go. You get that, right? You cross his threshold and as far as he's concerned, you're in Russia. And in Russia, nobody says no to him about anything."

"I just want to ask a few questions."

"And can you do that without pissing him off?"

I click my tongue in disbelief. "Of course I can. What do you take me for?"

"I don't take you for anything other than what you are: a pushy, stubborn, controlling pain in the ass."

"Now you sound like my editor."

Frank's mouth twitches. "Must be a smart and handsome man."

"No comment," I say and finish my coffee.

———

"You buying the gun?" Benny asks as I pay for the rental, ammo, and coffee. He has the Governor cleaned, oiled, and sitting pretty in its blue carrying case. "Take it now and I'll deduct the cost of the rental straight off the top. Even throw in a trigger lock, two boxes of ammo, and a bore snake."

"I'm tempted," I say.

"Paperwork is already done. You've got your license, so you can take it home right now."

"How much?"

"Six fifty all in. I eat the taxes. Best deal you'll find."

"That's a week's wages," I say.

"Because it's you, I can take installments."

I chew my lower lip and study the Governor. I like how it feels in my hand, but do I really want a gun in my house?

"Sorry, Benny, I'm just not there yet."

Benny shrugs and takes my cash for the rental.

"You've got the bug, Dix," he says. "I'll get you soon."

"We'll see." I head outside to catch a lift back downtown with Frank.

SIX

FRANK DROPS ME ON the corner a block from the *NOW* offices. The morning mist has turned to drizzle, but I don't mind. I'm one of those people who find walking in the rain to be one of the best ways to cleanse the jumble of my thoughts, sort out the mismatched ideas and see if there are any pairings to be made.

Which reminds me—I'm way behind on laundry.

As I near the restaurant, I pinch my nose, stare straight ahead, and make a dash for the stairs. Even with such precautions, I can smell the aroma of roasting lamb shanks with garlic and rosemary. If I didn't know better, I'd swear that Dmitri installed a fan in the kitchen to blow directly into the stairwell.

By the time I reach the third floor, I'm thinking someone should make a gum, like they do for smokers, for people who need their food cravings taken away. The heroin addicts I pass on the street are always skinny, so maybe we need a line of flavored gums with just enough poppy powder to take away the cravings without making us nodding zombies. The downside to that, of course, is that fewer things lower a woman's perceived intelligence like chewing gum. Men, on the other hand, can pretend they're baseball stars.

After letting Stoogan see my face so he can report what a loyal and agreeable employee I am, I head into the morgue and ask Lulu to pull any files she has on Krasnyi Lebed or clippings that mention Red Swan.

Her fingers dance across the keyboard.

"Not much here," she says when she looks back up. "Nothing under 'Red Swan' and only a couple of hits on Lebed. Man keeps a low profile."

"Pull me what you have."

"Sure, doll. Only take a minute. This to do with that Classified ad I mentioned?"

"It is." I smile. "Thanks for that."

Lulu beams. "I'm not just a pretty face."

"Preaching to the choir, sister."

Lulu bursts out laughing as she disappears into the archives to search for printed copies of the material. When she returns, she is holding a slim folder with Krasnyi Lebed's name on the cover.

Newspapers keep archives of prominent people so that when they die, obituaries are easier to write. The same is true of criminals who are likely to get in trouble with the law again. Nothing beefs up a breaking story on deadline than being able to quickly pull up a background full of previous run-ins and convictions.

I take the folder back to my desk and open it. There are only four clippings inside. Three are related to the case twelve years ago that Frank was involved in. Krasnyi had been charged with importing a shipment container from Novorossiysk, Russia, that contained a limited edition Rolls-Royce Phantom and enough pure heroin to get everyone on the western seaboard high.

Krasnyi was cleared of all charges when initial witnesses, including two undercover cops, recanted their statements about seeing him at the scene. This was despite him being pulled over and arrested six blocks from the docks while sitting in the back seat of the exact same silver Rolls-Royce that was on the shipping manifest.

No wonder Frank is pissed about it.

The fourth clipping is a photo and cutline that shows a younger Krasnyi as a pallbearer at a funeral. The cutline reads:

> Following the death of alleged crime boss Alim-zhan Izmaylovsky, police sources expect Krasnyi Lebed, right, to quickly take control of organized crime in San Francisco.

A low whistle escapes my lips. The clipping is unusual in that neither the name of the photographer nor the date it ran is printed anywhere on the sheet. I flip the clipping over to see if there's a date stamp on the back, but it's blank, too.

Whenever it ran, it was obviously in the days when *NOW* had a true independent heart and much ballsier staff. There is no way our paper's lawyer would ever let us run such a potentially libelous cutline today. I admire the cockiness of it.

Returning the folder to the morgue, I stop at the copy machine and make an enlargement of the photo. The faces of the other pallbearers are either out of frame or out of focus, and I wonder if that was the photographer's decision or the newspaper's.

I fold the copy and slip it into my back pocket.

"Find what you were looking for?" Lulu asks as I hand her the folder.

I shrug. "Just crumbs, but we keep archives of all our photos, right?"

"Sure."

"What about the negatives?"

Lulu's face wrinkles. "We're meant to, but there are definitely huge gaps. We lost a bunch when the roof leaked that one time, and photographers aren't always the best at returning negs after they've raided the archives for their portfolios, especially before I started here."

"Could you look up the photo in that last clipping? See if we have any hard copies or, better yet, the negatives? I'd like to find out who the photographer was and if more shots from that funeral are kicking around."

"What are you hoping to find?"

I shrug again. "You know me. I just pick at the scab until it bleeds."

Lulu winces. "Cute metaphor."

"That's why I'll never be a famous author; no time for pretty words."

Lulu laughs. "I'll see what I can do, but it might take some time. The photo archives aren't in the computer."

"Thanks. I'll check back."

For my next phone call, I head outside. The closest pay phone is four blocks to the south, but there are some calls I don't like to make within earshot of nosey reporters. Especially if they're anything like me.

I turn up my collar against the rain and walk.

His phone is answered on the sixth ring. There's no greeting, only silence.

"Pinch?" I ask. "You hungry?"

"What do you have in mind?" answers a voice that is so much deeper than you ever expect once you meet him in person.

"I'm thinking a cheeseburger at Pink Bicycle, but I'm also being tempted by a chocolate-chip mint sundae with rainbow sprinkles at Polka Dots."

"And these two disparate choices hold equal weight in your thoughts?"

"Yeah, I'm craving both, but I can't eat both, cause I already had a bagel and penis for breakfast. And if carbs went to your boobs, I'd be okay, but they don't. So…"

"I don't want to ask about the penis."

"Probably for the best. So which do you fancy?"

"Hamburger. Twenty minutes?"

"See you there."

SEVEN

THE PINK BICYCLE IS renowned for its great selection of *mini* sliders, but I haven't known Pinch long enough to be sure of how sensitive he is to the vertically challenged aspect of his stature. I mean, he's not *that* short. And as a girl whose Barbies preferred my neighbor's G.I. Joe with Kung Fu grip over the leaner and more emasculated Ken doll, I've always found shorter men to be more appealing.

Erring on the side of caution, however, I assume it's never smart to insult a hired killer—even unintentionally.

"What do you recommend?" he asks, looking up from the menu.

"There are no wrong choices here. It's all good."

"What about the sliders?"

I grin, relieved at the opening. "Fantastic. We could share the variety platter of six with yam fries on the side."

"And a salad?"

"If you need the roughage, sure."

Pinch's eyes dance with amusement although his lips barely twinge. He closes the menu. "So what's the ulterior motive?" he asks.

"Does there need to be one?"

"No, but there is."

The waitress arrives and we order. After she leaves, I lean across the table. My bust is so small that my shirt barely puckers. Disappointedly, his eyes don't even attempt a sneaky peek.

"You ever heard of the Red Swan?"

Pinch doesn't blink, but neither does he answer.

"Krasnyi Lebed," I continue. "He's—"

"I know who he is," Pinch interrupts.

"I want to meet him."

"Bad idea."

"It's for a story I'm—"

"Still a bad idea."

"He's a news junkie. He'll like me."

"He might, but it's better to be off his radar than on."

I lean back again. "You ever work for him?"

"No comment."

I narrow my eyes and shake my head. "No, you haven't, have you? If you had, you wouldn't be living here."

Pinch tilts his head to one side, a move that neither confirms nor denies my claim.

"People in your profession don't retire," I continue. "You disappear someplace where people don't know you. You picked San Francisco because you did most of your work on the East Coast. Am I close?"

"No comment."

I lean forward again. "I'm not expecting you to give me an introduction; I just need to know how I go about meeting him. Your name will never leave my lips. I hope that I've proven that to you."

Pinch nods. "You have."

"So will you help me?"

The waitress returns with our platter of assorted mini burgers and lays it on the table. A basket of crispy yam fries, chipotle mayo dip, and a carafe of ice water quickly join it. After she leaves, Pinch tucks his napkin under his chin and picks up the first burger: Angus beef with aged white cheddar.

I don't tell him the napkin makes him look darn cute.

"We'll talk after we eat," he says.

I agree and dive in.

———

I'm lifting my second slider—a teriyaki and green onion pork patty with pineapple—to my lips when a businessman in a bold pinstriped suit collides with our table and his elbow smacks my hand.

Like something out of a Max Payne video game, time slows. The burger leaves my hand, the top half of the bun accelerating faster than the bottom. In the same instant, the carafe of water is blasting off at an angle that would make NASA hit the self-destruct button.

I push my chair back in an attempt to avoid the worst of it, but out of the corner of my eye I see Pinch moving forward, his hands imperceptibly faster than the unfolding disaster. While his left hand plucks the glass carafe out of the air and lands it upright with barely a splash, his right hand intercepts the catapulted burger and slams it down onto the table. The only escapee is the top half of the bun that, like a miniature flying saucer that's low on fuel, loses altitude and crashes to the floor before reaching our neighbor's table.

The businessman laughs with such gusto it's evident he's indulged in several lunchtime martinis.

"Nice hands," he says to Pinch, then winks at his companions. "You'd make a good *short*stop for our company baseball team."

Pinch removes his hand from the ruined burger and wipes the sauce from his palm on a napkin.

"You owe the lady an apology," says Pinch.

Color rises in the businessman's cheeks and some of the glass evaporates from his eyes. "It was an accident," he snarls. "No damage done."

"Then a simple apology will suffice."

"Look, shorty, I—"

"Why do you choose to insult me?" Pinch asks in a calm voice. "I didn't call you a clumsy buffoon or a drunken asshole or even an arrogant prick. All of which, I might add, seem like a perfect fit. So why—"

"Hey, fuck you, midget! I bumped your table, big fucking deal."

I try to smooth the waters with a reasonable, "All we wanted was for you to say sorry."

Pinstripe glares at me like I've just farted in church and blamed the minister.

"Fuck you, too, lesbo. I'm tired of you freaks thinking you deserve equal fucking treatment every—"

The blood suddenly drains from Pinstripe's face and his throat releases a squeal that expertly imitates a hungry piglet that can't find its mother's teat. Pinch has left his chair and is standing with the man's crotch cupped in his hand.

54

Looking over at me, Pinch asks, "Remember what I taught you about the groin?"

"Ignore the penis, always go for the balls?" I answer like the star pupil I am.

He nods as the man continues to squeal. "And?"

"Don't tug," I answer. "Twist and squeeze like you're juicing a lemon."

Pinch rotates his wrist and the man's squeal hits a pitch so high that it becomes silent. He grabs the table as his eyes roll to the back of his head.

One of his companions steps forward, but Pinch lifts his free hand and wags one finger. The would-be rescuer stops dead in his tracks, a primitive part of his brain kicking into overdrive to warn him that, in this case, flight is a better option than fight.

I realize the waitress has appeared with our bill. She barely glances at the squirming suit.

"Umm, I don't want to call the police," she says. "But you're disturbing the other customers."

Pinch offers her a thin smile of apology before turning his attention to Pinstripe's companions.

"I believe your friend would like to pay for our lunch in apology for being such a jerk. Is that your understanding?"

"He-he's our boss," says one of the men. "Not really a friend."

Pinstripe finds his voice and utters a guttural moan of undecipherable meaning.

"Erm," continues the man, "but I'm thinking that means he would be happy to buy you both lunch."

Pinch turns to me. "Have you had enough to eat?"

I haven't, but I nod before adding, "Although I did leave room for dessert."

Pinstripe groans again and foamy drool drips from the corners of his mouth.

"But we could go elsewhere for that," I add.

A flicker of a smile creases Pinch's lips before he turns back to Pinstripe's employees. "Would you like to take a photo before I let him go? Might come in handy if the economy gets worse and he's trying to decide who to lay off."

"Ugh, no, that's okay, thanks."

Pinch leans in close to the boss's agonized face to whisper a final thought before releasing his grip. Upon release, the man's forehead jerks forward to hit the tabletop and his skeleton turns to rubber. He slides to the floor and curls into a fetal position with his bruised ego cradled in his hands.

Pinch removes a twenty from his pocket and hands it to our waitress.

"Sorry for the disturbance," he says.

"No worries," says the young woman. "That one's pinched my ass so many times, I've thought of doing the same thing. Twist and squeeze, huh?"

Pinch winks at her and holds the door open as we exit.

———

At Polka Dots, I order a chocolate-chip mint sundae with rainbow sprinkles and proceed to the vinyl booth where Pinch is already devouring a dark chocolate malt.

"Do you know what he did wrong?" Pinch asks as he licks his plastic spoon.

"Pinstripe?" I ask to make sure we're not talking about the pimply faced vendor behind the ice-cream counter.

Pinch nods.

"He underestimated you," I say.

"Worse. He overestimated himself. He's a big shot in whatever bullshit company employs him and he mistook that sliver of middle--management power for strength. He thought that because he gets away with being an asshole at work that he can be an asshole everywhere. The Red Swan isn't like that."

"What do you mean?"

"Krasnyi Lebed will come across as a gentle old soul who likes playing chess and inviting members of the symphony to play at his cocktail parties. He will be charming right up until the moment he sinks an ice pick into your neck. Power didn't make people fear him; fear made people give him power."

I swallow as the teenager delivers my ice cream. I notice that he's done an excellent job on the sprinkles. Nothing worse than a stingy sprinkler.

"If Pinstripe had crossed Lebed's path," Pinch continues, "ruptured testicles would be the least of his worries. The Red Swan does not bear insult or disrespect. He would have found out where the man worked and chained the doors closed before torching the entire building. Life means nothing to such a man."

"Then what does?" I ask.

"Nothing. He has no weakness because he has no conscience."

"So I can't appeal to his better nature?" I ask.

"He *has* no better nature. He is what he is, and what that is isn't pleasant."

"So you won't help me?" I ask.

"I just have," says Pinch.

EIGHT

Eddie is sitting in his usual spot at the rear of Mario's Deli when I enter. The door to the back room is slightly ajar and Eddie's talking to someone just out of sight in the shadows of its interior.

Before I reach the booth, the door closes.

"What's in there?" I ask.

"A room," Eddie answers.

"Yeah, but what kinda room? What goes on in there?"

Eddie shrugs. "It's just a room. You have too much imagination."

"Can't be a journalist without curiosity," I say.

"Can't be a runner without legs," he replies.

I recoil. "Jeez! Talk about ominous. It was just a question."

Eddie shrugs again. "See. Imagination. What did I say? You need legs to be a runner. A simple truth. But you, you take it another way. That's why I don't use imagination. People see a horse and they imagine it will run fast because it has a clever name. Is that logical? No. I get rich on imagination."

"So does your friend behind the door have a name?" I ask.

Eddie almost smiles, but it could be my imagination.

"What can I do for you, Dixie? Ready to make that big wager?"

"I have a question."

"Am I guru now? Does this look like mountaintop cave?"

"Not so much, but you're the closest to one I've got."

"I pity you then. Must not have many friends."

"Always room for one more."

"Not even your imagination is that vivid."

I smile. "You're a curious one, Eddie. You remind me of Yoda in that last Star Wars movie when he whips off his cloak to fight the bad guy and all of a sudden the old cripple is as spry as a teenager."

"If you're trying to confuse me, you succeeded. I do not know this Yoda. Now do you wish to place a bet?"

My smile fades. "I want to meet Krasnyi Lebed."

Eddie doesn't even blink. "So why come to me?"

"You know everyone."

"I know who's important to know, nobody else."

"And the Red Swan is important to know."

"True."

"So where can I find him?"

"It is not so difficult, but neither is it advisable."

"So I've been told."

"But still you persist."

"It's my job."

"Curiosity, they say, is lethal to felines."

I recoil again. "Jeez, Eddie. Enough with the doom and gloom. I just want to talk to the guy."

He releases a heavy sigh. "I can give you an address, but only on one condition."

"OK."

"Do *not* piss him off and do *not* mention my name."

"I can guarantee the latter, but I tend to have some trouble with the former."

"That you do."

He gives me the address anyway.

———

When the taxi arrives at the address, I release such a loud guffaw that it makes the olive-skinned driver with a boastful Seventies-era moustache jump in his beaded seat.

"Sorry," I say as I pay the fare. "Bumped my funny bone." When he doesn't smile, I point at the mat of wooden beads he's sitting on. "Are those comfortable or is it more like flagellation? I've always wondered."

He chooses to ignore me as he tucks the cash in his money pouch.

"I'll ask the next driver then," I say sarcastically. "Obviously, you've got places to be."

The taxi takes off as soon as I close the door, leaving me standing across the street from The Russian Tea House. Instead of harassing my contacts, I could have just looked in the phonebook under most likely place to find a Russian immigrant in need of an afternoon pick-me-up.

For a mob boss who likes to keep a low profile, Lebed certainly isn't hiding.

I cross the street and push through the front door.

The interior of the restaurant is first-class all the way: white linen, bone china, polished silver teapots and cutlery. The furnishings are antique dark woods against stark white walls with occasional touches of glittering robin's-egg blue, pomegranate red, and caterpillar yellow. The chandeliers are glistening crystal and gold, and I have a feeling the menu doesn't bother listing prices.

Dixie's Tips #14: *If you need to ask how much something costs, you can't afford it. To avoid embarrassment, head to the washroom and climb out the window.*

An expertly lit glass tower at the entrance holds four impressively bejeweled Fabergé eggs, although I doubt they're genuine; last I heard, an original is worth a minimum $10 million. And even if you can afford one, very few ever appear on the private market.

On the second shelf from the top is the largest egg at just over nine inches tall. It is light blue and held aloft by three golden lions. I'm intrigued by the domesticated elephant that crowns the fragile dome as the royal carriage upon its back reminds me of a scene from the third *Lord of the Rings* movie.

I lean forward to see if there are small figures of Frodo and Samwise running around.

"Table for one, madam?"

I turn to see a handsome maître d' dressed in an unusual stark white tuxedo with black bowtie and shiny black shoes. Despite the flattering cut of his suit, it's obvious he likes to hit the gym, and I wouldn't be surprised if I could scrub my delicates on his stomach on washday. (Which reminds me again of my need to do laundry.) His eyes are deep, dark, and chocolaty, but the perfect manicure, the closeness of his shave, and a posture that would make a ruler-wielding Catholic nun proud make me wonder if he's straight.

"I have an opening by the window," he offers.

The restaurant is completely deserted now that the lunchtime rush is over, so he can seat me anywhere, but the offer of the window is still gallant.

"I'm actually here to talk with Mr. Krasnyi Lebed." I dig in my pocket for a business card and hand it over.

When he glances up from the card, some of his charm has been replaced with a steely aggression that sucks in his cheeks to reveal sharp, angular bones beneath. A small tingle ignites in the base of my brain stem to tell me he's more than a head waiter.

"Do you have an appointment?" he asks.

"No, sorry. I wasn't sure how to contact him."

"Then I'm afraid—"

"I doubt you're the kind of man who gets afraid very often." I smile flirtatiously. "Especially not when it comes to women. Could you please show Mr. Lebed my card and see if we can set something up?"

My charms don't seem to have much effect.

"I'll wait here," I say. "And guard your eggs."

He glances toward the display cabinet, and out the corner of my eye I spot a tiny, almost imperceptible green light blink in the base of the topmost egg.

"You will wait here," he says.

I hold up three fingers with my pinkie trapped beneath my thumb. "Scout's honor."

The waiter scowls slightly before walking away, which makes me wonder if maybe they don't have Scouts in Russia and I've just given him the Moscow equivalent of our one-finger salute. That could be embarrassing.

When the waiter returns, his eyes and his mood are even darker.

"Mr. Lebed will see you," he says. "Hold out your arms."

I raise a quizzical eyebrow but comply, wondering if he wants us to play airplanes, which could actually be fun if we were both naked and the landing strip was a chocolate fountain.

The waiter moves in to pat me down. He's not shy about it either, but neither does he linger in the spots where I wouldn't mind some male attention.

"I usually get a man's name before I let him do this," I quip.

"And I usually get a woman drunk first," he says.

"That's disturbing," I say.

"It's meant to be."

Suddenly feeling more violated than aroused, I follow the no-longer-charming waiter through the deserted dining area to a private room in the rear, separated from the main restaurant by a pair of frosted glass doors.

The waiter knocks once before opening the door. He stands to the side as I enter, and I'm relieved when he closes the door behind me to return to his duties at the reception desk.

Inside, the room is half private-dining area and half office. Directly in front of me is a rectangular table sporting white linen, fine silver, and china place settings, but behind it is an elongated wood desk with two computers back-to-back that are being operated by what appear to be identical redheaded twins.

The twins are dressed smartly in black dress pants and white shirts with the sleeves rolled up to just below the elbow. Each has an identical pair of tortoise shell glasses. One is wearing a blue tie, the other green.

Neither of them flash me the top-secret Ginger Wink of Solidarity. Maybe they didn't get the memo.

I look to my left and see a mountain of a man with shoulders as wide as my legs are long. He's wearing a suit that must have been custom made in a tent shop, but it fits him well. The only flaw is a slight bulge beneath his left arm that tells me he's carrying a larger gun than the tailor intended. Then again, that could be on purpose, to give trouble pause before it starts.

The bodyguard is standing perfectly still, and even though he doesn't appear to be looking at me, I can feel his eyes probing every square inch of my intentions.

When I glance to my right, his shaved-head doppelganger is occupying a similar position. This mountain is darker and swarthier than his companion, but just as silent.

No one is paying any attention to me at all, which only makes me more nervous. I'm not a big fan of silence. I'm happy that Prince Marmalade the Purr Machine is in my life. Bubbles, the world's oldest goldfish, was never much for chatter, but then again I wasn't around for his final words. I can only guess they were cursing my name for leaving him alone with Prince when I went to work. Who knew kittens could jump so high?

A door connecting the private room to the kitchen opens and a razor-thin man enters in a tailored suit that matches the gray pallor of his skin. He smiles at me with teeth that have lost their luster, but none of their bite. His nose reminds me of a shark fin with a small bite taken out of one nostril. If he floated on his back in a pool, small children would scream.

"You are Dixie Flynn the reporter," he says with a Russian accent that has been refined and polished to remove the grit. "I am Krasnyi Lebed." He gestures toward the table. "Please, sit. I have ordered tea."

"Lovely," I say with a smile, and take a chair.

Lebed rests his elbows on the table and tucks his chin into his hands as he studies me. His wrists are so thin that half the links have been removed from the band of his platinum Rolex watch.

"I am surprised that our paths have not crossed before," he says, "but then, you do tend to spend more time in the gutter than the palace."

"I wouldn't necessarily say the gutter—"

"I would," he interrupts. "You may call it social conscience—I hear that is the buzz word people like to use these days—but really when you are writing about dumpster divers and injection clinics and former street walkers trying to go straight, the gutter is not below them, it is still all around."

"And what would you have me report on?" I ask, refusing to rise to the bait.

"What about political corruption?"

I blink. "Well, sure, if—"

"I could point you in the right directions."

My inner radar begins to beep with its *Lost in Space* mantra: *Danger, Dixie Flynn! Danger!*

"That's generous of you," I say cautiously. "I'm always open to reliable tips."

"Good." He unclasps his hands and stares at me through dull eyes that suck in light and make the whole room gloomier. "The tea is here."

Lebed sits up straight as the kitchen door swings open and a white-aproned server delivers a silver teapot along with a three-tiered tray of crackers, black caviar on ice, smoked fish, pickles, and sweet pastries. I begin to regret going for ice cream with Pinch, but then again I did only have time for one mini burger at the Pink Bicycle.

After the server departs, Lebed pours tea into two china cups and passes one over. He appears to take caution that our fingers don't accidentally touch.

"This is good Russian tea," he says. "Strong and hearty, like it should be."

I take a sip, control my shudder at the distinct smoky density of it, and smile. "Nice."

Lebed shakes his head. "Not nice. Russia does not have such a word. It is *khorosho*."

"*Khorosho*," I say, attempting to duplicate his intonation.

Lebed smiles for the first time and looks over at his two guards. "*Nyeplokho*."

The guards nod ever so slightly in agreement with whatever their boss has just said.

"Would you care for jam in your tea?" Lebed asks.

I shake my head while pretending that isn't one of the oddest things I've ever heard. "Black is fine."

He smiles again and wags a finger at me. "You may have some Russian in you. A Cold War infidelity, perhaps?"

I don't know how to answer, so I keep silent.

"Have you ever tried real caviar?" he asks.

"I'm not sure, but I do enjoy Greek taramosalata, which is—"

"Bah," he snarls. "Peasant food. That is cod roe, not caviar." He loads a small cracker with a spoonful of black fish eggs, places it on a china plate and slides it over to me. "Place the caviar on your tongue and savor it before swallowing."

I do as he says. The sturgeon roe is light and salty on my tongue, and as it warms within my mouth, each egg pops open like a champagne bubble. The taste is unusual and exquisite and thanks to the expansion of my palate at the hands of Dmitri, delicious. I scoop the remainder off the cracker with my tongue.

"This is amazing," I say.

"*Pryekrasno*! I'm pleased."

We eat and drink a bit more until I feel comfortable enough to say, "I want to ask you some questions about a missing person."

Lebed dabs his mouth with a cloth napkin and takes another sip of tea.

"A Russian?" he asks.

"No, but I think he worked for you."

"I am not missing anyone."

"This was twenty years ago."

"A lifetime."

"Maybe, but I have a feeling you possess a very good memory."

"Flattery," he says. "Only a woman can wield such a simple tool."

"I doubt that," I say with a smile, struggling to make it appear genuine. "I'm sure you charm the birds out of the trees."

"A man's skill. More complex."

I feel I've wandered onto thin ice, but nothing ventured… "His name is Joseph Brown."

Lebed glances over his left shoulder at the two redheaded twins, who haven't stopped pointing and clicking on their computers since I entered.

"That name is not familiar to me."

"Twenty years ago, you went to Joe Brown's apartment in the middle of the night and recruited him for a job. His family hasn't seen him since."

A shadow crosses Lebed's face to reveal the thug beneath the gentleman's veneer. "How do you come upon this information?"

"Does it matter? I'm not interested in whatever the job was. I only want to find out what happened to Mr. Brown."

"Why do you care?"

"So you do remember him?"

"No."

"Then why do you care why I care?"

Lebed flashes his teeth, but he's not smiling. "Because you are in my restaurant and I asked you a direct question."

"His family wants answers," I say. "So do I."

"The wife is dead and the daughter is a whore," he snaps angrily. "The past is the past."

I shudder and feel my own anger rise. "I'll take that as an admission then. So what happened to Joe?"

Lebed pushes away from the table and stands up. I notice his hands are clenching into fists and releasing, clenching and releasing. I'm suddenly, frighteningly aware that the only person who knows where I am at this moment is a small-time bookie with no reason to care what happens to me.

Lebed's voice becomes a hiss. "Do you know why Russian women get so fat?" Before I can answer, he continues. "Because they need to be able to absorb the blows of their husbands' fists. My mother was very fat, but my wife is fatter still. You are skinny; you would not survive."

I take this as my cue to stand up, too, and control the quiver in my voice. "I might surprise you."

"You would not."

"So I take it you're not going to help me find Joe Brown?"

"I told you before, I do not know who that is."

I swallow and look around the room. Neither of the guards has moved.

"Thanks for the caviar," I say.

Nobody attempts to stop me as I push through the door to the main dining room. It's still deserted of customers and I hold my breath all the way to the street.

NINE

Outside the tea house, I turn right and walk at a quick pace to put some distance between Lebed and myself.

Sweat trickles down my neck and an emotional tremor vibrates through my shoulders, but I'm determined not to cry. I tell myself the vicious little prick wouldn't be so frightening if he didn't have a muscle-bound golem standing in each corner, but I know I'm lying.

It's apparent, from reputation and demeanor, that Lebed has the granite heart of a killer and the itchy hands of a butcher who still needs to sink his fingers into bloody offal on occasion in order to feel alive.

I shake off the disturbing thoughts and look up from my feet too late to avoid running head first into an immobile iceberg wrapped in a beige trench coat and woolen cap.

"Sorry," I blurt as the man's hands grab me by the shoulders to steady my rebound.

"*Kto vas poslal*?" asks the man.

Confused, I look up to see a cruel visage with twisted lips. Before I can react, his grip tightens painfully and I'm jerked off my feet. My body is twisted in mid-air as though I weigh little more than an empty potato sack and I'm shoved hard against the red brick wall of a closed storefront.

Upon contact, the back of my head cracks the bricks, sending an explosion of pain to the front of my eyes, where stars are already dancing. I open my mouth to scream for help, but the man's a step ahead. He slaps one callused palm across my mouth, his fingernails black and smelling of rot, while his other hand pushes up on my breastbone to deflate my lungs and keep me glued to the wall. My feet dangle inches off the ground, making me feel as helpless as a child.

"*Kto vas poslal?*" he repeats.

Even if I understood Russian, which I don't, I can barely breathe behind his rough hand, never mind talk. Beneath the nail rot, his skin smells of shoe polish, leather, and engine oil, while his face has all the charm of a circuit gambler's pitbull. Livid burn scars crisscross his face; the worst is the left half of his upper lip, which is completely melted away. If he was a dog, he would be a shortsighted one who's had to survive by stealing steaks and chicken off lit neighborhood barbecues.

Instinctively, I plant one foot against the wall as an anchor and propel my other knee into his groin. It's a good plan, but I can't get enough force behind the strike to be taken seriously. The Russian grins through his ruined mouth, exposing the cigarette stubs of four teeth, laughing at my pathetic effort to break free.

Good, I tell myself in forced bravado, *I have him just where I need him.*

Pushing a vision of *Alien* into my head, I stab my teeth forward to latch onto the weathered flesh of his palm, scraping for purchase. At the same time, I swing my knee up again—but this time it has a passenger. The Russian releases a surprised grunt when my hitchhiking fingers grab hold of one withered testicle and clamp around it.

I don't waste time as my thumb seals the vise, and I use my remaining strength to viciously twist and squeeze. Blood squirts across my lips as he jerks his nipped hand away from my mouth.

A shriek of pain escapes his lips as his other hand slips from my chest and dives down to grab my wrist. In his panic to break my grip, he's forgotten about my other hand. Now that my feet are back on the ground, my free hand dives down, too, finds his testicular companion and applies eighty-plus pounds of pissed-off-female pressure.

The man roars and his face turns the color of borscht. As his knees start to tremble, I stab my face forward to make sure he's paying attention.

"If you understand English, tell your boss that I don't appreciate threats and I have friends who will appreciate it even less."

"*Sooka!*" he groans. "*Tebe pizd'ets.*"

"That doesn't sound nice," I say and twist my wrists to emphasize the point.

The man bellows and spits in my face. His own face is contorted by pain, but suddenly his hands release themselves from my wrists and find their way to my throat. I gasp as he finds the strength to squeeze my windpipe, his dirty nails digging into tender flesh.

Choking, I dig my own chewed-up nails into his balls and squeeze even harder, but it's as if I've taken him over the brink of pain so that he no longer feels it.

When my vision begins to blur from lack of oxygen, I make the decision to release my grip on his manhood and throw my hands skyward into the pressure points of his elbows. As I do, I also allow my body to become dead weight. The maneuver catches him off guard, and I break free of his chokehold to land on my ass.

He reaches for me again as I scramble on all fours to break away, but just as I'm getting to my feet, his fingers lock onto my suddenly-I-give-a-damn hair. Before he can slam my face into the wall and take all the fight out of me, I spin to face him and launch a palm strike to the base of his nose.

My hand connects instead with empty air as the large Russian unexpectedly tumbles sideways to collapse face first onto the sidewalk with a nasty crack of bone and squelch of flesh that makes me wince.

Gasping for air, my sight blurry from pain and exhaustion, I stare at the new arrival who has taken the Russian's place. This man is shorter than the Russian and skinnier, too. He's bald and unshaven and in his black-gloved hands is a short length of wood that still holds a splatter of blood and patch of hair from where it connected with my attacker's head.

I'm about to reach down for my boot knife when the man says, "You should get the hell out of here. It's not safe."

"You have a cellphone?" My voice is raspy from the bruised swelling on my throat where the Russian's thumbs had been trying to perform a tracheotomy on my windpipe.

When he shakes his head, his ears flap as if they have no cartilage.

"Where's the nearest pay phone then?" I ask.

The man jabs a bandaged thumb over his shoulder. "Two blocks. Same corner as Trusty's Pawn."

He says it as though everyone should know the local pawnshop.

"Do you know this guy?" I ask.

His ears flap again in the negative. "He was asking who sent you."

I touch my aching neck. "He could have asked nicer—and in English."

"Would it have made a difference?"

I snort. "No. None of his damn business."

I glance back down at the unmoving Russian. Inert, he resembles an old bear-skin rug that's molted and been tossed out with the trash.

"Thanks for the help," I say without looking up. "But you should make yourself scarce. This guy might have friends who are even uglier than he is."

When I don't receive a response, I lift my head to discover that I'm talking to myself. My Good Samaritan has vanished.

———

I reach the pay phone without further assault and call for a taxi. I tell Mo that I'm outside Trusty's Pawn.

"You short of cash?" Mo asks. "I've heard that Russian Tea House can be expensive."

I'm always a little surprised that Mo likes to keep an eye on my movements, and I suppose if I had any kind of a private life it might bother me. But as it stands, I'm grateful for his concern.

"I brought in a cow," I say, "but all Trusty could give me was a handful of magic beans."

Mo laughs and hacks up half a lung. "If you plant 'em, let me know. We'll go up the beanstalk together. You can distract the giant and I'll grab the golden goose."

"Why do I always get the crappy jobs?"

"You've got more elastic in you. Last time I tried to bounce, I threw my back out."

I chuckle through my sore throat. "Yeah, and what was her name?"

"Cab's on its way, Dix. Talk soon."

Mo hangs up before I can press him further. Obviously, I struck a nerve.

When the cab arrives, I gratefully slide into the back seat. An overwhelming desire washes over me to curl into the fetal position and pull a blanket over my head. Heck, I may even suck my thumb.

My neck and throat are throbbing to emphasize each pressure point of the Russian's indelicate fingers; my shoulders and breastbone ache; my scalp stings from where he yanked my hair; and my wrists feel like they've been crushed between two boulders.

Funny—but not in a ha-ha way—that I've managed to ignore the extent of my injuries until I finally feel safe.

"You heading back to the *NOW* offices?" asks the driver.

I think about it but slowly shake off the suggestion.

"Drop me at home, will you?" I say. "I could use a warm bath and a cuddle."

The driver raises an eyebrow in his rearview.

"Not from you," I add quickly. "I have a prince waiting at home."

The driver chuckles and weaves his way through traffic.

TEN

CLIMBING OUT OF THE cab, I wave to King William sitting regally in the street-level front window of Mrs. Pennell's apartment. He rewards me with a rare wink before I climb the short flight of stairs to the small lobby.

Inside, I optimistically check my mailbox for any secret Valentines that may have been stuck in the post office sorting room for the last four months or so but come up empty—less than empty, if you add in the bills.

The smell of Mr. French's pipe tobacco (whiskey, cherry, and chocolate Cavendish) lingers in the air, and the familiar comfort of it brings an unexpected tear to my eye. The Russian has shaken me up more than I care to admit.

I climb the stairs to the second floor, feeling every jar and bump in my muscles. A yellow note is stuck to the door of my apartment. It's in Mrs. Pennell's impeccable handwriting, and reads simply: *Please come down and see me when you get in.*

I leave the note where it is, so I won't forget, as Mrs. Pennell has become an important part of my handmade family. But just at this moment, I'm not in the mood for tea and gossip and anecdotes about King William's adorable behavior.

I ease into the apartment and shrug off my jacket as Prince Marmalade appears at the door to my bedroom. He yawns and stretches to make sure I know that I've interrupted his nap before padding over to wind his way around my feet, his loud purr practically vibrating the furniture in the room.

Scooping him up in my arms, I press my forehead into his fluffy face. His purr rumbles even louder as he places a paw on either side of my face and proceeds to lick my nose.

I give a half-laugh, half-exhale.

"You realize that's not soothing, don't you?" I ask. "You're not a dog and your tongue is a pumice stone."

Prince ignores me and licks off another layer of skin.

Laughing, I carry him into the bathroom, place him on the floor, and turn on the taps to fill the tub.

Instantly, Prince leaps onto the side of the tub and strolls over to examine the gushing spout. As I undress and try not to wince, he looks over as if to ask what madness has overcome me that I would possibly want to immerse myself in water.

I drop in a purple and yellow bath bomb that I found in a going-out-of-business sale from a store I had never visited before. Its magic ingredients promise to take away stress and calm a racing mind, which makes me wonder if I'm supposed to bathe in it or smoke it.

Once the tub is full, I step in and slide down until the warm water laps at my chin. Blood pulses to my wounds, alerting me that nothing is broken or cut, just bruised and sore.

Everyone was right: it would have been smarter to stay off the Red Swan's radar. But if it was my father who had gone missing, I would desperately want to know what happened. And I would want someone like me looking into it, too; someone who was too pig-headed and stubborn to know when she was out of her depth.

I had already made progress. Lebed slipped when he admitted his knowledge of Brown's family, and I'm sure he figured that all it would take to get me off his back was to deliver a bit of a scare.

And though I admit it wasn't pleasant and my body aches from fighting back, I don't scare that easy.

In fact, all Lebed has done is piss me off and make me even more determined to get to the truth.

There's a Father's Day story in there that replaces the usual cuteness factor with heartbreak, pain, and loss—possibly even murder. My publisher may not be thrilled, but hopefully, in the end, neither will Lebed. Physically, I may not be intimidating, but with a pen in my hand, I can make the mighty and powerful quake.

Now I just have to make sure that I grow an extra pair of eyes in the back of my head before returning to work.

Prince's tongue darts out and licks some bubbles off my bare knee. I open one eye to see him making a face as he scrapes the soapy foam off his tongue with his paw.

When he notices me laughing, he immediately spins around, throws his tail high in the air, and jumps from the tub's edge to exit the room in disgust.

I close my eye again and sink under the bubbles to the warm embrace below.

———

There's a quiet knock before I hear my apartment door opening and a voice call out, "Hey, Dix, you home?"

"In the bath."

"You alone?"

I laugh. "Completely."

The bathroom door opens wider and Kristy pops her head in.

"You okay?" she asks. "You realize you're taking a bath at three in the afternoon."

I sit up a little straighter. "Fine," I say. "Just needed a stress break."

Kristy glides over to the toilet, drops the lid, and sits. She's wearing baggy sweatpants and an oversized T-shirt with a neck hole that was designed for a claustrophobic linebacker. If I wore the same outfit, I would look like a shipwrecked hobo, but Kristy manages to pull off the whole *Flashdance,* Jennifer Beals, cute-and-sexy thing. Life, truly, isn't fair.

Kristy wrinkles her nose and sighs, which tells me that Sam has been at work all day and she's tired of being alone.

"Busy day?" I ask.

"No, just a bit dull. Computer work mostly."

"What are you researching?"

She wrinkles her nose in the opposite direction. "Bacon."

"That's an odd one. Which author wants that?"

Kristy is a freelance research assistant for fiction writers who want to get the facts straight but can't afford the time away from meeting deadlines. She researches everything from chicken farms and chocolate factories to handguns, sex toys, and race cars. She might seem a bit of a ditz, but when you consider her crazy research skills and insatiable curiosity, she's more like the absent-minded professor. If the absent-minded professor were a busty, blond lesbian.

"You know that's confidential, Dix."

"Bacon sounds like Stephen King or Stephen Hunter, maybe Karen Slaughter or even Matt Hilton. What does he or she want to know about bacon?"

Kristy rolls her eyes, knowing that I'm throwing out names to see if any of them cause a reaction. "Unusual things that are made from or contain bacon."

"Are there a lot?"

"You'd be surprised. I've already found maple bacon doughnuts, bacon salt, bacon toffee brittle, bacon lip balm, bacon chewing gum, bacon beer, bacon sex lube—even a bacon coffin. I've ordered samples of most of them, except the coffin, so I can describe the taste."

"Bacon beer sounds disgusting, but bacon brittle I could go for."

Kristy smiles. "You can help sample. The beer is from Portland and comes in a gorgeously tacky bright pink bottle."

"Wonder if vegetarians can drink it?"

Kristy giggles. "I'll make a note. My author will like that."

The water is beginning to turn cold, so I ask Kristy to hand me a towel. When I reach for it, she notices the deep welts, already an ugly shade of moldy mustard with hints of cabbage and beet, on my wrists.

"Dix!" She gasps. "Is some man being rough with you?"

"It's not what you think," I say quickly.

"Sam will kick his ass. Who is it?"

"It's nobody."

"We'll bury the sucker," Kristy continues, her face livid. "The Dixie Chicks ain't got nothing on us. If Earl's gotta die, we ain't gonna pussyfoot around."

"It's not a boyfriend," I interrupt, getting out of the tub with the towel wrapped around me. "It was more of a mugging."

"You were mugged?"

"Yeah, kinda."

"Did you call the police?"

"No."

"Not even Frank?"

"No."

"Why not?"

I shrug. "Well, the guy kinda ended up getting the worst of it. When I left, he was unconscious on the sidewalk."

Kristy's jaw drops before she breaks into a smile and holds up her hand for a high five. I grip my towel with one hand and high-five her with the other.

"That's the way to do it." She beams. "Wait till I tell Sam. She'll be so proud. Girl power!"

"Yeah," I say, remembering the Russian's hands around my throat. "Awesome."

ELEVEN

I SLIP INTO CLEAN underwear, fresh jeans, and a retro-inspired T-shirt from a Clash concert I was too young to attend but that makes me feel like I was there in spirit—and it looks cool.

When I emerge from the bedroom, Kristy uses a glass of white wine from a bottle she found in my fridge to lure me over to the couch, where Prince is already luxuriating in a personalized tummy rub and ear scratch.

"So tell me more about the mugging," she says. "Why were you targeted?"

I start at the beginning with the classified ad and end with the Good Samaritan translating what the Russian was after.

"That's odd," says Kristy. "What would it matter who sent you? This gangsta boss already admits he knew the missing man's family, even though he's lying to you about not knowing the guy. And after all this time, nobody but the family is really gonna care what happened to him, right?"

I nod. "True."

"It's also strange that he called the hairdresser a whore, don't you think? That sounds kinda angry, like personal angry."

I think about it. "Bailey admits her past was rough. She didn't go into details, but with her dad out of the picture—"

"And this creep asking to buy her," Kristy injects.

Goosebumps rise on my arms. "Exactly."

"Have you told the hairdresser what happened?" Kristy asks.

"I wanted to wait until I had something she doesn't already know."

"But you should warn her."

"Warn her?"

"Yeah." Kristy leans forward, her eyes wide. "If this Russian mob boss is so paranoid about you snooping around that he sent a thug to threaten you, what's he gonna do to the people he thinks actually *did* send you?"

The blood drains from my face. "Oh shit!"

"Come on," Kristy says, getting to her feet. "My car's downstairs. Grab your coat."

———

Scissors & Sizzle is still open for business when Kristy pulls to the curb and I hop out. Kristy doesn't want anyone to see her in less than pristine condition, so she tells me she'll keep the car running, as though I'm about to rob a bank and will need a quick getaway.

When I burst through the salon doors, the receptionist with the bruised eyes takes one look at me and says, "Bailey couldn't help, huh? Shame."

"Is she here?" I ask urgently.

"Bails?"

"Yes!" I snap.

"Whoa. Chill." She holds up both hands in a calming motion. "We can't work miracles, you know? Sometimes you just have to let it grow out."

I step forward and flash my angry face. "I'm not here about the goddamn hair. Is Bailey Brown here?"

The receptionist gulps. "She's in back."

"Can you get her for me?"

"Yeah, yeah, sure."

She lifts the phone and talks into the mouthpiece. When she hangs up, she looks sheepish. "Bails isn't there, but she's probably just in the alley having a sneaky smoke."

I point to the rear of the shop. "You have a back door?"

"Yeah, but we don't allow customers—"

I don't bother to let her finish before I'm running through the salon. When I burst through the rear exit, I'm not sure what I'll find, but I prepare for the worst.

Fortunately, my imagination is more active than reality.

"Hey, Dixie," Bailey says as she exhales a lungful of smoke from a sweetly scented cigarette. "Cloves and a little sprinkling of pot. Helps the anxiety, you know?"

"Has anyone been to see you?" I ask.

Her eyes narrow. "Just customers, why?"

I tell her about the Russian with the rotten nails.

She takes another drag on the cigarette and holds it in her lungs for a long time. I watch the tremor in her fingers and think she should've gone with less cloves and more weed.

"I didn't think he knew I was back," she says.

"Back?"

"I've been living in Boston for the last ten years, but I missed home, you know?" She takes a deep breath. "I shouldn't have come back."

"What about your sister?" I ask. "Did she leave, too?"

Bailey's eyes ripple with moisture as she shakes her head. "Roxanne stayed here. I tried to take her with me, but ..." Her voice fades.

I think back to what Lebed said. He only actually mentioned one daughter; one whore.

"Do you know where I can find her?" I ask.

A sharp pain creases Bailey's face as she lifts the medicinal cigarette to her lips and takes a deep pull. Her hands are shaking so badly that ash drops from its tip until it's little more than a yellowed nib.

"I asked around when I first got back, heard she's working a low-rent hotel on the eastside. But I haven't had the courage to find her. She was such a pretty girl, but that life quickly goes from five-star to the sewer. I didn't know if my heart could take it."

"Do you know which hotel?"

"The Sandford. You know it?"

I do. By reputation. A short cab ride from the transport docks and popular with the international cadre of merchant seamen whose English vocabulary consists of two words: *pussy* and *whiskey*. It's the kind of place where if the doorman doesn't find any weapons on you, he hands you one.

"I'll find her," I say. "But you be careful. Don't go anywhere alone."

Bailey shrugs and wraps her arms across her bosom in a protective hug. "Nothing much left that Lebed can do to me."

I reach out and take hold of her trembling hand. "Then do it for me. I don't want it on my conscience if you get hurt."

Bailey squeezes my hand and smiles. "That's actually one of the nicest things I've heard in awhile."

I squeeze back. "I'll take that as a promise."

Bailey smiles and lifts the cigarette stub to her lips again, but there's nothing left to puff. "This needed more pot," she says.

I leave her with a wink as I turn around and head back through the salon to Kristy's waiting car.

TWELVE

I MAKE KRISTY PULL over at the first pay phone we see, and I hop out to make a quick call.

Pinch doesn't answer, but I leave a brief message on his machine just to let him know where I'm heading in case he's in the neighborhood and feels like joining me for a drink in the unfriendliest hotel bar in town.

Admittedly, it won't be the most appealing offer he's ever received, but I knew every patron's comprehension of English would be instantly forgotten if I invited Frank along instead. Frank is so much a cop that even a blind drunk can tell when he walks in a room.

As we near the hotel, Kristy studies both sides of the street and says, "Lock your door."

"We're in a convertible," I say. "A locked door isn't going to help. If someone—"

"Stop talking, Dix!" Kristy yells.

"Sorry," I say sheepishly.

Curious eyes follow us as we travel the last two blocks; shadowy faces appearing from doorways and behind the windows of last-stop bachelor apartments with a bird's-eye view of the liquor stores, porno vendors, pawnshops, and moneylenders. Kristy's electric-yellow VW Bug is a spaceship here—an alien visitor from a different world.

Every other vehicle is some shade of gray, as if this part of the city can only be seen in black and white. Even the people on the street are dressed in monochrome: black hoodies, black jeans, black boots. It reminds me of a Frank Miller comic book where the only color comes as the result of violence—an angry slash of red.

"You should head home after you drop me off," I say.

Kristy glances over, her eyes wide with panic.

"I'll be fine," I add. "I can blend in; you can't."

"If you're sure," Kristy says bravely.

I nod. "The Bug belongs in a happier place."

Kristy smiles and pats the dashboard as if stroking a pet. "She does prefer the sunny side of the street."

Kristy pulls over outside the Sandford Hotel. "Let me know when you're safely back home," she says.

I put on a brave smile and open the door.

———

Even though I know it's likely a waste of time, I start at the reception desk. The lobby smells of cigarettes, beer, and something fouler that was mopped up using a lot of industrial bleach; but whoever did the job missed a few spots, rubbed it into the carpet with the toe of their shoe, and hoped nobody noticed.

The disturbing part is that the hotel's usual clientele likely wouldn't.

The clerk behind the reception desk could be anywhere from thirty to sixty; his eyes say the latter, but the lack of wrinkles on his sallow face beg to differ. He's tall and scarecrow lean with an unflattering haircut that reminds me of a monk, as though someone stuck a bowl on his head and simply cut off whatever dangled below the rim.

He also holds his head at a 45-degree angle with his left ear practically stitched to his shoulder, which makes meeting his gaze unnervingly difficult.

"I'm looking for a girl," I say. "Twenty years old, possibly blond, called Roxanne."

"She black, chink, or vanilla?" the man asks. A nametag on his shirt reads *Hello, my name is Warrick* just in case some customer gives a damn, which I'm guessing most don't.

"Caucasian," I say.

"Cock Asian, that's a new one. You mean chink she-male?"

He grins. I don't.

"She's white," I say.

"And who's asking?"

"I am."

Warrick grins again, the upper half of his mouth opening wider than the lower half to form a toothy comma.

"And who are you?"

"A friend of her sister."

"I like sisters," he says.

"Yeah, who doesn't?" I snap impatiently. "Do you know her or not?"

Warrick moves his head from side to side, but because of the angle of his neck, I can't tell if he means it be a shake or a nod.

"What room is she in?" I press.

Warrick shrugs. "I take the money and hand out keys. I don't peep."

Which tells me straight away that he's a peeper.

"So you have cameras in the rooms."

He looks horrified. "No!"

Which means yes. I lift my chin to indicate the door behind him. "You keep the monitors and video equipment in there?"

"NO!"

"Good to know. Thanks."

He begins to panic. "I didn't tell you anything."

I smile cruelly. "That's exactly what I'll tell Red Swan when I'm talking to him."

If it is possible for his face to become any paler, it does. "I-I-I didn't say anything," he insists.

"Not a thing," I agree, but my eyes say different and he's reading my eyes.

He looks away and begins chewing his fingernails. It's not a new habit. "What do you want?"

"Just one girl. You'll hardly even miss her. Is she here?"

His eyes flash around the lobby as if he's expecting an army of ninjas to drop from the ceiling or spring from hidden cavities in the walls. I'm guessing he's been watching too much *Scooby-Doo*.

"Which room?" I ask.

He glances down at a small computer monitor on his desk, which tells me he's not as thick as he's letting on.

"She's in the bar."

"Thanks."

I turn to head for the connecting doors to the bar but stop and turn back before I push through.

"Is she still blond?" I ask, since the only photograph I've seen of her was when she was around five years old.

"Pink," he says. "This week she's pink."

———

The bar is noisy and filled with enough testosterone to make me worry I'm about to sprout hair on my chest and start scratching my balls.

A few heads turn my way, and I suddenly feel thankful that my breasts are discreet and I decided to wear a bra today. I just hope the manly pheromone stench doesn't make my nipples pop out to say hello, because I have a feeling that would be like taking a match to a tinderbox doused in white gas.

I try to remember how it is that Sam can enter a room and make everyone instantly aware that she's a butch lesbian who won't put up with any homophobic shit. But when you love someone as a sister, it's difficult to see her through anyone else's eyes.

Instead I channel Clint Eastwood with hard cowboy eyes and an unfriendly scowl. Pity I don't have a cigarillo and a poncho to complete the look.

I make my way to the bar, since standing still is attracting too much attention. I ignore the first hand that lands on my ass; the second is more difficult, as it's eager to explore and I'm forced to quicken my pace; the third makes a pinching move, catching a piece of flesh between finger and thumb.

I spin, grab the offending finger, and force it in a direction it was never designed to go. The jarring snap of bone is like a gunshot that silences the room. The finger's owner—a gristly longshoreman with bad teeth and overgrown mutton-chop sideburns—screams in agony before jabbering in a long string of Polish that, even to untrained ears, has the meaty weight of profanity.

None of the men at his table move an inch as Mutton Chop fixes murderous red-rimmed eyes on me and I wait to see if he wants to take it further.

Unfortunately, he does, and it's too late for me to explain that I hadn't actually planned to break the offending digit; I was aiming for a dislocation or serious sprain, but I'm still learning. However, as Pinch has been teaching me: If you have to put a man down, make sure he doesn't want to get up again.

I hear Mutton Chop's chair scrape backward as he prepares to rise, but I don't want him to get to his feet and make this a fairer fight. As his knees begin to straighten and he's in that awkward, top-heavy and unbalanced state between sitting and standing, I blindside him with a straight-armed strike containing all the strength of my shoulders and back.

This time I connect with the back of his skull, the heel of my hand sliding into the nerve cluster where bone meets neck; my fingers dig through greasy hair to latch onto his scalp. In the same instant, I yank his supporting arm to one side and lift off my feet to focus all my weight behind the head slam.

Mutton Chop doesn't even have time to scream again before his remaining support buckles and his face crunches into the table with enough force to crack the wood. His companions push away from the table in the nick of time to save their beers and avoid most of the blood spray.

I hold my breath, tense and more than a little afraid, but none of them rise in defense of their friend as he turns his head to the side to blow blood bubbles through his nose.

No other errant hand makes an attempt to molest me when I continue to the bar and order a draft beer and shot of Jack Daniel's.

I keep my back to the crowd as I down the Tennessee whiskey in one gulp so that only the bartender witnesses the tremor in my hand. He refills the shot glass without being asked.

"On the house," he says. "Gerek's an asshole."

"Think his friends will let me walk out of here?" I ask.

The bartender shrugs. "I wouldn't go to the john alone if I were you. Too much privacy is never healthy."

I down the second shot and take a sip of beer. I have to stop myself from spitting the beer back out; it's cheap and wet, but that's the only good thing I can say about it.

I leave the glass on the bar and surreptitiously scan the room. I spot a young girl with pink hair standing near the jukebox. A slobbering ox has his hand up her short skirt while an imposing bouncer stands nearby awaiting word that an exchange of money is needed to go any further.

Abandoning the liquid insult to craft brewers everywhere, I move around the edge of the room until I'm beside the jukebox with the drunken ox between the helium-filled bouncer and myself.

"Roxanne?" I ask.

The pink-haired girl looks over at me, and I instantly see the family resemblance to Bailey. Despite being five years younger, her face wears similar scars. If I had to say who looked older, Roxanne would win hands down.

"Can we go somewhere?" I ask.

The ox's hand is still moving under her skirt, but his eyes are so glazed he doesn't appear to be in the same room.

"Don't usually get that request from girls," she says. "Not in this dump at least. Used to when I worked the classy joints."

"We need to talk."

"Oh shit! What are you, a social worker? Cop?"

"Neither. I'm a friend of your sister's."

"Bullshit. She's gone."

"She's back in San Francisco. She wants to see you."

Roxanne snorts. "Get lost. I don't have a sister anymore."

"She misses you," I press.

"Now I know you're lying. Bailey can't miss anyone; you need to have a heart first."

"Maybe she's changed?"

"Yeah, and maybe ducks will shit rainbows."

I smile at the crude expression. "That would be something to see, wouldn't it?"

Roxanne surprises me by smiling back, briefly exposing the young girl within.

"You're an odd one, but I like how you handled Gerek back there. None of these Polish freaks can get their rocks off unless it's anal and you're in pain. What the fuck is up with that?"

I shrug and try to make sure I'm not cringing.

"Can we get out of here?" I ask.

"I'm working."

"I think you might be in danger."

"What? Why?"

I tell her about my meeting with the Red Swan and her face glows livid.

"You stupid bitch! Why would you go looking into that?"

"Don't you want to know what happened to your father?"

"No! I don't even remember him, and that's the way I like it."

I notice that people are starting to pay attention to us, and that's never a good thing.

"Look at your life, Roxanne. Is this really what you want?"

"Fuck you!" she explodes. "You don't know me or what I want."

"I can help," I push. "I know some great people who can get you back on your feet."

"Yeah, yeah, and off my back. I've heard the sermons before, sister."

"Damnit. Listen to me: you're in danger here."

"No." Roxanne shakes her head. "The only one in danger here is you."

I look beyond the ox and see the bouncer moving in toward us. I glance over my shoulder and see a second bouncer coming from behind the bar.

"Please, Roxanne." I hold out my hand. "Just come with me. Give me a day. We'll see your sister."

Roxanne's eyes are hard and dry as millstone. "You really think I have that choice?" she says. "Don't be so fucking naive."

The first bouncer pushes past the ox, telling him to back off or take it upstairs, and advances on me.

All I have is my boot knife, Lily, but I know it won't do me any good. A smart fighter knows when a brawl is lost before it's even begun.

I raise my hands to show they're empty and that I'm willing to go peacefully.

THIRTEEN

"The exit is back that way," I say as the two bouncers lead me in the opposite direction. "My friend is waiting for me outside. She'll probably be getting worried. Wouldn't want her calling the cops simply because you have a lousy sense of direction, would you?"

"There's nobody waiting," the first bouncer says. "Think we don't have eyes on the street?"

I try a different tactic: "So are you two lovers?" I ask.

"Fuck you, bitch!"

"Kinda quick to anger there," I press. "Strike a nerve? One-way love affair maybe? He's straight, you're—"

I yelp as my arm is twisted behind my back and the bouncer's thumb presses into the existing bruise on my wrist.

"You don't have to hide your feelings with me, boys," I groan. "I'm a live-and-let-live kinda gal."

"Shut your mouth," the bouncer snaps.

At the end of a short, dilapidated hallway, we reach the rear of the hotel and a room labeled *Storage*. The first bouncer opens the door and flicks on the overhead light; the second one shoves me through the doorway.

The room is mostly old boxes, forgotten luggage, stained mattresses, and dusty stacks of wooden chairs. I'm just happy that it's not a torture chamber, complete with dentist chair and crazy Nazi with a drill à la *Marathon Man*, which I watched on Netflix last week.

"This your secret love nest?" I sniff the air. "Smells like it."

The lead bouncer shakes his massive head and I can see his muscles tense with rage. "The boss'll want me to hurt you. I look forward to it."

"Deny, deny, deny," I fire back bravely. "It'll eat you up inside."

The bouncer makes a move to rush me, but his partner holds him back, cluing me into the fact that they're not allowed to do anything until the boss shows.

They both retreat into the hall before slamming the door closed, leaving me alone inside the windowless room.

I allow a small smile to break through my secret terror, knowing that if I hadn't made them so angry, they might've engaged their brains and searched me. As it is, they couldn't wait to get out of earshot. Typical.

I touch the pearl-handled switchblade in my boot to reassure myself it's still there before studying the room in more detail. The wooden chairs are old and uncomfortable, built in an age when craftsmen wanted them to last.

I lift one off the stack, lay it on its side, and kick at a point where one of the legs meets the seat. The ancient glue crumbles into powder, and two more kicks reward me with a skull-crushing club of solid oak.

Next I check the abandoned luggage, cutting through any locked straps with my knife. Unfortunately, I don't find anything of interest except for an antique hand mirror in a solid silver frame. If I was up against a vain werewolf it could be a lifesaver, but my enemies appear to be human, if just barely.

With my club and knife at the ready, I move to the door and study the hinges. All three hinges are on my side. I slip the blade under the bottom hinge pin and wiggle it up and down. The pin creaks and lifts about an eighth of an inch before stopping. I flip the blade over so that its thicker, stronger edge is now resting under the head of the pin and ease it up with both hands.

It takes some muscle and sweat, but eventually the pin pulls completely free.

I move to the middle pin.

———

When the handle turns and the door starts to open, I leverage the opposite side with my wooden club to knock it off its hinges. The heavy door falls into the room, yanking my captor with it and eliciting a startled grunt.

Standing on a chair beside the now-open doorway, I capitalize on the confusion by swinging my club toward where I expect the first bouncer's head to be, but I misjudge. The club smashes into the doorjamb instead. Wood splinters and the vibrations send a shockwave of pain down my arm, causing me to drop the club.

I leap off the chair and instantly make a dash for freedom down the hallway, my knife ready to slash anyone who gets between the exit and me. But as I run, I see the two bouncers slumped on the floor.

And just as I realize that they're both unconscious, I hear my name being called by a familiar voice.

"Dixie! Wait up."

I skid to a halt and turn to see Pinch brushing wood splinters out of his hair. He grins as he says, "You just about knocked my head off."

I smile in response, realizing that the only reason my plan didn't work was that I was expecting a taller man.

"So I take it we're not getting that beer?" he says as he closes the gap between us.

"Beer's lousy here anyway. I couldn't even finish mine."

"Good to know," he says. "They don't do karaoke either, and jam night is sea shanties only. Pitiful."

I can't help myself as I rush forward and wrap him in a hug, fighting not to collapse onto my knees in a fit of sobbing. Pinch squeezes me back until I feel my strength and resolve returning.

When I'm ready, I let him go and wipe my eyes.

"How did you find me?" I ask.

"You left a message, remember? And when I found myself being stood up, I asked the bartender if he'd seen you. Man was nice enough to point the way."

I glance down at the unconscious bouncers.

"And these two?"

Pinch shrugs. "Nap time."

"I shouldn't have called," I say. "But I'm so glad you're here."

"Let's find a nicer bar. You can buy me a drink to say thanks."

"I can't leave yet."

"Oh? It would seem like the prudent thing to do."

"I know, but I need to take someone with me."

"Who?"

"A young girl with pink hair."

"I didn't spot her in the bar."

"Then she's in a room."

"No shortage of those."

"The guy at reception will know which one."

Pinch raises an eyebrow. "Will he tell you?"

"I can be very persuasive."

Pinch grins again and gestures for me to lead the way.

———

Unfortunately, the only route I know to get to the lobby is back through the bar.

"This could get ugly," I tell Pinch.

"I've been in there." He smirks. "It already is."

Despite everything that's happened, I burst out laughing just as I push open the door.

The roomful of men turn to stare, but when they see that it's me, they all swivel back around and instantly find the interior of their beer mugs fascinating. All, that is, except one.

Pinch squeezes my shoulder and whispers, "You leave a lasting impression."

The one exception is a Polish dockworker with a swollen and dis-colored finger, flattened nose, and blood-encrusted muttonchops.

Pinch winks at the dockworker as we move past, and while scarlet blooms in every burst blood vessel in his cheeks and nose, Gerek makes no attempt to stop us.

In the lobby, Warrick holds up his hands and mutters, "I didn't do, do— I d-d-don't know nothing."

"What room is she in?" I ask.

"Uh, uh, uh."

"I don't have time." I jab my thumb in Pinch's direction. "Tell me now or my friend will remove your fucking spleen through your anus."

Warrick gulps and blurts, "Twenty-two, on the second floor."

I nod. "Is Lebed here yet?"

Warrick gulps again and moves his head in the same useless gesture that doesn't answer my question. I head for the stairs, deciding and/or hoping that he means no.

———

"I like the spleen via anus threat," says Pinch as we climb the stairs to the second floor. "Mind if I borrow that sometime?"

"Be my guest."

He chuckles. "You surprise me, Dixie."

"In what way?"

"This," he says. "You're normally so passive, but I just saw you leave a room full of hard men quaking in their salty boots. I like it. You'd make a good contractor."

"Uh, I'll take that as a compliment."

"You should."

On the second landing, I open the door and peer down the hall. There are no bouncers standing guard outside any of the rooms, which is likely because of the video surveillance inside. If anyone starts trouble, whoever monitors the cameras will sound the alarm.

We head down the hall to Room 22. Outside, I stop and tell Pinch about the cameras.

"You shouldn't be seen," I tell him. "No point you getting on Lebed's radar, too."

Pinch's grin practically breaks his face in half. "Curiouser and curiouser, Alice."

I wrinkle my brow in confusion, but don't want to waste time asking exactly what he means. Instead, I try the handle. The door is unlocked.

Inside, Roxanne is on all fours on the bed while the drunken ox is mounting her from behind. The man still doesn't quite appear to know where he is, as his eyes roll around his skull and ribbons of drool drip from the corners of his mouth. He's operating on autopilot, pure primal instinct. He also has the hairiest ass I've ever seen outside of a zoo.

"Get dressed," I tell Roxanne. "We're leaving."

She rolls her eyes at me like a teenager caught kissing a boy in her bedroom. "I told you, I'm working."

"Red Swan is on his way and he's not happy."

Roxanne pales but tries not to let her fear show. The ox, oblivious to anyone else in the room, continues to thrust into her in a rhythm that would confuse Ringo Starr.

"This isn't open for debate," I say, cutting off any argument. "We're leaving. Now."

She stabs a thumb over her shoulder. "And what do I do about him?"

The ox shows no sign of finishing anytime soon. I turn to Pinch, who's standing in the hallway.

"Any advice?" I ask.

He reaches into his pocket and tosses over a scuffed leather black-jack. I catch it and instantly feel the weight of a lead core surrounded by dense sand. Pinch points to a soft spot just behind his ear, indicating that I should swing the weapon with everything I have.

I move behind the ox, careful to avoid the sweaty slap of hairy buttocks. Then I wind up my pitching arm and let loose with the sap. It lands with a heavy thud that stops the ox's eyeballs from rolling in all directions. In a brief respite of clarity, he turns his head. His pupils center and his lips curl into an angry grimace before his eyes roll skyward and his body begins to fall.

I quickly shove him from the side so that he lands on the bed beside Roxanne rather than crushing her beneath him.

"You have ten seconds," I tell her. "Move."

This time she doesn't argue.

FOURTEEN

PINCH DROPS ROXANNE AND me in front of my building after co-ercing a promise that I'll call if I need assistance.

"It's been fun," he says. "I didn't realize how much I missed the rush."

"Personally," I say, "you can keep it. Forget rush, I'd rather lie on a sandy beach with a handsome mute waiter bringing me Long Island ice teas and touching up my sunscreen with strong but amazingly soft hands."

Pinch grins. "You have such specific fantasies."

"Details are important."

"Like I said, you'd make a good contractor."

"I'll keep it in mind."

After Pinch drives away, I take hold of Roxanne's arm and lead her up the stairs to my apartment. Inside, she takes one look around and asks if she can take a bath.

I point the way while slipping off my jacket and heading for the kitchen phone. Before reaching it, however, I'm distracted by the unfinished glasses of wine still standing on my coffee table. I make a detour to pour both half-sipped glasses into one and carry the full glass to the bathroom. The door is ajar, but I knock softly anyway.

"Come in," says Roxanne. "It's your house."

I enter to find her naked again, leaning over the sink and scrubbing the makeup off her face. Cigarette burns and bruises, both old and new, run the length of her body from shoulders to ankles amidst a confection of tattoos that I didn't have time to examine in the hotel room.

Two of the circular burns form the eyes of a lifeless baby curled above her right hip, while the largest tattoo is a length of barbed wire that wraps around her spine. The artist has created the illusion that the wire cuts into and under her skin on one side of the spine before appearing on the other, continuing in a series of intertwining loops. Growing from the wire in three random spots are delicate red poppies.

On the back of her left calf, the tattoo is of a partially open zipper. Peeking through the zipper's gap is the green eye of a black cat. Her right calf is bare, but her right buttock is inked with a small rectangular sticker that reads: *Your ad goes here.*

"Is that for me?" Roxanne asks.

My gaze lifts from her body to her freshly scrubbed face, and as I hand over the wine I can't believe how old she still looks for being barely twenty. The spider web wrinkles around her eyes and mouth are not from laughter or joy; they go so much deeper.

She sips the wine and sighs before brushing past me and stepping into the tub. After switching off the taps, she leans back, closes her eyes, and balances the lip of the glass on the lower lip of her mouth to take long, noisy sips, as if attempting to filter errant grape seeds through her teeth.

Leaving her to it, I head for the kitchen to call her sister.

———

There's a knock at the apartment door just as I hang up with an excited Bailey. The door opens before I get to it, and Kristy rushes in to give me a big hug.

"You survived," she squeals. "I was so worried. That neighborhood is scary."

Releasing me, Kristy steps back to study my face. "No new bruises," she says with a smile. "That makes a change."

"It went fine," I lie. "No problems."

"Did you find the sister?"

I nod toward the bathroom. "She's taking a bath."

I flash back to when I was in the bathroom earlier and suddenly realize what is missing.

"Have you seen Prince?" I ask urgently. "He never misses a chance to get under my feet as soon as I get home."

"He's with me," says Kristy. "It's OK. I was lonely when I got home, so I took him over to our place."

I exhale in relief but still jump in alarm when the phone rings.

"Relax, Dix," says Kristy. "Where's that bottle of wine gone? We deserve a glass."

With a chuckle, I reach for the phone and lift it to my ear.

On the other end of the line, Frank says, "Did you piss him off?"

"Who?"

"Krasnyi Lebed. Your Russian."

"How do you know that I met with—"

"There's a car downstairs," Frank interrupts. "Hate to disturb your evening, but I need you to join me."

"Where?"

"I'll tell you when you arrive."

I glance toward the bathroom. "I have company."

"Just you. The driver's waiting."

"But, Frank—"

The line goes dead in my ear.

With an irritated sigh, I cross the room to the front window and glance down at the street. An unmarked patrol car is idling at the curb. The driver—a young, handsome man in a two-piece suit picked off the rack by his mother and sporting a ten-dollar haircut from the same barber as his father—looks up and tilts an invisible hat in my direction.

I hold up five fingers and he nods in acknowledgment.

"Everything OK, Dix?" Kristy asks.

"I need to go out," I say.

"But you just got in."

"And I need a favor," I add.

"So long as it's not babysitting the naked prostitute who is currently butchering Lady Gaga in your bathtub."

"Just don't let her leave," I say with an apologetic grin. "Her sister is on her way over. Keep both of them here until I get back. Please?"

"I'll need more wine."

I grab my jacket as I head for the door. "I'll pick up a bottle on my way back."

"Make it two," says Kristy.

FIFTEEN

THE DRIVER ROLLS PAST The Russian Tea House and I notice the place is packed. From the few tables I can see through the lace-draped windows, most of the clientele appear to be older gentlemen with a penchant for moustaches, tailored finery, and escorting much, much younger women.

"Father-daughter night at the tea house?" I ask the driver, who introduced himself as Detective Russell Shaw. Before getting in the car, I asked to see his badge just to make sure it wasn't made of cardboard and crayon.

Dixie's Tips #15: *Just because a police officer looks like a high school hall monitor doesn't mean that we ladies are getting older. Men use moisturizer now, too. We're still young and gorgeous.*

Shaw smiles. "I had to observe that place for three weeks last year. Every night is like that except Thursdays."

"What happens on Thursdays?" I ask, intrigued.

"The same men come, but with their wives. There are so many mink shawls and coats that I kept worrying some PETA fanatics would show up with buckets of red paint."

I picture it in my mind. Scantily clad vegans throwing fake blood over spouses of the Russian mob. It wouldn't be any animal's skin they'd have to worry about after that.

We turn left at the next intersection and head down a few blocks to where the neighborhood starts to shed some of its old-world charm in favor of modern survival. Shaw pulls to the curb and points to a nearby alley.

"Detective Sergeant Fury's down there," he says.

I look around at the absence of streetlights and police activity, the bars and metal shutters on the store windows, and the unnerving stillness of it all. It's like everyone is huddled indoors in expectance of a storm. Had I missed the weather warning?

"This isn't a crime scene?" I ask, figuring that's the usual reason Frank calls me after the sun goes down.

"It is, but the sergeant wants it kept low-key for now."

I study the deserted street and the yawning mouth of the dark alley. After the day I've had, I'm not in the mood for any more surprises.

"Er—not to sound too girly, but are you planning to escort me down there?"

Shaw flashes a smile and his teeth are like bleached corn niblets on a summer's day. I wonder if he tastes of salt and butter, but then quickly blink the thought away. He must be ten years my junior. But then again …

"It wouldn't be gentlemanly not to," he says.

"That's what I was thinking."

I climb out of the car and breathe in the night air. Somebody's boiling cabbage or old socks nearby, and a neighbor has burned a frying pan of ground beef and onions. The air also carries the scent of fresh rain and soggy garbage left too long between pickups.

It makes me think it's been too long since I left the city and went for a walk in old-growth forest where the oxygen is so thick you can almost slice off a piece and slip it into your pocket for later.

I make a mental note to do something about that soon.

"This way, Ms. Flynn," says Shaw.

He's slipped on a blue rain jacket with *SFPD* printed in yellow on the back. For some reason, the jacket makes me feel better.

I follow him into the alley.

———

Halfway down the brick-sided and puddle-strewn corridor, Frank is standing over a blue tarp that's being lit by two battery-operated lights on aluminum tripods. His car blocks the far end of the alley and several long strands of crime scene tape are strewn on the ground.

I point at the discarded yellow tape. "Trying to stop the cockroaches from gawking?"

Frank's lips twitch. "Just the media," he says.

"Most of us stand erect now," I say. "Evolution."

"Hmmm. Who knew?"

"Guess the tape didn't stick," says Shaw. "Sorry, sir. I'll fix that."

"String it at each end," says Frank. "Coroner's on her way over. Make it look nice and official."

I smile as I glide over to stand beside him. "I'm surprised Ruth's not already here," I say. "Tittle tattle says you've been spending a lot of time together."

"Never listen to gossip."

"Normally, I wouldn't, but this was pillow talk." I grin wickedly as Frank's eyebrows arch upward. "My pillow," I say teasingly, before adding, "but I was talking to myself."

Frank's lips practically do a rumba as he shakes his head. "We enjoy each other's company," he admits, "but we also need our own space. She's still Audrey Hepburn, while I prefer John Wayne."

"Now there's a surprise."

Frank snorts and nods toward the tarp. "Aren't you going to unwrap your present?"

"For me? You shouldn't have."

"I want to see if you know him."

The smile leaves my face as I read the seriousness in Frank's. This isn't about tipping me off to a story.

Bending down, I take a deep breath and reach for the corner of the tarp.

"Prepare yourself," says Frank. "It ain't nowhere near pretty."

I've developed a fairly strong stomach from covering grizzly crime scenes over the last decade or so. Admittedly, the first few haunted my dreams—especially the burnings and the smell, each stage of decomposition so different—but over time even olfactory memory can fade.

I lift the tarp and make a noise halfway between a squeal and a gasp.

"Jeez, Frank, what the hell is that?"

"Look at his wrists."

I lift the tarp higher and look down at the body's wrists. His arms end in bloody stumps. I return to the deformed head and see that what I first thought was some kind of alien sea creature bursting out of his stretched mouth is actually both of his hands, bound together with twine and stuffed, wrist first, down his throat. Bloodless blue fingers crawl out of his mouth, while the force needed to lodge them there has broken and distended the man's jaw.

"He was holding this in his fingers."

I drop the tarp and turn to see Frank holding a plastic evidence bag containing one of my business cards. Disturbingly, a circular burn has removed most of the picture of my face.

"He was really holding that?" I ask.

"It was sticking out between his fingers. We were meant to see it."

"And the body was here?" I ask. "Just lying in the open? Not stuffed in a dumpster or anything?"

Franks nods.

"How did you discover it?" I ask.

"Anonymous tip."

"Convenient."

"Do you know him?" Franks asks.

Despite my repulsion, I lift the tarp again to exam the body in more detail. Even in its altered state, it's not an easy face to forget. And if I look past the crisscross of scars and melted lip, the stench of rot wafting from his black fingertips is a dead giveaway.

"*How* do you know him?" Frank asks, reading my body language.

"He tried to kill me."

"What?" Frank's voice is tight, angry. "When?"

"This afternoon," I say. "After … " I pause and wince.

"After you went to meet Krasnyi Lebed?"

115

"Yes," I admit. "I know you told me not to, but—"

"Start from the beginning," Frank growls.

"But just so we're clear: you know I didn't do this, right?"

Frank's eyes crinkle. "It doesn't fit your usual MO."

"Maybe we could go for a drink," I say as a shiver runs through me. "The Dog House or—"

"I need to wait for Ruth. Tell me here."

I stand and wrap my arms across my chest in a self-comforting hug. The night is colder than I'm dressed for, and I suddenly feel so incredibly tired. I wish I smoked cigarettes just for something to do with my hands.

"You don't have a cigar do you?" I ask.

Occasionally, Frank and I smoke a cigar while strolling homeward after a late evening of beers and bullshit at the Dog House. Frank introduced me to this brand from the Dominican Republic called Macanudo Maduro that is dark leafed, wet, and smooth with subtle caramel undertones.

No wonder I have trouble getting a date.

"Quit stallin'," says Frank.

I sigh and tell him the whole story, ending with the Good Samaritan who came to my rescue by cracking the Russian's skull with a piece of lumber. I pull my collar to one side to show him the bruising.

"These marks will match his fingers," I say.

"You should've called me."

"I know, but I was just relieved to get away. Who knew he'd end up dead in an alley?"

"And the guy who stepped in to help you?"

"Took off before I did. I have no idea who he was."

"Cutting off the hands is a message," says Frank. "I'm just not sure who it's directed at."

"But whoever killed him wanted me to know about it?" I say. "That's why he left my card."

"Yeah, but if the message is meant to let you know that this guy won't be laying his hands on anyone else, then why burn your face off the card?"

I wince. "That *is* unsettling."

"It could be both an apology and a warning in one, but I've never seen the like."

The young detective returns from stringing a line of tape across both entrances to the alley and says, "Coroner just pulled up."

Frank tilts his chin toward me. "You need Ruth to take a look at those bruises?"

I shake off the suggestion. "I'm fine. Nothing a bath and a good mattress can't fix."

"Go home, then. I'll be in touch when I know more. And if you think of anything else—"

"I'll call. Promise."

"You better." He turns to Shaw. "Take her home and then come straight back. It's time to get this circus started."

SIXTEEN

THE PAINTED LADY IS quiet when young Detective Shaw drops me out front. Both Mrs. Pennell's and Mr. French's apartments are in darkness, as are the two apartments on the top floor. In the middle, however, lights are glowing. I take it as a hopeful sign that my reluctant guest has stayed put.

I didn't mention Roxanne to Frank because I don't want him thinking that I'm involved even more than he already knows. One butchered corpse is enough for him to be concerned about without adding angry Polish sailors, unconscious Russian henchmen, and the reluctant abduction of a prostitute to the mix.

I tell myself that I'm being thoughtful.

When I enter the lobby, Mrs. Pennell's door creaks open and she pokes her head through the gap. Her hair is wrapped in baby blue curlers and she's draped in a flowery nightgown that reaches almost to the ankles of her compression stockings and sensible rubber-soled slippers.

"Oh, hello, dear," she says. "I hoped it was you. Kristy said you had gone out again. Long day?"

I nod and smile, not wanting to get corralled into a long conversation.

"I left a note on your door earlier, did you see it?"

I blanch. "Sorry, I completely forgot. It's been one of those crazy days. Did you need something?"

"Not to worry, dear. It's just a package that was dropped off for you. I took it inside because the man said it shouldn't be left unattended."

Curious. I'm not expecting anything. "What kind of package?" I ask.

"A box wrapped in brown paper." She holds out her hands to indicate its approximate width. "Little bit heavy and doesn't rattle. Not that I was shaking it, of course."

"When was this?"

"This afternoon."

I have no idea what it can be, and a shiver of paranoia makes stiletto-heeled ants march down my spine. Had my handless Russian been missing any other parts? Or . . . I think of my card gripped in his fingers with my face burned off.

"Did you recognize the delivery man?" I ask.

"No, but he was older than usual. Normally they're young men on bicycles with their hats on backward and smelling of marijuana, but this man was more like one of their dads."

Panic rises, but I try to keep it out of my voice. "Did he have an accent? Russian maybe?"

"Not that I noticed."

"Do you still have the package?"

"I took it upstairs when I thought you were home, but you weren't there again. Kristy answered the door though and said she'd leave it on the counter for you. I hope that's alright?"

I attempt a smile. "That's just fine, Mrs. Pennell. Thanks for taking care of it."

"Any time. You sleep tight now."

"You, too."

As soon as Mrs. Pennell closes her door, I rush up the stairs, taking them two at a time.

———

I push open the apartment door and take in the room. Kristy and Sam are cuddling on the couch with Prince Marmalade nestled on Kristy's lap. His purrs are vibrating like a subwoofer set on happy.

The door to my bedroom is open and I see Roxanne and Bailey sitting on my bed. They've both been crying.

A brown paper–wrapped package sits on the kitchen counter. Undisturbed. Innocent in its plainness.

"You OK, Dix?" Sam asks. "You look pale."

I point at the package. "Anything about that look suspicious?"

"There was no address on it," says Kristy. "Just your name … " Her eyes widen and she stands up. "But it's not ticking or anything, if that's what you mean."

Sam stands up beside her and slightly forward, protective. "Er, is there something we should know?"

I cross the room to examine the package. I sniff the paper, but it smells simply of paper. There's no lingering petroleum smell of crude explosive—nor of fresh human blood or decomposing flesh.

I place my ear close to it and listen. Everything is quiet. I reach down to my boot, pull out my knife, and flick open the blade.

Kristy pulls Sam down behind the couch. "Tell us if we need to run," she says.

Prince, thinking it's a game, rubs his furry body across Sam's and Kristy's faces, purr increasing in volume.

Being careful to look for hidden wires, I slice open one end of the brown packaging and carefully peel back the folds. There is a blue plastic box inside.

I open the other end and unwrap the paper to fully expose the box. Only it's not a box. It has a foldaway handle. It's a protective case, and I recognize it.

Two snaps hold it closed.

I unsnap the latches and carefully open the lid.

Inside, nestled in custom-cut foam, is a gleaming Smith & Wesson Governor handgun, two boxes of ammo, a trigger lock, and a bore snake for keeping the barrel clean. Resting on top is one of Frank's business cards. I flip the card over and read: *Happy Birthday. I know even you must have one—Frank.*

"What is it?" asks Kristy. "Is it safe? Can we get up now?"

I laugh to release the tension and lift the gun from its cushioned rest.

"Sorry," I say over my shoulder. "Paranoia. It's a present from Frank that he didn't tell me he was sending."

"But you thought it was, what? A bomb," asks Sam. "What kind of story are you into now?"

I turn around and show them the gun. "Obviously one that has Frank a little worried about my safety."

Sam holds up her hands in shock. "You're not *keeping* it are you?"

"Of course I am. It's a lovely gesture. I was shooting one at the range earlier today and—"

Sam shakes her head. "I don't like guns, and I don't like the idea of you having one. More people in this country are killed from their own guns turned against them than other people's." She heads for the door. "I don't want it here."

"I'll get a gun safe," I say. "And I'm being properly trained."

"Come on, Kristy," Sam calls. "We're not staying."

"Sam," I call after her. "I promise I'll get a proper safe. Tomorrow."

Sam stops at the door and holds out her hand until Kristy arrives to take it. Her eyes lock onto mine and there is an anger there that I've never seen before.

"Until you do," she bristles, "and that weapon is locked inside it, we won't be back."

"But, Sam—"

She holds up her free hand again to stop me. "I can't be any clearer, Dix. Good night."

They pull the door closed behind them as I replace the gun in its case.

———

"Problem?" asks Bailey as she appears in the bedroom doorway.

I close the gun case and snap the latches before turning to her.

"They're tired," I say. "It's been a long day for everyone."

Unexpectedly, Bailey rushes forward and wraps me in a lung-deflating hug.

"I can't thank you enough for getting my sister out of that place," she says. "I was so..." She struggles to find the word; to admit it to herself. "So scared, I guess. How did you do it?"

"I had help."

Bailey releases me and looks into my eyes. "They'll come for her though, won't they?"

"Eventually," I agree. "But they'll need to negotiate. They don't want the publicity that I can bring down on them, and now they can't hide her away. All we need is the price of her freedom."

"And what will that be?" Bailey asks.

"I don't know."

"Money?"

I shake my head. "The Red Swan has little need of money from the likes of us."

Bailey pales. "Then what?"

I shrug. "I think your father is the key. If he's alive, he must know some valuable secrets that have kept him that way."

"And if he's dead?"

"Then we'll think of something else."

Bailey blinks away a spattering of tears. "I'm sorry I got you involved in all this."

"You didn't." I smile. "I jumped in with both clumsy feet and splashed half the water out of the pool like the baby hippo that I am."

Bailey wipes her eyes and laughs. "Hippo?" she asks. "I think *you're* a swan."

"Then clearly you are over-tired," I say. "Why don't you and Roxanne spend the night in my room? I'll crash on the sofa and we'll make a fresh plan in the morning."

"Are you sure?"

"I insist."

Bailey wraps me in another hug before returning to the bedroom and gently closing the door.

———

Alone, I bring the gun case over to the coffee table and open it again. The Governor feels good in my hand, solid weight and comfortable grip. I open the boxes of ammunition and load it in an alternating pattern of one shotgun shell and one .45 until all six chambers are filled.

I make sure the safety is on, a matter that can be confusing for gun virgins because there is no visual indicator to say the gun is safe. It's only when you flick the thumb safety off that a painted red dot appears to let you know the gun is ready to fire. That's why gun instructors tell you, "Red means dead." I slip the Governor under the arm cushion that I'll be using as my pillow.

From the hall closet, I grab a spare blanket, strip down to my underwear, and eat a few mouthfuls of peanut butter out of the jar until my eyelids become heavy and my mouth too lazy to chew.

Prince jumps onto the couch and curls his furry body around my butt as I succumb to the dark, hoping I can bypass REM and sink blissfully into dreamless oblivion.

Pity it's to be so short-lived.

SEVENTEEN

THE SOUND IS MORE like scratching than anything sinister.

I move my hand toward my butt and feel the warm fur still pressed against it. If Prince isn't in his litter box ...

The scratching stops and there is a clunk and scrape of metal sliding back into its stainless-steel sheath. My upgraded security locks have just failed their first test.

I slip off the couch and ease the Governor from beneath the pillow. It feels heavier in my hand than it did at the range, but the rubber grip holds secure despite the film of perspiration that coats my palm.

I thumb off the safety, revealing the ominous red dot, and cup my shooting hand with my left to form a triangular support. My eyes never leave the door as I move sideways toward the armchair, its antique solidity making it the most protective piece of furniture in the room.

By the time the door begins to swing open on whispering hinges, I am steely-eyed, petrified, and concentrating on my breath. Unlike at the range, I am having trouble keeping my inhalations calm and steady.

When the door is three-quarters of the way open, I see a silhouette straightening up from a crouch in the doorway. The ever-burning hallway light is dark, but loose strands of moonlight entering through the small street-side window are enough to let me know that whoever is standing there is a solid object.

When the silhouette steps forward, I thumb back the Governor's hammer with a click that sounds more like a thunderclap.

The dark figure freezes in place and its head turns in my direction.

I wonder if I should speak or if it's better not to let the intruder know that I'm alone. If he has an imagination like mine, he might wonder if the room isn't filled with ninja assassins or a ruthless biker gang that owes me a favor and plans to use his limbs as baseball bats.

Neither of us moves, but I wonder if he can hear my heart on its thudding journey from chest to throat.

Perhaps deciding the sound was in his imagination, the intruder lifts his foot to take another step.

"I will shoot," I say, hoping I sound more like *24*'s Jack Bauer than *Three's Company*'s Jack Tripper.

"We need to talk," says the silhouette.

"I have a phone for that."

"I can help you."

"If that were true, I doubt you'd be breaking into my apartment in the middle of the night."

The silhouette moves his head, surveying the room. He doesn't appear to be wearing night-vision goggles. In the movies, they always glow green, and no part of him is glowing, but the longer he stands there, the clearer he's becoming as my eyes adjust to the dark. Which also means his eyesight is improving, too.

"Are the sisters here?" he asks.

"What sisters?"

I see his lips bend in a smile and it worries me. Soon, he'll be able to tell that I'm alone, in my underwear, hiding behind a chair.

"You won't be able to protect them by yourself. Mr. Lebed is far too powerful to take on alone."

This catches me off guard, since I assumed it was Lebed who sent him.

"You don't work for Lebed?" I ask.

"I didn't say that."

Now I'm even more confused. "I want you to leave," I say.

"If you answer one question."

"What's that?"

"Who sent you?"

The bedroom door creaks open as the question sinks in and I realize it's the same one that the dead Russian had been asking me on the street.

"Dixie?" calls out Bailey. "Who are you talking to?"

The silhouette moves forward and turns toward the bedroom in the same instant that I call out for Bailey to get back inside. I see the intruder's arm rising, the shape of a gun in his hand.

I fire.

The Governor booms, unleashing one of its shotgun shells in a spray of lethal force.

The intruder spins and curses, his own gun firing in a rapid succession of trigger-twitching anarchy. Plaster rains from the ceiling and stuffing flies from my protective armchair.

I crouch down low and roll to a new position behind the couch. From this vantage point I still have a clear view of the bedroom door. Ears ringing and eyes stinging from dust and sweat, I've lost sight of the intruder. But I know what he's after.

The sisters.

So with eyes fixed on the closed door to his targets, I allow my ears to scan the room.

They come up empty.

I wait in silence until Sam's voice calls from the hallway outside.

"Dixie? Are you OK?"

I don't want to call back and give away my position, but I can't let Sam walk into danger.

"Stay in your apartment, Sam," I yell back.

"I've called the police," Sam yells. "They're on their way."

"You hear that?" I say to the darkness as a rush of relief ignites the adrenaline pumping through my bloodstream. "If you're still here when Detective Fury arrives, he'll fold you in half and stuff your head so far up your ass you'll need a snorkel to breathe."

The darkness doesn't answer.

EIGHTEEN

FRANK HANDS ME A coffee mug and tells me to drink. Expecting coffee, I shudder slightly as ice-cold vodka splashes over my tongue and burns my throat.

"You have a lousy liquor selection," says Frank. "But that'll help with the shock."

"I should have one, too, then," says Kristy. "My whole body is shaking."

Kristy and Sam are beside me on the couch. After making sure that I was alive and uninjured, Sam has been silently fuming on the far cushion. She's in full-blown I-told-you-so blame mode in her belief that the mere presence of the gun brought armed trouble to my door. Kristy sits close and rubs my arm, making comforting cooing noises like a dove in its nest.

When Frank doesn't move to fetch Kristy a drink, she nudges Sam into action.

"And get Dixie a refill," she tells her. "This is a lot of shock. A shoot-out in our own home."

"It wasn't a shoot-out," I say.

"It was," insists Kristy. "He had a gun, you had a gun. The clock struck midnight—"

"Who fired first?" Frank interrupts as he hitches his pants and crouches down to eye level.

I hear his knees crack.

"I did," I say.

"Because you felt your life was in imminent danger," says Frank. He's not asking the question, but guiding me on the proper response.

"He came for the sisters," I say. "I'm sure he was planning to kill them. He had a gun. He was aiming..."

Sam returns with the vodka bottle and a second cup for Kristy. As soon as she splashes a mouthful into my cup, I swallow it. Hole in one. Doesn't even touch the sides.

I hold up my cup for another, but Frank takes it away instead.

"I need you sober," he says.

"I don't," I answer.

Frank's lips twitch. "There's blood on the wall, so we know you wounded him. None of it appears arterial, but I've put out an alert to the local hospitals and walk-in clinics."

I shake my head. "He's smarter than that. Lebed will have his own doctors."

"You don't know that this man works for Lebed. You told me you didn't see his face."

"No, but he didn't deny working for him, either."

"Did he have an accent?"

"No. Not everyone in the organization does."

Frank glances in the direction of the bedroom, where young Detective Shaw and an attractive female officer with flawless Halle Berry skin are interviewing Bailey and Roxanne.

"Why would Lebed want the sisters dead?" he asks.

"Roxanne belongs to him. I took her away."

Frank dismisses the statement. "He keeps a large stable. One misplaced girl isn't going to mean much, and he definitely doesn't want me on his case when—and I hate to sound crude—but a flash of cash can make these girls come running back to work much easier than a threat."

I want to argue, to stand up for Roxanne, but I know Frank's right. Roxanne didn't exactly plead with me to get her out of the hotel. I look over to the bedroom and meet her gaze. She's barely listening to the two officers as they interview her sister. Her eyes are focused on me, and they're hurting. A pain that I'll likely never fully comprehend is pulsing behind aqua blue jewels clouded in a crimson mist.

I wonder if, despite her denial, she knows the gunman. What if she made a secret call while I was out? Told him where she was.

She didn't know I had a gun. Neither sister did.

"What are you thinking?" Frank asks. "I can see the gears working from here."

"I need better locks," I say.

"Best locks in the world won't keep out a determined man," says Frank. "We have a guy on Entry Squad named Dozer who can swing a battering ram like nobody's business. If Dozer can't get it done, we switch over to Gently, an explosives' expert who makes holes in walls any size and shape he wants. I saw him enter a crack house through a hole that, I swear, looked just like the Death Star."

"That's not comforting," I say.

Frank shrugs. "It's reality. A good deadbolt does the job ninety percent of the time. For the other ten, you need something better than a lock." He glances over at the blue case resting on the coffee table. "Good job you opened your birthday present early."

"I forgot to thank you for that."

Frank's lips dance and his hand stretches out to squeeze my knee. "The best thanks I can ask for is seeing you sitting here in one piece."

"Awww," says Kristy as she reaches out to pat Frank's hand. "That's so sweet."

Frank's face instantly returns to a block of unyielding granite as he retrieves his hand and stands up.

As soon as they see their boss standing, Detective Shaw and the female officer leave the bedroom and approach.

"Anything?" Frank asks.

Shaw glances down at me, obviously wanting to take the conversation out of earshot.

"It's OK," says Frank. "If she doesn't hear it now, she'll just annoy the hell out of you until you tell her later anyway."

Though pretending not to be listening, I smile, pleased with the compliment.

"Neither of them saw his face," says Shaw. "The younger one is a piece of work though. She's fighting it, but she's riding a snake."

"What does that mean?" I ask. "Riding a snake?"

"Snakes and ladders," injects the female detective. "Your friend is sliding into withdrawal. Judging by the track marks, I'd say heroin is her main course, but she's also smoking a between-meal snack of either crack or crystal."

Her tone is factual rather than judgmental, which I appreciate. Pity she's so attractive, as I'm already halfway to my quota.

Dixie's Tips #16: *Super attractive friends are fine, but never have more than two at one time—otherwise your odds of being the sacrificial "ugly one" for the handsome boy's "wingman" increase to a seriously depressing level.*

She holds out her hand. "I'm Betty. Detective Betty White."

"Like the actress?" I say.

"Except younger, darker, and nowhere near as funny."

I grin—too late, I like her—and shake her hand.

"How do I treat withdrawal?" I ask.

"Two ways," says Betty. "Cold turkey, which means tying her to a bed, taking a shitload of verbal abuse, and cleaning up puke for a week. Or take her to a clinic and get her enrolled in a methadone program."

"But?" I sense the unspoken words in her tone.

Betty meets my gaze. "She thinks she's handling it, which means she isn't ready to admit there's a problem. She's injecting between her toes because she believes that if no one sees the injection points, no one can tell. I've known addicts who inject themselves in the corner of their eyes, nasal passages, and moist places you don't want to think about, and they still think they don't have a problem."

"So, option one," I say.

"Both options get them clean, but neither one keeps them that way. That's a bigger step."

Frank interjects. "Are we done here?"

Both detectives straighten up and nod.

Frank turns to me. His face is weary and disappointed, like a father who's found a condom wrapper in his teenage daughter's nightstand drawer.

"I'll leave a uniform in the lobby until morning. Get some sleep, Dix. We'll talk about this mess later."

———

After everyone has left, Bailey and Roxanne return to bed, while I curl into a ball on the couch.

I resist the urge to suck my thumb and pout, though I do keep the gun case on the coffee table close at hand.

I doubt I'll be able to get any sleep, but I surprise myself by drifting off.

When I open my eyes again, darkness has been replaced by morning light and Bailey is gone.

NINETEEN

"Did she say anything?" I ask.

Roxanne is in the armchair; a bullet wound bleeding antique white stuffing inches from her head. She's drowning in a borrowed pair of fleece pajamas with her knees pulled up to her chin. Her bare feet are bruised, a purple-yellow cancer spreading from between her toes. Tension pulses in waves through her undernourished frame making her eyes practically bleed, and her dripping nose is that of a pouting child rather than a woman hardened in the kiln of neglect.

She sniffs and shakes her head.

"No note?" I press. "Nothing?"

She glares at me, angry at the repetition.

"OK." I back off. "We'll find her."

The glare intensifies. "You think she's gone to *him*, don't you?"

I shrug, but there's a reason I bet on horses and dogs rather than play poker.

"Don't!" She hisses. "Don't you treat me like a child. I grew up a long time ago."

"I know you did."

"Don't do that either."

"What?"

"Act like you give a damn. I don't need nobody to care for me."

"We all need someone—"

"I don't! So stuff your caring. You think you can—" She looks away and scrapes at her eyes, but her skin is impermeable to tears. "You think you know me? You have no fucking clue. Do-gooders like you think it's about sex. That sucking a dick is sucking a dick, and you can just put it behind you." She laughs, but there's no humor in it, only pain. "Fucking, sucking, pissing, whipping... that's the least of what I do."

"I don't understand," I say.

"And you never will. You think that pen in your hand gives you a right to dig into my life and try an' fix things? Well, it don't. It's just a fucking pen."

"This isn't my fault," I say.

Roxanne snorts. "Then whose is it? If you hadn't stuck your big nose in, Bailey would still be cutting hair and I would be... where I'm meant to be."

"And where's that? Screwing sailors and sticking needles between your toes to pretend you're not dead inside?"

Roxanne blanches and tugs the pajama cuffs over her exposed feet but instantly punishes herself for the flinch by nipping her inner cheek with her teeth. It's something I've noticed her do before, but I didn't realize it was on purpose. Her inner flesh must be a transit map of repressed pain.

"Yeah," she snarls, her head turning away from me to focus on the front window. "Cause that's what I am, daddy's little junkie whore."

"Who calls you that?" I ask in a gentler tone.

She doesn't answer.

"Lebed?"

Her eyes fix on mine again, but their intensity is sputtering, like a fire that's consumed most of the oxygen in a room and has nowhere left to go.

"You can't help yourself, can you?" she says. "Always questions."

"It's the only way I know to get answers."

"And why do you need them?"

"Because I want to help."

"Why?"

My words stumble as I struggle with the question. "I'm not sure I—"

"Why do you stick your nose in other people's shit? Why write stories?"

"I guess it's how I make a difference," I blurt. "I don't want to fight in a war, I don't want to run into a burning building when everyone else is running out or make my mark in public office, but I want to connect—to let people see what and who is behind the headlines. I still believe that reporters make a difference. Our stories open eyes, keep most politicians honest, and act as the community's watchdog. It's the storytellers who are tasked with not just reporting history as it's made, but being a public voice to stand up for injustice and shine a spotlight on corruption. It'd be easier not to give a damn, but we're made this way—too flippin' curious."

"Then maybe this is how I'm made," says Roxanne.

"No!" Once ignited, my anger burns hot. "No woman, and especially not a child, is born to be a whore."

Roxanne actually smiles. It's almost pretty.

"I'm glad you used that word," she says. "I hate it when people say 'sex worker'. Makes it sound like I jerk off chickens for a living. I'm a whore, plain and simple. Give me cash and you can use my body as a fucking ashtray."

I blanch. "Who calls you daddy's little whore?"

She smiles again, but it's thinner and sharper than before. "You guessed right, but it was a long time ago. I was Lebed's plaything until puberty hit. Soon as my tits started showing, he threw me out of his house and onto the circuit."

"The circuit?" I ask.

She hugs her knees tighter and wipes her nose on the fleece. "It starts out okay: private clients, five-star treatment, nice clothes, pedicures and manicures; a lot of threesomes, fantasy games, deflowering the sons of important men. That's actually a word they use: *deflowering*. As if the horny little pricks haven't been jerking off for years. Some of the boys were sweet, though, especially those who were too scared to tell their daddies they were gay. Others were assholes, turning their fathers' disapproval into a cruel streak. I fell from top-tier to bottom faster than most after I stuck a letter opener through one idiot's cock. He was threatening to cut off one of my nipples as a souvenir at the time and I panicked."

"What were you supposed to do?" I ask. "Let him cut you?"

Roxanne releases her knees and lowers her feet to the floor as Prince jumps off the couch and onto the arm of her chair. With a warm, fleece-lined lap exposed, Prince steps onto her thighs and kneads a little before turning around three times and curling into a furry cinnamon roll.

Roxanne pets the purring cat without answering my question.

I ask another. "Is the hotel where I found you the bottom rung?"

She shakes her head. "It might look like it, but there's lower. Lots lower."

"Why haven't you left?"

"And go where?"

"Your sister loves you. She'd take you in."

Fresh tears glisten in swollen eyes. "Until last night, I wouldn't have believed that."

"And now?"

"We need to get her back before it's too late."

"You agree she went to Lebed?"

Roxanne nods.

"To bargain for you?"

She nods again.

"And what will he ask in exchange?" I ask.

"There's only one thing he's interested in."

"What?"

"My father."

———

"So, your father's alive," I say.

"He has to be."

"Why?"

"Because if he isn't, Lebed wouldn't give a shit about us. He'd have used us and tossed us without a second thought, but he's always kept close watch—we're his bait."

"You and your sister?" I say. "Even when Bailey was living in Boston?"

Roxanne nods. "He'd tell me. Lebed. When he was lying beside me, making me do what he wanted, he'd tell me about my sister, where she lived, who she saw, what he would do to her if I ever tried to run away."

"Jesus, what a bastard."

Roxanne grins. "Oh yeah."

"Bailey thought she escaped."

"There is no escape. He has eyes everywhere."

"And why does he want your father?" I ask.

"I tried to ask, but he would never get into specifics and always got angry if I pressed too hard. But it has something to do with that night before I was born; the night Bailey remembers when Lebed came to my parents' apartment. He hired my father to do something, but I think Dad was supposed to die, too. Only he didn't, and Lebed's been looking for him ever since."

"Twenty years is a long time to stay in hiding. He could be anywhere. South America? The North Pole?"

Roxanne shakes her head. "No, he stayed close."

"How do you know?"

Her voice is barely a whisper. "I've seen him."

"What? Where? When?"

"Just … glimpses. Sometimes at the hotel; sometimes in the street. He's never talked to me, and at first I thought it was my imagination putting my father's face on other men's shoulders. After all, I only know him from pictures, but it's him. I'm sure of it."

"Did you tell Bailey this?"

She shakes her head and chews at her nails.

I stand up and run fingers through my unkempt hair. "She's got nothing to bargain with. What the hell was she thinking?"

There's a crack in Roxanne's voice. "She's trying to be a big sister again. After all these years, she still thinks she has to protect me."

I glance down at the blue case on the coffee table. "I need to see Lebed."

"Why would he see you? He holds all the cards."

"Not all of them," I say.

"No?"

I lock eyes with Roxanne. "I still have you."

TWENTY

AFTER SHOWERING AND PULLING on fresh clothes, I phone Stoogan at the *NOW* office to let him know I'm still pursuing the Father's Day piece.

"Care to share any details with your stressed-out, death-by-a-thousand-meetings editor?" he asks. "Just so I'm not throwing out random cover-my-reporter's-ass, made-up-bullshit promises of content forthcoming."

"You'll love it," I say with a chuckle. "Adoring daughters searching for their missing father. Kittens and balloons."

"Kittens and balloons?"

"OK. Maybe not balloons."

Stoogan sighs. "Why don't I believe you?"

"Because you're a distrusting and cynical man?"

"With a nose for bullshit," he adds.

"Have I ever steered you wrong?"

"You've never steered me straight."

I guffaw at the same time there's a knock on the apartment door.

"I have to go, but keep the cover slot open. I have a lead on the missing dad to give you that squishy, feel-good ending the publisher craves."

"Squishy?"

I chuckle. "That's why you're such a good editor, boss, you pick up on words like that."

Stoogan sighs heavily again and hangs up.

———

Roxanne is in the shower with the door closed. No radio, no singing, just running water. I find it oddly unsettling, like sleep without dreams.

A shower is my favorite part of the day, a time to align my mind and set the mood. Upbeat music helps get the blood flowing and replace some of the worries with fresh and positive thoughts. Bathing in silence, or alone for that matter, does nothing helpful—except get you clean.

I answer the knock at the door to find Mrs. Pennell standing in the hallway.

"I didn't want to bother you last night," she says without preamble. "With all the police and such. The nice officer downstairs filled me in and told me everybody was all right, and I'm so glad to hear that. Last time there was trouble, you had that great big knife stuck in your hand and what a mess that was." She tuts. "But guns? Guns! What's going on, Dixie?"

"Sorry, Mrs. Pennell." I squirm. "I don't know what to say. The police are looking for the man who broke in."

"Why is it always your place?"

I shrug, not wanting to get into the whole story and cause unnecessary panic. "Maybe they think a single woman is an easy target."

She clucks her tongue louder in disgust.

"Well, I hope they find him and throw away the key. I'm lucky I have King William on guard, but a gun in my home! Indeed."

The sound of the shower clicks off.

"Do you need anything else?" I ask.

"Yes, one thing. And I don't want you to get too self-conscious, but Derek and Shahnaz have asked if they can move across the hall to the empty apartment above Sam and Kristy."

"Oh? Why? It's not any bigger."

Mrs. Pennell points over my shoulder to the ceiling, and when I turn around I immediately see a ray of light from the apartment above shining through a stray bullet hole.

"I can patch that," I say sheepishly.

"I don't think that's exactly their worry, dear," says Mrs. Pennell.

"No," I admit. "Guess not."

———

The phone rings as Roxanne opens the bathroom door in a barely there towel. She's at the age when all awkward teenage plumpness should have turned into luscious, head-turning curves, but the woman in front of me is little more than a skeleton wrapped in grayish flesh.

The barbed wire tattoo on her back has companions on her front that make her look like a sadistically stitched doll. The ink speaks to me in a voice that pricks at my heart and sends electrical filaments of doubt deep into my soul. There are wounds here too deep to heal.

The phone continues to ring.

"Do you have clothes I can borrow?" she asks. "My old ones feel dirty."

"Of course." I lead the way to the bedroom. "Let's see what we can find."

The answering machine clicks on. It's Stoogan.

"Dix, pick up, what the hell? I just received a police report on a shooting last night—at *your* address. You didn't think to mention that? Are you OK? What's going on? You need to get a cellphone. Jesus, call me."

I don't.

TWENTY-ONE

KRISTY ALLOWS ME TO borrow her precious VW Bug in exchange for not asking her to look after Roxanne again and a promise that I won't leave it unattended anywhere near the Sandford Hotel.

I park around the corner from The Russian Tea House and get out to feed the meter. When Roxanne opens the passenger door, I tell her to stay in the car.

"She's my sister," argues Roxanne. "I want to come."

"And what good will that do?" I squat down beside the car to meet her at eye level. "Lebed's men will take you back, and there's nothing I can do to stop them. The only leverage we have is the worth he believes you offer as bait for your father. If Lebed decides you're no longer worth keeping alive, then walking into his hands is suicide."

"Maybe he'll take me in exchange for Bailey."

I shake my head. "He already had you and your father didn't come."

Her voice rises in alarm. "What the fuck does that mean?"

I wince, wishing I had a better filter between my brain and mouth.

"Tell me," she presses.

"OK," I relent. "But this is just a theory and I could be completely wrong."

"Tell me," she repeats.

"It's what you said this morning about Lebed keeping an eye on both you and your sister. He left Bailey alone while he set you on a destructive path to the gutter. Any father worth the name would have tried to rescue you; but if he felt he couldn't, he might reach out to the daughter who had already escaped. Your father did neither, so now it's time to switch things up. Lebed lets you go free, but—"

"He punishes Bailey," Roxanne finishes.

"It's just a theory," I repeat.

"But you're smart. Like him."

"Not like him. Not like that."

"You're wrong." Bailey's eyes fill with warm tears and she can no longer hold my gaze. "That's exactly how he thinks."

———

The handsome maître d' isn't trained well enough to keep the look of surprise off his face when I walk through the front doors of The Russian Tea House.

"We're not open yet," he barks, moving quickly to block my progress.

"Then you should lock your doors," I quip. "Gals like me get desperate for a good pot of tea and a Russian crumpet in the morning."

I flash him one of my get-down-on-your-knees-and-beg smiles, but it bounces off his crisp white T-shirt as though it's made of Kevlar.

I like the way his shirt suctions to his abs to form a six-pack of kissable muscle, although the tightness also reveals a wide patch of some kind underneath that covers his left side. I wonder if it's used to hold a gun against the small of his back, but figure he won't give me a twirl—even if I ask nicely.

Last time we met, he was in a white tuxedo that made him look good enough to take home to meet the parents; this time his tight jeans and T-shirt say forget the parents and let's head straight to the bedroom.

"Are you straight?" I ask before the professional side of my brain can kick me in the kneecaps.

The question flusters him. "You have to go," he says.

I straighten my shoulders to fix my posture, which also makes my breasts ride high and proud, but his eyes don't flicker below my neck. Admittedly, they're small breasts, but they still deserve a glance.

"Do you remember me?" I ask. "I gave you my card last time I was here."

"I know who you are." His eyes shift nervously and his hands clench and unclench at his side.

"You didn't call," I say. "So, I thought—"

"You're here to see me?" he blurts, his confusion deepening.

"Relax, it's just an ice-breaker. I need to see the Red Swan." I smile again, but with a little more innocence this time. "I just love that moniker, don't you? I was thinking of calling myself the Ginger Fawn. What do you think? Too threatening?"

The skin on his nose furrows into deep wrinkles and his voice is laced with fire. "Mr. Lebed isn't receiving visitors at this time."

"No offense, cute cheeks, but I'd rather hear that from him."

"You are making a mistake."

149

I unwrap a chocolate mint from a bowl on the reception desk and pop it in my mouth. "Wouldn't be the first time," I say.

"I need you to go."

"Not gonna happen." I crack the candy with my teeth and suck out the chocolate filling.

He moves around the reception desk, but he's walking stiffly and I can see ripples of pain moving across his face.

"What'd you do?" I ask. "Try to clap your hands and stomp your feet at the same time? Tell me you didn't go for the hat trick and throw in gum chewing, too."

He doesn't smile as he clears the desk and puffs up his chest to appear more intimidating. He points at the door.

"Leave. Now!"

I stand my ground. "Your body is beautiful, but your vocabulary seems somewhat limited."

His face flushes with anger, but it's tempered by the pain. I glance down at the patch around his kidneys and see the outline of thick tape holding it to his flesh. My eyes drop to below his belt and notice that his jeans are also stretched tighter against his left hip than his right.

It's not a belt to hide a gun, I realize.

It's a bandage. And it's fresh.

With a snarl, I curl my right hand into a fist and jab it into his left kidney, aiming, as Pinch has taught me, for the center of his core.

The shock on his face is quickly replaced with a bone-white queasiness as he reaches for the counter and drops to his knees. The bandage on his side blossoms in a Rorschach stain of blood. I've torn his fresh stitches where shotgun pellets ripped into his flesh.

"You were in my apartment last night," I hiss. "With a fucking gun. Were you ordered to kill us?"

With one hand gripping the counter, the maître d' grabs my wrist with his free hand and squeezes so hard my bones rub together.

"Quiet your tongue," he says between clenched teeth. "You have no idea what is going on."

"Then tell me," I hiss back. "And let go of my fucking arm before I punch you again in the same spot."

He immediately releases my arm, which means I've made a good impression.

Dixie's Tips #17: *Don't make a threat you're not willing to follow through on. It's vastly more effective if even you believe you'll do it.*

"Where's Bailey?" I ask.

"I don't know."

"Bullshit!"

"No." He holds up a hand to stop me lashing out. "She arrived earlier, but I didn't see her leave. I-I don't know where she is now."

"Then let me talk to Lebed."

From his knees, he looks up into my eyes. Fear glistens within dark blue orbs, but beneath it is a lead-lined layer of defiance. His voice is low, just above a whisper.

"Mr. Lebed doesn't know."

"Doesn't know what?"

"About my visit."

"Last night?"

He nods.

"He didn't order you to kill us?"

He shakes his head.

I curl my fist again and let him see it. "Then why?"

He swallows. "I need answers."

"What answers?"

"To who sent you."

A puzzle clears in my brain.

"The last time I left here, I was attacked in the street. It wasn't Lebed who sent him either, was it?"

He shrugs. "He was told not to hurt you."

"So you cut off his hands?"

"It sends a message."

"No shit, but why did you send him after me?"

"I need to know if the man's alive."

"Who?" Another puzzle piece meets its mate. "Wait a minute. The sisters' father?"

He nods.

"Why?" I ask.

"He has evidence."

"What evidence?"

He swallows again and pulls himself slowly to his feet. Despite myself, I help him stand.

He leans in close, his mouth next to my ear. "He can bring the Red Swan down," he whispers. "He's the only one who can."

I push him away.

"And why would you want that?" I ask.

His eyes burn as color returns to his cheeks. "That is for me to know."

"So the enemy of my enemy is now my friend?" I ask.

He doesn't smile. "Perhaps."

"Then get me in to see Lebed and maybe we can work together."

He hesitates, but then nods. "Give me a moment to replace my bandage and I'll see if Mr. Lebed is available."

"There," I say, unwrapping another chocolate mint, "that wasn't so difficult, was it?"

TWENTY-TWO

THE MAÎTRE D'—WHO TELLS me his name is Mikhail, which is so stereotypical, I don't know if I believe him—leads me across the restaurant to the doors of the same private room where I met Lebed before.

"Wait here," he says. "And I mean it. Unless invited, the guards won't hesitate to break your neck."

I remember the two guards, so I stay put.

When Mikhail reappears, he flashes me a look of warning before holding the door open to allow access. He doesn't follow me inside.

Krasnyi Lebed, aka Red Swan, is sitting behind the immaculately dressed table with his twin computer geeks busy being nerdish with numbers at his back. He's eating a lump of pungent blue cheese with a curved knife, its tip split into a two-pronged fork, while sipping black tea from a china cup rimmed in gold.

Lebed stabs his knife in the direction of an empty chair at the table.

"Sit," he says.

I observe the mountainous guards, one on either side of the door like Orcs guarding the black gates of Mordor, as I move to take the chair. Neither seems particularly worried or concerned about my presence.

"Are you hungry?" Lebed asks. "My chef is preparing fresh anchovies straight from the boat. Cherry smoke salt and lime zest." He kisses the tips of his fingers. "Delicious."

Although intrigued, I decline.

"I'm here to collect Bailey," I say.

"Do you prefer smoked fish?" he asks as if I haven't spoken. "There is a town in Scotland named Arbroath where a man of Scandinavian origin prepares smoked haddock that has to be tasted to be believed. I have a box flown in every week."

"Where's Bailey?" I ask.

"I know not of whom you speak."

"Yes, you do. She stupidly came to visit you this morning. I want her back."

He slices off a chunk of cheese and lifts it to his mouth on the tip of the knife. A pale pink tongue darts from between coral lips, its tip encircling the cheese like a snake before drawing it into his mouth.

"You intrigue me, Ms. Flynn," he says, swallowing the cheese. "You seem to think that being a reporter offers you some kind of protection. It does not. With a simple command, my guards will bend you over this table, strip you naked, and rape you in unison. They will not care about your screams or whom you write for. If I invite more men, they will join in, too. If you do not have enough holes ... they will make new ones."

He stabs the knife into the chunk of cheese and twists the blade to cut out a cone-shaped plug. Placing the plug of ripe, veined cheese on a small plate, he pushes it toward me.

"This is neither a boast nor a threat," he says. "This is truth."

I want to say something tough and defiant to show that I can't be intimidated, but I worry that if I even breathe, my bladder will release.

I push away from the table and stand. My eyes are glowering, but my legs are weak. I plead for them not to buckle. Turning around, I walk to the French doors, keeping my head high and my fear hidden beneath an immovable mask.

As my hand turns the knob and pulls the door, I catch a glimmer of movement out the corner of my eye. It's immediately followed by the sound of the two guards unzipping themselves.

I lose all dignity and bolt from the room. If the guards are laughing, I can't hear it over the sound of my own internal scream.

TWENTY-THREE

OUTSIDE THE RESTAURANT, I ashamedly dart into a nearby alley and shake. Tears flood down my cheeks and I hate myself for the weakness. I'm a mess, a blubbering, choking, sniveling pile of oozing estrogen.

The smug bastard scared me with words. That's supposed to be my domain.

An alarming screech of metal stops my heart and makes me swivel to study the dark recess of the alley as I suddenly realize that like a choking victim flushed with embarrassment, I have run away from the safety of others to a dangerously isolated spot.

A rusted sheet of corrugated iron slides off its greasy perch atop a foul-smelling dumpster to hit the alley floor, scaring a family of rats. Ten alarmingly blood-red eyes stare back at me before scurrying away. Their bald tails are what make them so disgustingly creepy, and each one twitches like the silenced rattle of a desert snake.

As my heart returns to its hollow beneath my ribs, another movement makes it leap again. From behind the dumpster, a shadow unfolds to form the shape of a man. There isn't enough light to make out his features, except that he's painfully thin with a wiry, unkempt beard.

A growl grows in the back of my throat as my right hand instinctively reaches for the knife in my boot.

The shadow holds up a pair of gloved hands to show he means no harm.

"You shouldn't be here," he says. His words are all rough-edged and stiff as though he doesn't use them much.

"No shit," I growl defensively. "Who the hell are you?"

"No one."

A flicker of light catches his eyes and there is a shimmer of pale blue within murky puddles of rat red.

He pulls a black knit cap off his head to reveal a bald pate, the gesture as stiff as his words, as though gentlemanly politeness was once driven home to him by a mother who never expected he'd end his days hiding in alleyways.

"You should go."

Recognition dawns.

"You're my Good Samaritan," I say. "Why'd you step in the other day? Wasn't your fight."

He begins to back away from me, moving deeper into the alley, deeper into the shadows. "That was a mistake," he says.

"Not from where I'm standing. I wanted to thank you."

"No need." He lifts an arm and points over my shoulder to the mouth of the alley where light still dares to shine. "You need to go. Don't come back. These are bad men."

I cast a glance to where he's pointing in case he's trying to warn me of someone else approaching, but there's nobody there.

When I turn back around, he's gone.

———

Returning to the car, I reach in to grab the box of tissues that Kristy always keeps on the back seat. I need to blow my nose and wipe my eyes and get a grip on—

Shit! Roxanne is missing.

Cursing, I stand on my tiptoes and scour the street. She couldn't have followed me to the tea house, I realize. I would have seen her.

Just as panic is threatening to make my head explode, I spot her half a block away. She's exiting another unseemly alley and stops by a lamppost to spit into the gutter. Between the two of us, we set women's good graces back a hundred years.

When she looks up, she spots me standing by the car. A smile broadens on her face and she waves as if we had plans to meet for a girly lunch and, hey, isn't this neat to bump into each other on the street beforehand?

I slide back into the car before I call her something that women aren't meant to call each other.

When she reaches the Bug, she has trouble with the door, like she's forgotten how to work her thumb. I reach over and open it from the inside.

She slides in with a goofy smile wider than her face and I know exactly what she was doing in the alley. I grab her arm and spot a fresh bead of blood in the crease of her elbow. Guess she didn't want to take her shoes off.

"What are you on?" I ask.

"Life, baby doll," she answers, her voice growing distant and dreamy.

"How'd you pay for it?"

She licks her lips. "Got gum?"

"Christ, did you share a needle with someone? Are you out of your goddamned mind? What would Bailey say?"

"Where is she?" Roxanne asks, twisting her head to take in the Bug's cramped interior. "Where's my sister?"

"I don't know," I snap.

"You were supposed to get her."

"I know. I failed."

Roxanne's lip curls into a snarl, but she can't maintain it. Her words slur. "Where ish she then?"

I shake my head and start the engine. "I'll find out," I say.

"Yeah." She reclines her chair and closes her eyes. "You d'tha."

I pull into traffic, wondering when a simple FOKing story had taken such a wrong turn.

———

I leave Roxanne buckled and oblivious in the passenger seat as I plug the parking meter and dart across the street to Mario's Deli. Wherever the heroin is taking her mind, it left her body behind.

Inside the deli, Mario takes one look at me and suggests a cinnamon raisin bagel with plain cream cheese and large coffee with an added double shot of espresso. The drink is called Two Shots in the Dark, which seems apropos.

"I look that bad, huh?" I ask.

"You are such a beauty," he says with honey on his tongue, "you could never look less than angelic. But a little sugar, some wholesome fiber, and a jolt of caffeine will bring the light back to your eyes."

How can I not smile in response to a line like that?

"Sounds perfect."

Mario grins and gets to work on my order.

At the red vinyl booth in the back, Eddie the Wolf is gnawing on a hangnail while still operating his laptop one-handed. I slide in across from him.

"Working on a remix?" I ask. "I saw a great one the other day that an engineer from PBS did. He turned some old Mr. Rogers clips into a great song called 'Garden of Your Mind'. Best use of Auto-Tune I've heard. And if you know anything about me, you know I despise Auto-Tune."

Eddie stops chewing on his nail and stares at me through wrinkled, narrow slits that remind me of newborn mice.

"Every time, you confuse me," he says. "Was what you just said even in English?"

I wink. "More like Geeklish."

"Ah. I don't speak that."

I glance at his laptop and array of smartphones. "Why don't I believe you?"

He frowns. "You want to place a bet?"

"Actually, I need some help."

"Try Craigslist. It's very good."

"This is more specific."

"I'm just a humble bookie."

"Yeah, and I make Beyoncé look homely."

"Again with the Geeklish?"

Mario brings my order to the table. "Don't let him fool you," he says. "I've seen him rock out to 'Single Ladies.'"

Mario and I share a grin, but Eddie doesn't join in. I take a gulp of my coffee and feel a layer of skin peel off my tongue. It's exactly what I need.

"I've been hearing about you," says Eddie, growing tired of the silence as I shove pieces of warm bagel into my mouth. "You are swimming with sharks, and there's blood in the water."

"And?" I prod.

"In a horse race between you and the Russian, you would not leave the gate. Hell, you wouldn't even make it out of the stables."

"Good thing I'm a gambler then, and not a pragmatist."

This time, Eddie's eyes dance despite the lack of curvature on his lips. "What kind of help do you seek?" he asks.

"Red Swan has a friend of mine. She went to him voluntarily, but I don't believe she was planning to stay. I need to know where he's keeping her."

"And what makes you think I can find such information?"

I smile as though butter wouldn't melt in my mouth. "I'll bet you five hundred that you can."

Eddie leans back in the booth and folds his arms across his chest. Despite his humble claims, he has the upper body of someone who has done his fair share of manual labor. Under his shirt, I wouldn't be surprised to find a lot of black and green ink from amateur artists without access to any sterilization equipment apart from a burning match or the occasional welding torch.

"You realize," he says, "you just lost the fifty dollars you wagered yesterday?"

I nod.

162

"And your new bet is that if I *find* the information you seek, I lose another five hundred."

I nod again.

"But if I do nothing, I win five hundred from you."

I nod for the third time.

"That is the most ridiculous wager I have ever heard."

"Can I get in on this?" Mario chirps in.

Eddie shakes a large-knuckled hand in frustration to shoo him away. "No. Stay out. One crazy person is enough."

"So you'll take the bet?" I ask.

Eddie sighs. "I think you are smarter than I give you credit for."

"I'm not sure if that's a compliment or an insult," I say.

"Good," says Eddie. "That's how I meant it."

TWENTY-FOUR

I RETURN HOME AND knock on Kristy and Sam's door. There's no answer, but before I turn away, a loud bang and a muttered curse drops down the stairwell from above.

I climb the lone flight of stairs to find Derek sitting on the corner of a couch, resting on the landing between two apartments, and licking a bloody gash across his knuckles.

He looks at me and winces. "Sorry, did I disturb you?" he says. "Damn thing got stuck in the doorway."

"Need a hand?" I ask.

"Sure. This is the last of the big stuff."

"Where's Shahnaz?"

"She had an assignment for work and I had the bright idea to move this stuff before she got back."

I wrinkle my nose. "Sorry you have to move."

Derek shrugs and a flush of embarrassment darkens his olive cheeks. "It's just, you know? Guns." He struggles to find the words.

"We still like you, Dixie, but your life gets crazy at times. You attract trouble like sugar attracts wasps. Last time, you were stabbed, and now … a bullet came right through our *floor*. What if we had kids? What if it was our bedroom?"

"I know," I say. "And I don't know how to apologize enough."

He attempts a smile. "Just help me move the couch and we'll call it even."

"OK," I say, "but I also need a favor."

"Seriously?"

"I wouldn't ask, except—"

Derek sighs. "Just spit it out. What do you need?"

"I have a friend downstairs who I need help getting upstairs and into my apartment."

"He can't walk?" he asks.

"It's a she, and right now I'm just happy that she's remembering to breathe."

Derek sighs louder. "Dare I ask?"

"Probably best not to."

"Right." Derek stands and grabs one end of the couch. "Let's move this first."

———

After Derek leaves my apartment, I roll Roxanne onto her side and prop a pillow behind her back. She's oblivious to it all, but the last thing I want is for her to have a seizure and choke to death on her own vomit.

I place a bucket on the floor and a glass of water on the nightstand.

Dixie's Tips #18: *If you're going to do drugs, stick with marijuana. It might make you stupider but, unlike everything else, it doesn't try to kill you.*

In the living room, I slip into my green leather trenchcoat with the oddly placed zipper that runs down the back. A friend of Mrs. Pennell's installed the zipper after I ripped the coat so badly that a regular repair wasn't possible. To be fair to myself, it wasn't my fault that my favorite coat very nearly ended up in the trash; I blame the driver of the car that tried to run me down. I pause.

Maybe Derek is right. I do attract trouble.

Knowing I should go to the office and check in with Stoogan, I lock the apartment door and head downstairs.

———

At my local watering hole, the Dog House, Bill the bartender takes one look at me and says, "Shouldn't you be at work?"

Bill is a former wrestler who gained notoriety as the Biting Bulgarian Bulldog, and his role as the villain shows in a face that only his friends can love. I count myself as one of those friends.

Before I can answer in the guilty affirmative, Bill has pulled a cold bottle of Warthog Ale from a basin of ice behind the bar and placed it on the counter.

I take a long swallow and then another. The third and fourth empty the bottle. A fresh one instantly replaces it.

"You working a story?" Bill asks.

I nod and take a sip on the new bottle.

"It kicking your ass?"

I shrug and take another, smaller sip.

"You'll beat it," he says. "You always do."

I look over at the empty stool on my right that is reserved for the ghost of Al Capone and raise my bottle to the empty space.

"He's not there," says Bill, who's the only one to ever see the ghost.

"Yeah, but he's probably watching," I say. "Some people have angels; I like to think I've at least got a dead gangster on my side."

Bill grins, and if you didn't know him, it would make lesser beings flee in terror.

"He's got a soft spot for you, Dix. But ghosts can't stop bullets."

"You heard about that, huh?"

"Frank told me. Also said you kept a cool head and returned fire to scare the bastard off. I think I even saw his chest swell with pride as he was telling it."

I grin. "Only Frank could find the silver lining of being shot at."

"That's how we get through life, Dix. Shit is gonna happen, but it's how we handle it that matters."

I raise my beer. "To assholes with guns."

Bill raises a glass of flat ginger ale and clinks it against my bottle. "And to making the fuckers duck."

TWENTY-FIVE

WHEN THE PHONE BEHIND the bar rings, Bill picks it up and listens before tucking the receiver under his chin and fixing me with a concerned gaze.

"You cheating on me?" he asks.

Not sure where he's going, I quip, "How could anyone else compete?"

"Eddie the Wolf?" he says. "I thought I was your bookie."

I flush slightly and hold out my hand for the phone. "It's not what you think. I needed information."

"He's dangerous."

"So are you."

"Not to my friends. A wolf may entice you with a smile, but inside he's always thinking how best to eat you."

"Thanks for the advice," I say impatiently, still holding out my hand, "but I'm a big girl."

Bill shrugs and hands me the phone.

"Eddie," I say, "how did you track me down?"

"Second phone call," he says. "You walk a small circle."

"And here I thought I was a wild and crazy young thing."

Eddie grunts.

"So did you find her?" I ask, turning serious.

"Of course."

"And?"

"The Russian wants someone to come for her."

"What do you mean?"

"He has her on the third floor of a four-story flophouse with one guard on the door. The guard likes to take long smoke breaks. That part isn't a secret. Every junkie and whore in the neighborhood knows the score."

"But?" I inject.

"There is also a small team camped out on the fourth floor. They're waiting for someone. I don't believe even the Russian would go to that much effort for you."

"No," I agree. "How's Bailey?"

"OK for now, but the Russian doesn't sweeten a trap with sugar. Whoever he's baiting will need to act soon if he wishes her to remain in one piece."

"Do you have an address?"

"You sure you want it?"

"Yes."

He tells me the address.

"Thanks. Guess you owe me five hundred now," I say.

"Minus my fee."

"Ahh, and your fee is—"

"Five hundred."

"Of course it is."

———

I hand Bill the phone and decline the third beer he pulls out of the cooler.

"Bad news?" he asks, returning the bottle to ice.

"Let's call it mixed."

"Anything I can do?"

I think about it. "Are any of your old wrestling pals living in town?"

Bill grins. "There's six of us who play cards once a week."

"They all as big as you?"

Bill grins wider and the pectoral muscles beneath his shirt do a little dance. "They wish," he quips, before adding, "but they're still pumping iron if that's what you mean. Why?"

The seed of a plan stretches for the light.

"Think they'd be up for causing a little chaos to help a lady?"

This time, Bill's grin sends a shiver down my spine. "You ring that bell," he says, "and they'll cause all the trouble you want."

TWENTY-SIX

I ARRIVE IN THE newsroom to let Stoogan catch a glimpse of my unconcerned, I-have-everything-under-control-and-still-look-marvelous face, then immediately detour to the morgue before he can pick up the phone and summon me to his office.

Lulu brightens at seeing me.

"The newsroom is buzzing over your FOK note, Dix," she says.

I'm puzzled. "Why?"

"You're our shining star, sweetie. If you can't tell the publisher to stick his notes where the sun don't shine, what chance do the rest of us have?"

I grunt. "If they're looking for Norma Rae, they need to get their eyes tested. I have all the leadership qualities of an expired corner store sandwich. Hell, I don't even *like* most of the newsroom."

"So you're still doing the Father's Day piece?" Lulu's painted eyebrows arch to new heights.

"Of course," I say with a smile. "But that doesn't mean the publisher will get exactly what he wants."

Lulu sticks her tongue in her cheek and makes it pop, while her eyes sparkle mischievously. "Uh-huh. See, you don't have to be a leader to inspire, you just have to remain true to you."

"Well, I don't know how else to be, but if I was recruiting for J-school, I certainly wouldn't pick me as the poster child."

"Of course not," Lulu agrees. "You'd want somebody sexy." She strikes a hooker pose. "Like me."

We both grin until I say, "You know they'd be more likely to put Mary Jane on the poster with the slogan *Journalism: It's not that hard anymore.*"

Lulu erupts into such a loud gale of laughter that she has to sit down, while several people in the newsroom across the hall stand up at their desks to see what is going on.

After calming down and giving me heck for wrecking her eye makeup, Lulu asks, "So what can I do for you?"

I hand her a piece of paper with an address written on it. "I want blueprints for this building," I say. "I need to know the layout of every floor, fire exits, any recent renovations, the works."

"And this is for your FOK note?"

I shrug. "The story has become a little more complicated than I counted on. How soon can you have the plans?"

Lulu glances at the clock. "I have a friend at City Hall who can sweet talk the engineers in Planning. End of day?"

"Perfect. If I'm not back, leave them on my desk."

"Count on it, but I have something else for you, too."

Lulu hands me a large brown envelope with a waxy, waterproof coating that looks like it's been stuck behind an outhouse for a few decades.

"What's this?" I ask.

"The photos from that funeral that you asked me to dig out from the archives. I also found the photographer. His card is inside, although I tried his phone number and it was disconnected."

I beam. "This is brilliant. I could kiss you."

"If I wasn't a straight woman, I'd take you up on that."

A witty retort raises its hand from the back row in my brain and begins to call "Ooh, ooh, ooh", but I ignore it. There's a good reason it's in the back row.

"My loss," I say instead.

I turn around to make my exit, but the doorway is blocked by Ishmael's nemesis.

"Hey, boss," I say. "I was just coming to see you."

The look on Stoogan's puffy white face says he doesn't believe me.

If I wasn't lying, I might be insulted.

———

After reassuring Stoogan that I have everything in hand and he shouldn't give the cover away to one of Mary Jane's sex-themed masterpieces of investigative spanking journalism, I slide into my office chair and open the waxy envelope.

Inside are half a dozen photographs, a creased business card that looks as if every corner has been used to remove kernels of corn from between somebody's teeth, and a rectangular cardboard sleeve.

The photos had originally been in color, but newspapers never aim for museum quality when they're only one day away from lining a birdcage. The pre-digital lab techs were trained to print the best images circled on a contact sheet and get them to the photo editor ASAP. So long as the image lasted long enough to make it into print, the editors could care less about historical value.

Thus, the photos are cracked, faded, and water damaged. Superimposing my memory of the newspaper clipping that showed Krasnyi Lebed as a pallbearer at the funeral of the man he replaced as boss, I can tell these were shot at the same funeral, but the poor quality makes even that much a deductive leap.

I open the cardboard sleeve to find the film negatives stuck together in a celluloid blob. Useless.

With a sigh I push the envelope away and close my eyes to think. What was I really hoping to find? A concrete connection between Joseph Brown and Krasnyi Lebed, the Red Swan, of course. But I already have that, don't I? Bailey told me her father was doing a job for Lebed when he disappeared, and the tea house maitre d', Mikhail, said Brown—*if he's alive*—has evidence that could bring down the Red Swan.

The trouble is that every question leads to another question; to write a story, I need answers.

I pick up the cardboard sleeve again and notice the date penciled in the corner. It's faded but still legible.

I pull my own notepad out of my back pocket and write it down. The year of the funeral is the same year Joe Brown went missing—the same year that Lebed came into full control of the city's Russian mob.

Could Brown have been more than he seemed?

Instead of being an underling, could he have been an equal? A threat to Lebed's throne, even? If so, he would surely have been one of the pallbearers.

I need a better look at the funeral photographs. I also need to know the exact date when Brown went missing, and the only person who accurately knows that information is Bailey.

TWENTY-SEVEN

THE TAXI DROPS ME in a part of town that smells of home. Not *my* home—too often filled with the static undertone of bickering and not-quite-good-enough—but home just the same. The humid air promises doughy perogies on the boil, onions in the frying pan, smoked ham on the bone, and hand-rolled cigarettes.

I find the photographer's shingle on a blink-and-you'll-miss-it doorway nestled between a Korean convenience store and a Ukrainian import food emporium with jars of jellied pigs feet displayed in the front window. I'm not sure if the display is meant to entice customers inside or scare them away.

There's no buzzer or bell in the entrance alcove, so I try the door. It's unlocked but not necessarily inviting. Inside, the narrow landing at the foot of the stairs is littered with broken glass vials, burnt squares of aluminum foil, and dead disposable lighters. The air is heavy with the stench of urine, rancid body juices, and no shortage of despair. Fortunately, the stairwell dwellers are out on their daily rounds.

At the top of the stairs, I'm given the choice of two doors. The one on my right has a discolored plastic sign that boasts *Mavis's Makeovers and Alterations*. The sign on the other door is etched metal, but the black paint that once made the letters stand out has cracked and peeled to the point where you need imagination rather than good eyesight to read what it says.

By process of elimination—i.e., I don't currently need a seamstress—I knock on the left-hand door.

When there's no answer, I knock again. Harder. And press my ear to the door.

A distant grunt and cough from inside is followed by a shuffling of feet and the *click-clack-click* of something solid hitting a wooden floor.

The noises continue until I can sense someone standing on the other side of the door, catching his breath. There's no peephole, so I don't have to fix my hair or put on a friendly smile.

Finally, a hoarse male voice calls, "Who's there?"

"Dixie Flynn. I'm a reporter with *NOW* and I'm looking for a photographer who used to work for us."

"You got ID?"

"Business card OK?" I pull one of the few cards that I carry with me and slide it under the door.

After a moment, the voice asks, "How old are you?"

"Same as my bra size, how about you?"

The man grunts again, but he must have liked the quip, since a bolt slides back from the other side of the door.

"Watch your step," he says as the door swings open to expose a maze of newspapers, magazines, books, and camera equipment of every vintage.

The passageway between the piles of fermenting pulp is deliberately wide to allow the man room to move as he sways from side to side like a penguin. Neither of his legs appears to work that well, and he relies heavily on a metal cane with a stabilizing tripod end. One of the rubber stoppers has fallen off the tripod, exposing a sharp-edged metal point. I glance at the floor and notice the scars it's left along the hallway—a trail in inverted Braille.

I close the door behind me and follow him through the warren into a cluttered room where two armchairs rest in front of two large windows with a view of the street. One of the chairs is indented in the shape of the man, while the other looks barely used.

He plops himself into the worn chair with a grateful sigh before pulling a pouch of loose tobacco and a pack of rolling papers out of a well-used pocket sewn into the chair's side.

The man jabs his chin in the direction of the other chair as he expertly rolls a thin cigarette and slips it between his lips. He lights it with an ancient steel Zippo and the smoke drifts to a gap at the sill of the window closest to him. I patiently wait for him to settle and open the conversation.

"I still read them," he says between puffs, "the newspapers...but I can't say I'm impressed. They've turned photojournalists into photographers and dulled their teeth with rubber caps. The only one with any guts anymore is that young punk up in Seattle, Hackett I think his name is, who stood his ground when a vigilante gang assassinated that murderer in the middle of the street. That took nerve. Everyone else is shooting grip 'n' grins and puppies licking ice cream. Even you"—he points his lit cigarette at me—"with that dead artist piece. The narrative was great, but the paper didn't run the crucial photo— the headless body and bloody canvas. Where's the balls?"

"The publisher keeps everyone's testicles in a jar," I say. "Kinda like those pickled feet downstairs. Break open only in case of emergency."

The man grins and holds out a hand. "I'm Victor Hendrickson. My shriveled jewels are locked in that jar, too."

I lean forward to take his hand. The skin is softer than I expect, like well-oiled calfskin.

"So, what're you looking for?" Victor asks. "Something for an anniversary piece? A look back at what *NOW* published before it became scared of its own shadow and everybody else's checkbook?"

I remove the photocopy of the funeral clipping from my pocket and hand it over. "I'm wondering if you still have any more shots from this day."

He blanches when he unfolds the paper and looks at the image. "Alimzhan Izmaylovsky's funeral," he says with perfect pronunciation.

"Good memory."

"Not really." He rubs his left leg. "That photo cost me both knees. The docs were able to replace my right one, but the left didn't take and the bastard insurance wouldn't let them try again. Too expensive, they said. Some fucking number cruncher refuses to tick a box and that's me, screwed for life. Sweet land of liberty? Bullshit! Only if you can afford it."

"How did the photo cost you your knees?" I ask.

Victor crushes the damp stub of his cigarette into the photocopied face of Krasnyi Lebed.

"Musta shot his bad side, I guess. Not that he has a good one. The same day the paper hit the streets, I was jumped by two guys and driven to a warehouse near the docks. The Swan was there, but the bastard didn't say a word. Just watched with those dead eyes of his as his goons took an axe handle to both my knees. When they were done, they drove me back to the paper and dumped me on the street. It took awhile for people to realize I wasn't a homeless drunk sleeping off a bender and needed medical help. But I got off easy."

"In what way?" I ask.

Victor sighs. "The copy editor who wrote the cutline—just a young guy in his twenties—he had the tops of all his fingers snipped off. They generously left him his thumbs and cauterized the stubs with hot tar."

"Jesus!"

Victor nods. "The Red fucking Swan knows how to send a message. I was warned he would take my eyes next, so I never did go back to the paper. Not sure what happened to the editor."

"I'm sorry."

"Yeah, me too—sorry I couldn't nail that son-of-a-bitch with something that would stick."

"Did you keep any of your photos?"

"Silly question." Victor grins. "Of course I did. He took my mobility, not my ego."

"What about from Izmaylovsky's funeral? The ones in our archive are ruined."

"Newspapers may write our history, but I've never trusted them to preserve it." With some effort, Victor pulls himself out of the chair. "Heat up some water for coffee and I'll dig out my scrapbooks."

I smile. "Deal."

———

Over cups of instant coffee, Victor and I flip through a dozen scrapbooks filled with photographs and newspaper clippings. Although he has blessedly arranged his lifetime's collection by year, with at least a dozen scrapbooks dedicated to each one, he hasn't organized the photos into any subcategories beyond that.

Victor comes across the funeral first.

"I hid inside a crypt," he tells me. "I knew the Russians would post guards at each entrance to keep the media away, so I paid the groundskeeper to unlock one of the family tombs on a small hill near the gravesite, and I spent the night. Good job I don't have much of an imagination, 'cause that place was on the spooky side. But the next morning, the view was perfect for a long lens and steady nerves. None of the goons spotted me." He chuckles. "I even took pics of the cops setting up their surveillance, but they weren't exactly trying to go unnoticed."

I sit beside him and look closely at the photos.

"Anyone in particular you're looking for?" he asks.

"A man named Joe Brown. I'm wondering if he was one of the pallbearers."

Victor shakes his head. "No chance. Every pallbearer was pure Ruskie. If you're born in America, you can only go so high in this organization. And with a name like Brown, he wouldn't even make it to middle management, but—"

Victor flips forward a few pages and stabs his finger at a photo. "This could be your man."

I look down to see a plain face frozen in time, unkempt hair and an ill-fitting suit, standing beside a giant oak. The picture is grainy, obviously shot from a long distance and enlarged, but I can see Bailey in the shape of his face—especially the eyes, which are tired and forlorn.

"Looks like he wasn't invited," I say.

"Nope. He was standing quite a distance away, but you can see in his face that he wants to be there. That's why I snapped it. Curious, huh?"

"This didn't run in the paper, did it?"

"Nope. No reason to. Is that your man?"

"I think so. Any chance I can get a copy?"

Victor peels back the plastic sheet that's holding the photo in place. "Take this one," he says. "Not even sure why I held onto it."

I take one more look. The face, apart from its passing resemblance to Bailey, is that of a stranger. A small romantic part of me had secretly hoped Joe Brown and my Good Samaritan would turn out to be one and the same. It would have made my next step so much simpler.

I slip the photo into my pocket and stand up to go.

"One more thing," I say. "I forgot to check the story, but how did Izmaylovsky die?"

"Heart attack," says Victor. "Died in his sleep. Not the way a bastard like that should go."

I nod. "Thanks for your time," I say. "It's been helpful."

"Anytime." He takes my hand and holds on to squeeze it with tight sincerity. "And if you ever get a chance to bring the Swan down, give me a call. I'll bust open that jar, strap on my balls, and join in."

"You know, Victor," I say. "I just may take you up on that."

TWENTY-EIGHT

THE LAST PERSON I expect to bump into is coming down the stairs as I enter my building's lobby from the street. We both freeze in place, uncomfortable and awkward.

The bastard is still handsome in that stormy-eyed, kissable-lipped kind of way that normally makes my heart flutter. Unfortunately, the last time I saw this man, we had a little misunderstanding in which I held a knife to his throat after trashing the art gallery he owns.

"Declan," I say to cleverly show I haven't forgotten his name even though I've tried. "What are you doing here?"

His eyes are more hazelnut than almond, in both shape and color, which tells me he was hoping to avoid exactly this situation. His loss for words is worse than mine.

"You didn't come to see me, did you?" I say.

"I … well … I was—"

Bare feet patter on the stairs behind him and Kristy bursts around the bend like Sonic the Hedgehog coming out of a loop. With a tiny eek, she grasps the handrail to stop herself from slamming into Declan.

I fold my arms across my chest and flash a look of annoyance that is too close to my mother's for comfort, yet seems to fit as though custom made.

"Oh, hey, Dix," says Kristy with a fake and awkward smile. "Thought you'd be at the office."

"Why's he here?" I ask. "Does Sam know?"

Kristy sticks her lower lip out in an impressive pout. "Yes, Sam knows. We weren't doing anything inappropriate."

"Such as?" I ask.

"Such as … anything," Kristy jabs back weakly.

"I suppose he's consulting on your art collection."

"No! We were … we're just—"

"I'm standing right here," says Declan. "You don't need to talk around me."

I lock onto Declan's gaze. His eyes are smoldering yet cold. "Were you having sex?"

He blushes slightly, and I wish he wouldn't. "No."

I move my gaze to Kristy. "Were you?"

"No."

"But even if we were," declares Declan, "it's of no concern of yours."

"I disagree," I say. "Kristy and Sam are my friends. Anything that affects them, affects me."

"That's sweet, Dix," says Kristy. "We love you, too."

"So what were you doing?" I ask.

Kristy sighs. "Declan's agreed to be our donor."

"Sperm donor?" I ask.

"Of course," says Kristy, her brow knitting in confusion. "What else would we need a man for?"

"Why?"

"Look at him," says Kristy. "He's got good genes, and he's smart too."

I look at Declan. "I've done nothing wrong," he says.

"Don't be mad, Dix," says Kristy. "It's just, you know, business."

Declan takes the rest of the stairs until he's standing directly in front of me. "Can I go now?"

I keep my eyes locked on his as I step aside. "Keep it business," I say as he brushes past. "I'm protective of my friends."

"Except when you get your wires crossed," Declan snarls back. "Then it's just Dixie for herself."

I almost rabbit punch him in the back of the head as he pushes through the door, but I clench my teeth instead.

When he's gone, I turn back to Kristy. "Really?" I ask.

Kristy shrugs. "I want my baby to look that cute. Did you notice his dimples?"

I sigh. Yes, I had noticed the dimples, and the eyes, and the way his jeans ...

"You want a glass of wine?" Kristy asks. "I've just opened a bottle."

"Maybe later. I have some work first."

"OK, just knock, I'm gonna watch *Ellen*."

———

I knock on Mr. French's door and hear his parakeet, Baccarat, begin to chirp from inside.

"Is someone at the door?" I hear Mr. French say as he clomps down the hall. "Oh, what a smart girl you are. Yes indeed."

When he opens the door, all three feet, ten inches of him twitches with delight. He's impeccably dressed, as always, in tweed pants and sporting one of his many colorful sweater vests. Between his lips is the stem of a briar pipe carved in the shape of a busty mermaid, and the smoke has the distinct aroma of licorice and orange.

But there's something new. Dusting his upper lip is the beginning of a platinum moustache.

I point at it and ask, "Errol Flynn?"

Mr. French beams. "To begin with, perhaps, but I'm planning for a bit more length so that I can twirl the ends à la Rollie Fingers. I've even bought a lovely jar of French moustache wax in anticipation."

"I can see that on you," I say.

His eyes twinkle. "Come in, come in, Miss Flynn—any relation to Errol?"

I only shake my head.

"Pity. Anyway, Baccarat must have known it was you, his chirp was particularly robust upon your knock."

After following him into the main room and making appropriate kissing/cooing noises to Baccarat, I settle into the couch but decline his offer of tea.

"I'm afraid," I begin, "that time is of the essence."

"Intriguing, Miss Flynn. Do go on."

"I need you to do a bit of spying for me."

"Certainly. I have my walkie-talkies all charged from our last adventure, and I can get Clifford to help out if—"

"I have another assistant for you this time," I interrupt. "A photographer named Victor who knows the people involved and why it's important to be careful."

"Ah," he says, "sounds ominous."

I nod. "The people I want you to watch are dangerous. So your job, should you choose to accept it, is simply to observe and report back to me. You are not to engage them at any time and you are not to be seen."

"Stealth is my specialty, Miss Flynn. When do I start?"

I give him a copy of the address where Bailey is being held. "I need to know what's happening there now. I've filled in Victor with what faces to look out for."

Mr. French grabs a pair of two-way radios off the bookshelf and hands one to me.

"Channel seven," he says. "If you can't reach me, drop to channel three. We'll be set up within the hour."

TWENTY-NINE

IN THE APARTMENT, I shake Roxanne awake and show her the photo of the uninvited guest at Izmaylovsky's funeral.

"Is this your father?" I ask.

Roxanne snarls at me and pushes the photo away. She tries to bury herself beneath the sheets again, but I yank them away.

"I've had enough of this," I yell. "Look at you. You're killing yourself with this junk and you don't give a damn. People want to help—let them."

Roxanne glares at me, her pupils enlarging and dilating as though attempting to journey back from a dark pit, until her throat suddenly bulges, then she grabs the bucket I left by the side of her bed and vomits into it.

"Charming," I say before heading into the bathroom and retrieving a cold, wet cloth.

When I return to the bedroom, I press the cloth against her forehead as she dry heaves into the bucket. When she's done, I use a corner of it to wipe the sticky edges of her eyes and mouth.

"How is this helping?" I ask. "Your sister is being held by a Russian mobster and you're shooting poison into your veins."

"Don't fucking judge me," Roxanne croaks.

"Somebody has to. And better it's someone who gives a damn."

"Why?" she snarls. "What the fuck do you care what happens to me or my sister? You're nobody to us."

"I'm involved."

"Who asked you to be?"

I shake my head. "No one."

"Exactly."

She sits up and attempts to swing her legs over the side of the bed, but her lower body doesn't cooperate and she ends up flopping back onto the pillows.

"What I do," she continues in frustration, "is none of your damn business."

"So you like being a whore and a junkie and a waste of space?" I growl.

"Maybe I do."

"I don't believe you."

"Well, too bad, because you don't know me from spit on the ground."

"And yet I want to help you."

"That's your problem."

I sigh and show her the photo again. "Is this your father?"

This time she studies it. "Yeah. So what?"

"Do you know when he went missing? Was it before or after Alimzhan Izmaylovsky's funeral?"

"Who? I wasn't even born yet, how would I know?"

"Bailey never talked about it?"

Roxanne shrugs and looks away. "Yeah, OK, she did."

"Did she mention a date?"

Roxanne's lips curl with the full intent of telling a lie, but then relax as though deciding the truth is easier.

"June twenty-first," she says. "Bailey baked these chocolate cupcakes on the anniversary every year. They were supposedly dad's favorite and she thought if he smelled them baking, he would come home." She wipes at her eyes. "For a while she even had me believing it, too."

I flip the photo over to reveal the date of the funeral. June 28.

"He was alive when this photo was taken," I say. "That's seven days after he left the apartment."

"So?"

"If he was alive a week after his disappearance, there's no reason to think he isn't still."

Roxanne's laugh is soft, dark, and laced with bile. "Maybe you should bake some cupcakes, then," she says snarkily. "He might smell them and come running."

———

When Pinch arrives, he's dressed in pristine head-to-toe black and sporting a fashionable pair of Winklepicker boots with pointed toes so sharp they look dangerous.

His eyes are hard as he steps through the door and takes in the room, and I worry that I've pissed him off by asking for yet another favor. Without saying a word, he brushes his hand over the shotgun-shell damage to the left of the door, his index finger flicking off traces of dried blood. My attacker's blood. Mikhail's blood.

Next, he glances up at the bullet hole in the ceiling as though calculating the angle, and finally he fixes his gaze on Roxanne, who's sitting on the couch nervously chewing her nails. I can read the same concern on his face that crossed mine when I wondered how Mikhail knew where to find us.

"The fresh air isn't doing you much good, darling," he says. "You looked better with a three-hundred-pound sailor on your back instead of this monkey."

Roxanne flashes him the finger.

Pinch turns to me. "Never trust a junkie, Dix. Ever. They'll take your good intentions and sharpen them into knives to throw back in your face. If she's involved, I'm not."

"She's not involved," I say, making the decision on the spot.

"Like hell I'm not! You're going after my sister. I need to be there."

Pinch glares at me. "Have you told her what you're planning?"

"None of the details."

"What about the address?"

I shake my head.

"I am still here," Roxanne shouts.

"That's a problem we need to fix," says Pinch.

"Hey, fuck you, shorty!"

I grab Roxanne's arm and yank her to her feet. "I need you to go next door—"

"Fuck you, too," Roxanne snarls. "It's *my* sister."

"But Pinch is right. You can't be trusted." My voice breaks slightly, but I batten down the hatches and lock them tight. "I should have known better. I wanted to believe that nobody could possibly choose to live like you do. But you never wanted to leave, did you? That's why Bailey had such a difficult time finding you. The sister she remembers died a long time ago."

"You have no right to keep me here."

"I know," I say. "But I can't risk you roaming free. Not yet. Once Bailey is back, you can choose your life. I won't stop you."

I march her across the hall and knock on the door. When Kristy answers, I push Roxanne inside.

"Sorry," I say, "but I need a favor. You still keep a set of handcuffs? Good ones?"

Kristy nods and Roxanne's eyes widen as I relate what needs to be done.

THIRTY

On the drive over to the *NOW* offices in Pinch's vintage Jaguar, I ask why he's acting so pissy.

"'Cause if it's PMS, tell me now," I say, "and I'll bail. Hell, there are some months when I can't even stand myself."

A small grin creases his mouth. "I'm not used to doing favors," he says. "And I'm also not used to"—he pauses—"not used to finding that I enjoy them."

"Awww," I say. "Is that a compliment?"

"Yes. And that's unusual, too."

"Why?"

"Because I don't like anyone."

"Me either."

His grin widens. "That's not true. Your problem is you like too many people."

"I do?"

"You have a big heart."

"And you don't?"

He shakes his head with minimal energy, barely a twitch. "I keep it small and wrapped in a full-metal jacket. Makes it harder to hit."

I reach over and stroke his arm. "I don't believe you."

"You should."

———

The office is deserted when we walk into the newsroom and cross to my desk.

"You actually work here?" Pinch asks, taking in the rows of cluttered desks; low-walled, no-privacy cubicles; and lack of natural light.

"I'm out a lot," I say. "Some reporters can work a phone like it's an extension of themselves, but I need to look people in the eye. I'm an adolescent dog stuck in the muck between the old newshounds and Facebook pups." I chuckle. "A few months back one of the interns asked if I was tweeting, and I thought she was accusing me of being high."

Pinch grins. "It's not like you see on TV shows, is it?"

I laugh. "Not even close. No smoking, no drinking, no swearing or cracking jokes. Hell, laugh too loud and the publisher might accuse you of creating a disturbance. The last fistfight I witnessed was back in my *Chronicle* days, and that was between the news editor and the ME over a front-page headline. As fucked up as it sounds, I sometimes miss that passion."

"I'd go crazy."

I wink. "Most of us do."

Lulu has come through again, and the building's blueprints are waiting on my desk. I unroll them and weigh down the corners with the various odds and ends—empty stapler, Mickey Spillane and Raymond Chandler bobbleheads, etc.—that litter my desk.

"Bailey is being held on the third floor," I say. "There's one guard with her as bait, but four gunmen waiting on the fourth. Their plan is to lure Bailey's dad into the trap when the guard goes out for one of his frequent smoke breaks, and then the four move in for the capture or kill."

"Who tipped you off?" Pinch asks.

"A gambler."

"Can you trust him?"

I shrug. "Not really, but this has the ring of truth to it. He's not a fan of Lebed."

"Money doesn't require friendship or loyalty, Dix, only opportunity. Never trust anyone where greed is the only binding factor. There's always someone who can outbid you."

"Yes, Yoda," I quip.

Pinch studies the blueprints, his finger running up and down the center staircase. He turns the page and studies the aerial view, too. The building has a flat roof, three exterior fire escapes, and another in the center that connects with the interior staircase.

"The Swan is too clever to set only one trap," he says. "Four men can provide enough firepower for what he's expecting, but their location isn't ideal. Seconds will be wasted getting down those stairs."

"He doesn't want them being seen," I say. "Joe never showed up for Roxanne. Lebed obviously wants to make this choice look easier."

"Maybe." Pinch sighs and turns his back on the map. He closes his eyes for a second, then turns back and studies the map once more.

When he's satisfied, he straightens up, brushes some invisible lint off his sleeve and looks at his watch. "Ready?"

I nod, gulp, and follow him back to his car.

———

We park a short distance away from the building and I switch on the walkie-talkie. The static hisses for a second before clearing.

"Mr. French?"

"We're here, Miss Flynn. Eyes in the sky. All clear."

"Any movement?" I ask.

"The guard appears to be trying to kill himself with a smoke break every twenty minutes. Regular as clockwork. If my bowels did that, I could cut back on my morning prunes."

I grimace. "Any sign of the father?"

"None, I'm afraid. Victor has been scanning the streets with his telephoto lenses, but nothing yet."

"When is the guard due to take his next break?"

"Twelve minutes. He exits the front door, lights his cigarette, and walks half-a-block to either the north or south. He's very predictable, which means he'll go north next time."

"Any movement on the fourth floor?"

"Quiet as a church mouse, although Victor has noticed occasional wisps of smoke drifting over the roof. He thinks somebody is sneaking onto the rear fire escape for clandestine smoke breaks."

Having heard enough, Pinch slips out of the car and opens the trunk to prepare.

"Is Bill here?" I ask.

"Mr. Bulldog is in position," answers Mr. French. "And he's brought friends. Very large friends."

"Give him a two-minute heads up when the guard is about to show."

"Roger that. Where will you be?"

"You'll see me."

"Be careful."

I swallow. "Stay out of sight. I'll be fine."

I switch off the walkie-talkie and slip it under the passenger seat. If anything goes wrong, I don't want Lebed to know that I had any help.

Outside, I walk to the rear of the car to join Pinch.

"Change of plan," he says, handing me a gun.

By the time I find my voice to protest, Pinch is dashing across the street and vanishing into the shadows.

THIRTY-ONE

"Change of plan?" I mutter to myself. "What the hell!"

We had discussed the plan over a dozen times and agreed that Pinch was to accompany me into the building to make sure I didn't get my ass shot off.

Now I was on my own and having second thoughts about not involving Frank. Of course, he would have been thrilled with that conversation: "You *think* a friend of yours is being held captive by Russian mobsters. And based on a tip from a back-street bookie, you want me to get a SWAT team and execute a search warrant?"

Despite his great fondness for me, there's only so much rope Frank is willing to wind out. At least Pinch, until he deserted me, hadn't questioned my twisted logic.

I study the gun: Italian-made Beretta 92FS semi-automatic with a non-reflective black finish. I eject the magazine and count fifteen rounds of 124-grain 9mm jacketed hollow-point. It's a nice gun—not as comforting as my own, which Pinch told me to leave at home—but solid and reliable. I just hope I don't need to use it.

After double-checking the safety, I slip the gun into the rear waistband of my jeans and move to the corner of the building opposite the one where Bailey is being held. I work on my breathing as I wait, trying to slow each inhale as though I'm running a marathon or swimming laps in a pool. My lungs convulse, fighting me, wanting to race like greyhounds with an electric rabbit in their sights.

Across the street, a broad-shouldered man with distinct five o'clock stubble and nicotine-fueled eyes steps out of the doorway and lights a cigarette. His gaze takes in the breadth of the street—mentally ticking off the junkies, whores, welfare bums, and storeowners that he knows on sight—before heading north for a casual stroll. If he's bored, he isn't showing it. Every muscle moves like a coiled spring.

I wait two heartbeats before stepping out of the shadows and crossing the road. Out the corner of my eye, I notice the guard turn his head to check me out. I'm dressed casually in dark jeans, leather boots, loose T-shirt, and my long green trenchcoat.

I don't hold his interest for long, especially when the wrestlers turn the corner ahead of him.

Bulldog's boys are boisterous, pushing and shoving each other as they fight over a glass jug of Tennessee whiskey. I watch the guard's pace falter as he takes in the collective size of the encroaching group.

I reach the doorway but freeze in place when the guard suddenly swivels back toward me, a silent alarm tripped somewhere in his brain. Time slows and my panic rises when he tosses his cigarette aside. I watch it spin and spark as it bounces into the gutter.

When our eyes meet, I sense recognition, and wonder if Lebed has warned him about me. But how could the Red Swan possibly believe I would attempt this when even I think it's crazy?

The guard's right hand reaches inside his jacket, but whether to grab a phone or a gun, I'll never know, because in the same instant the gang of rowdy wrestlers swallows him whole.

I immediately push through the door and head up the stairs.

———

Nobody blocks my way to the first landing and I waste no time in rounding the bend and moving swiftly to the second. *This is all part of Lebed's plan*, I remind myself to keep my confidence in check. Lebed *wants* Joe to make it to the third floor.

It's getting back out that'll be the problem.

As I round the second floor on my way to the third, I hear a steel bolt sliding back from one of the closed doors on either side of the stairwell.

I don't stop to look. That'll come later.

On the third floor, I stop on the landing to catch my breath. There are four doors to choose from, but the guard has made it easy by leaving one of them slightly ajar.

Sweat beads on my scalp, pools under my arms, and runs between my breasts. I smell my own fear leaching from my pores. It's sour and unpleasant.

As soon as I go through that door, everything changes. Does Lebed want a dead journalist on his hands? I'm betting heavily that he doesn't. But even if that's the case, has he told his team of hired thugs in the room above?

You should have thought of that before you came this far, says an inner voice with such sarcastic clarity that I almost look around to see who's spoken.

"Shit!" I curse under my breath and move closer to the door. "Now or never, Dixie," I tell myself.

Now or never.

I push open the door and vanish inside.

THIRTY-TWO

EASING DOWN THE HALLWAY, my eyes and ears alert for any sudden movement, I'm surprised to find the Beretta back in my hand with the safety flicked off and a bullet in the chamber. I don't remember grabbing it, but apparently another part of my brain has kicked into survival mode.

The first door I pass leads into a bleak bedroom with little more than four walls and a single unmade bed. The air holds the flophouse smell of hired men—body odor, masturbation, and gun oil—but the space is all ghosts and no threat.

At the end of the hall are two more doors before I reach the living room. The one on the left is for a toilet and stand-up shower that would make Mr. Clean weep, while the other opens to a barely used galley kitchen. I make sure both rooms are unoccupied before passing.

Entering the living room, I see a woman tied to a wooden chair in front of a small portable television that's broadcasting QVC without sound. And if that doesn't count as cruel and unusual, I'm not sure what does. The rest of the room is empty.

When I appear in front of her, Bailey's eyes grow four times their normal size. Her face is red and puffy with signs of bruising on her cheeks and forehead. At one point, she must have struggled.

I wink at her, slip the Beretta into my pocket, and replace it with my switchblade, Lily. Vivid blue tape has been wrapped in a thick band around her head, sealing her mouth. I slide the thin blade into the gap behind her ear to slice an opening before attempting to peel it off. Freeing her mouth, I leave the tape that's become stuck firmly in her hair to be removed when we have more time.

Bailey works her jaw, wincing as her tongue tends to the dried and broken skin of her lips, while I slice through the rope and plastic straps that hold her to the chair.

When I'm done, I ask if she can stand.

"You shouldn't have come," she says as she pushes herself slowly out of the chair. Her body is stiff and her muscles tremble from fatigue and stress. "This is a trap."

"I know," I say, "but it's a trap for your father."

"You think Lebed's gonna care?"

"I'm banking on it."

Bailey stands up straight and groans as electric pins and needles course through her muscles.

"You're either very brave or very stupid," she says.

"Yeah," I agree. "I was just thinking the same thing."

Bailey cracks a smile, but it fades just as quickly as it bloomed. "My dad was never going to come, was he?"

I slip the knife into my boot and retrieve the Beretta. "Let's talk about that later. Preferably over a beer in a nice little pub run by a very large and protective friend of mine."

With a grimace, Bailey swings an arm around my neck so I can hold part of her weight.

"I could really use the toilet," she says.

"No time. Sorry."

A boisterous cry erupts from the street, followed by the unmistakable crunch of something overly large and metallic being overturned.

"What's that?" Bailey cries out.

I grin. "Just some friends causing havoc."

A whoosh of gasoline catching fire is followed by the sound of breaking glass. Voices begin to rise in chants and protest. Every riot begins as a party.

"That's our cue," I say.

Apparently, it's also somebody else's: bursts of automatic gunfire erupt on the floor above us, followed by the stomping of panicked feet, screams of pain, and loud Russian voices. More glass shatters, and the downward concussion of a second explosion nearly knocks us to our knees.

Bailey looks at me in blood-drained panic, her face reflecting what I already know: we're in a war zone.

"We need to move," I say, trying not to show that I'm just as frightened as she is.

With Bailey leaning against me for balance as her legs work out the kinks of being strapped tight to a chair, we head quickly down the hallway toward the apartment door and the stairwell to the street beyond.

Two feet from the end, the door is suddenly kicked open by an ugly thug armed with an MP5 submachine gun. His scalp is partially singed and the only thing that delays him from squeezing the trigger is his surprise over seeing two women rather than the man he was likely told to expect.

Everything in that moment screams at me to run and hide, pull the covers over my head and pretend there are no monsters under the bed—but I'm expecting it. Pinch warned me about the overwhelming impulse for flight and how, in times of war, we need to disable that core hard-wired instinct. He also said that was why so many battle-weary soldiers have difficulty returning to civilian life; once that switch is disabled, it can be a difficult thing to reset again.

Shoving Bailey behind me, I snap the Beretta into a two-handed grip and fire three shots in rapid succession at the intruder's center mass. Each bullet hits the man's chest and expands to nearly double its size, sending him flying backward into the door across the landing.

My first thought is, *Oh shit!*

But my second is, *No blood.*

The man sits up, his chest oozing white stuffing from a ballistic vest. If I'm lucky he'll have a broken rib or two and find it difficult to catch his breath, but that will only slow him down.

Cursing in Russian, the thug recovers faster than I'd like and, still sitting, brings his MP5 to bear.

I immediately grab Bailey's hand and rush back toward the living room before throwing her screaming, terrified body onto the ground as if she's a skim board and we're going to do a little sand surfing.

Bullets zip inches above our heads as I desperately shove Bailey around the corner, where the large appliances in the kitchen next door will offer some protection.

Not giving her time to catch her breath or allow panic to freeze her in place, I point at the window that overlooks the street.

"Open the window," I yell.

"There's no fire escape on this side," Bailey protests.

"Just get it open," I yell back. "Smash it if you have to."

Bullets are racing down the hallway, spraying the far wall and destroying everything in their path. The living room begins to fill with white dust from disintegrating plaster as the gunman slowly makes his way up the hall toward us. He's angry, injured, and firing without discretion, knowing that we have no place to run or hide.

Before reaching us, his magazine runs empty. I hear it eject and hit the floor with a metallic clang. In the next instant, a fresh one is snapped into place.

Knowing I have to act before he can slap the charging handle forward to fire again, I launch myself across the floor directly into his path. He's standing in the middle of the hall, staring directly ahead, not down, but when he spots me on the floor, he smiles through bloody teeth—until I fire.

The hollow-point round hits his ankle with such explosive force that his foot is nearly ripped clean off the bone.

I don't wait to watch him crumple to the ground—the piercing intensity of his scream tells me I've bought a little time.

I scramble back to Bailey's side and help her shove the window open to its full height. Below us, the wrestlers are cheering the fiery destruction of an overturned car. The smoke is thick and black. In the distance I can hear sirens approaching from all directions.

The heat in the room is too intense to be coming just from the burning car, however. I glance up and see the entire fourth floor also ablaze.

Pinch.

Change of plans.

That's why only one gunman appeared at our door and not four. Pinch must have scaled the fire escape and entered via the roof to take on the Russians before they moved on me. Pity one got away.

Pressing two fingers between my lips, I release an ear-splitting whistle—the same one my mother always gave me hell for and which my father taught me to perfect.

Two of the wrestlers look up and wave.

"Form a net," I call down. "I need you to catch someone."

Bailey looks at me in abject terror. "You're not serious."

"The police are on their way, the hall is blocked by an angry and armed Russian, and we need to get out now. You're first."

"But—"

I don't let her finish as I drag and push her to the window ledge until she's balanced precariously on her knees.

Down below, the wrestlers have linked their arms to form a human net. Their bulging biceps make it resemble a small inflatable bed.

"Close your eyes."

Bailey's eyes grow wider.

"Close them," I say. "It'll be over soon."

Bailey closes her eyes and I shove her out.

"Don't move, bitch!"

Shit!

I turn around to see the Russian thug sitting on the floor, a river of blood leading from his right foot into the hall. His submachine gun is aimed directly at me, and despite the pain glistening on his face, his aim seems true.

"Drop the gun."

I drop the Beretta.

Smoke is filling the room from above, but I'm beginning to doubt I'll have to worry about it.

"Who are you?" His accent is thick and cumbersome, the English words practically choking him.

"A journalist," I say. "Your boss doesn't want me dead."

The man spits on the floor. "My orders are clear. No one leaves alive."

"That why he killed your friends?" I glance up at the ceiling. "Leave no witnesses?"

The man looks confused for a second before clarity returns to his eyes. "That is not Red Swan. It is short bastard in black. His corpse will be crispy by now."

"Just like yours, then," I say.

The thug's finger twitches on the trigger as I dive to one side and pull the knife out of my boot. The first spray of bullets misses me completely, finding the open window where I stood and sending a shower of glass and lead over the street like lethal fireworks.

But as the gun circles back, I realize the distance between us is too great for a knife to give me any advantage.

The Russian realizes this, too.

"I would rather kill you with bare hands," he says as ripples of flame suddenly burst across the ceiling. "But we run out of time."

He raises his gun again just as a black blur bursts through the doorway and slams into him with a shoulder block that would make any NFL couch proud. The gun sails out of the Russian's grip as the blur circles behind him and locks a skinny forearm around his throat.

The Russian's eyes bulge as the intruder squeezes tight.

"You should leave," says the blur. "Now."

To my surprise, it isn't Pinch.

It's my Good Samaritan.

"What are you doing here?" I ask.

"Does it matter?"

"I find it odd."

"Odder than standing here while a building burns to the ground around you?"

The Russian thrashes his legs in panic as the life is slowly squeezed from him, my Samaritan's boney forearm locked in a merciless vise.

"Don't kill him," I say. "He's only a gun for hire."

"He wouldn't give you the same courtesy, and I don't like who hired him."

"We need to talk," I say.

The man nods. "But let's pick a better time. The stairwell should be clear if you go now."

"Are you coming?" I ask.

"Right behind you."

I find the Beretta and slip it back into my jeans as I take off down the hall. The cracking timbers sound like breaking bones, and the fire cackles at my back.

THIRTY-THREE

I RUSH DOWN THE concrete stairs, taking them two at a time, grabbing the sticky handrail to propel me across each landing and down toward the next. At the same time, pounding feet are rushing up from below and I wonder if it's Frank, and if so, what his face will reveal when he sees that it's me.

I hope he's not too disappointed.

I round the next bend just as an armed Russian comes into view on the stairs below.

He raises his gun before I can reach the Beretta, and I know he's going to shoot despite my hands reaching for the sky in a sign of surrender.

His trigger finger whitens in the moment before his right eye implodes and the back of his skull is smeared across the wall.

I only hear the gunshot's echo, no louder than a cough, after I watch him die.

It came from behind me.

As I turn, Pinch reaches underneath my coat and removes the Beretta. He's holding a silenced pistol in one hand as he pockets the Beretta and hands me a lemon-scented disinfectant wet wipe.

"That's the last one," he whispers into my ear. "Everything go OK with Bailey?"

"She's outside," I say, struggling to find words.

"Join her," he says. "And use the wipe. It's best to have clean hands."

I feel him move away. By the time I complete my turn, he's vanished again.

Not entirely knowing why, I use the napkin to clean my hands. The ritual is oddly soothing and I rub the disinfectant deep into my flesh as I quickly finish my descent.

———

Outside, I take hold of Bailey's hand and tell the wrestlers to disappear.

"You're sure?" one of them asks.

I nod. "I appreciate all you've done, but I don't want you getting in trouble with the police. I've set up a tab at Bulldog's, but just remember that I'm a poor working stiff."

Red and blue lights are rushing toward us from both ends of the street.

"You just want all the firemen to yourself," says the wrestler with a smirk.

I can't help but smile. He could be right. Looking around at the chaos they've created, I ask, "Where's the other guard?"

The wrestler returns my grin and winks. "The cops'll find him."

As the wrestlers disperse in one direction, Bailey and I cross the street to vanish into the open-mouthed crowd.

Better nobody knows we were here than try to explain why we were.

THIRTY-FOUR

BAILEY INSISTS WE STOP at Scissors & Sizzle before continuing on to the Dog House. The owner, Marjorie, lives above the salon and after one look at Bailey and her tape-strewn hair, opens the shop without question.

Bailey sprints to the bathroom then joins Marjorie at one of the sinks at the back. I make sure the front door is locked and the window blind is firmly closed to block out interior light.

I have no idea what the Red Swan is going to think of the mess we've made of his building or what he'll do about me springing his trap, but I know it's best if we're surrounded by friends rather than on our own.

With Marjorie busy tutting her tongue and snipping her scissors over the mess of tape in Bailey's hair, I pick up the salon's phone and dial Kristy.

"It's me," I say. "You can let Roxanne go now."

"I've been watching the news," says Kristy in a tone that manages to mix both concern and uncertainty. "Is that you?"

"Depends. Is it about a lottery winner who's moving to the Bahamas to soak up the sun and be fawned over by half-naked sex gods who make a bottomless Long Island iced tea?"

"No, it's about a street riot that seems to have set fire to a building containing an illegal arsenal. The police are warning everyone to stay clear because bullets keep going off in the blaze. And there are bodies inside, but it's too dangerous to retrieve them. Even the firefighters are having to wear bulletproof vests."

"Now why would that make you think of me?" I ask.

"Roxanne was talking about her sister while you were gone. Well, I say talking, but it's more like ranting. You didn't tell me she's possessed. I'm scared to get too close to her in case she tries to bite. Is she on drugs?"

"Open the door and unlock the handcuffs; she'll run away."

"You sure?"

"Yeah. But first, tell her that her sister is safe, and if she wants to see us we're heading down to the Dog House. But also tell her to be careful. You too."

"Me?"

"Just don't talk to any strangers. Some bad men might come looking for me."

"Oh, Dix, what are you into?"

"It's OK. I'm handling it."

"Not very well! A man tried to shoot you in your own apartment!"

"That's dealt with."

"So this is *new* trouble?"

I hesitate. "Kinda."

"You need to talk to Frank."

"Yeah," I agree. "It might be time."

"Keep safe, sweetie. Our baby needs an auntie."

I inhale sharply, my voice filling with unexpected emotion. "Are you—"

"Not yet," says Kristy, cutting me off. "But I will be."

So long as I don't bring angry Russian mobsters to your door, I think. *Jesus, what have I done?*

I hang up the phone and walk to the sink where Bailey is having the last of the gunk washed from her hair. Looking down at her, I suddenly begin to laugh.

"What?" Bailey asks, horrified.

"You've just escaped the clutches of a mad Russian mob boss and what's the first thing you do?" I ask. "Go to a hair salon. How frickin' girly is that?"

Bailey's mouth is caught between a pout and a smile. "I'm a hairdresser," she says. "Besides, some of those wrestlers were cute."

I laugh even louder.

"I like you Ms. Bailey Brown," I say. "You're my kind of gal."

I turn to Marjorie. "Is there a TV around?"

She points to a small flat-screen mounted near the row of industrial hair dryers that still look like they belong in the 1950s. The remote is attached to the wall beside the TV with Velcro.

I tune into the local news and am rewarded with a full-screen image of black smoke and steam billowing from the building we recently exited. Firefighters pour on the water. The fire appears to be mostly extinguished, but the top two floors have been gutted. The camera pans down to focus on an attractive Asian woman with perfectly symmetrical eyes, seductive lips, and overly wide shoulders. Her face is serious to let us know this isn't the weather report.

I notice her lips moving before the words scroll across the bottom of the screen. Because of the noise usually generated by the full-helmet hair dryers, Marjorie has the TV set to display closed captioning.

Authorities are saying they have no explanation for what started the initial melee that is believed to be responsible for spreading the fire to the building. One witness has described the events as spontaneous hooliganism, and indeed the police did find one man hog-tied and stuffed in a nearby garbage can. We're told that man has been taken to the hospital in police custody and will be facing several weapons charges after his injuries have been treated. Despite rumors currently trending on Twitter under the hashtag SFAttack, police are adamant there is no terrorist connection being considered at this time. However, authorities on the scene are also reluctant to offer any explanation for the large arsenal of ammunition that has been igniting inside the building. Nor are they saying anything about what are believed to be numerous bodies still inside. One reliable source has claimed there may be as many as twelve—

The reporter touches her ear as a question comes in from her anchor.

That's correct, Clive, she says when the captions catch up to her lips again. *When we asked about a possible gang connection, Detective Sergeant Frank Fury blanked us with a strict "no comment."*

The fiery twinkle in her eye tells the viewer that she doesn't appreciate Frank's unhelpfulness. She touches her ear again and nods.

Drugs have not been ruled out either, Clive. In fact, one bystander who didn't want to go on record has informed me that the building housed at least one illegal meth lab. And as you'll remember from my award-winning investigative piece last year, crystal methamphetamine is an extremely dangerous drug to produce exactly because of its flammability. This, she indicts the building behind her with a subtle hand gesture, *could quite easily be the result of a drug cook gone wrong.*

I switch off the TV. When the on-the-spot news teams aren't spoon-fed information, they tend to ramble and hope nobody notices. *Drug cook gone wrong?* Good grief.

I turn to Bailey. "You nearly ready? I could really use a beer."

THIRTY-FIVE

THE TAXI PICKS US up in front of Bailey's apartment, a short walk from the salon, and takes us to the Dog House. While I look like I've gone three rounds with a bruise-knuckled smoke monster, Bailey is practically glowing with a freshly scrubbed face, new haircut, clean underwear, and fresh clothes.

If this were a fairy tale, it would be called *The Princess and the Ugh*.

"You sure know how to make a girl feel good about herself," I grumble as we push open the doors to the bar.

A loud cheer erupts as soon as we step inside, shattering my feelings of inadequacy and sweeping them off to a corner. The bar is packed with gorgeous, muscled men with too much alcohol diluting their blood and enough scar tissue to show it isn't a new experience.

Before I can speak, two of the wrestlers hoist me on their shoulders and parade me around the tiny bar as if I've just bagged the Snitch to win a Quidditch match. Despite a brief flush of embarrassment, I find

I enjoy it—especially when I reach the bar and Bill hands me an ice-cold Warthog.

The men quickly turn their attention to Bailey, and a fresh round of beer is soon flowing as I slide into my usual spot beside the stool reserved for the ghost of Al Capone. I clink glasses with Bill.

"I take it the boys did alright," he says.

"Couldn't have been better," I say. "Overturning the car was a nice touch. Brought the cops running."

"How about inside? Any trouble?"

I shrug, unable to be glib. "Any trouble you can walk away from..."

"I hear that, but—" Bill's large forehead furrows. "Dix. I've been watching the news. You're wading in some deep muck here. They're talking terrorists, gangs, arsenals, drugs?"

"Would you believe me if I said it's supposed to be a nice little upbeat story for Father's Day?"

Bill's mouth splits into a wide grin before a rumble erupts from deep in his belly to become a room-filling guffaw. He still has tears running down his cheeks when the door bursts open and Frank shoves inside with a face like he's been chewing a nest of wasps.

The crowd quiets slightly as Frank pushes his way through to the bar and sits next to me.

Bill wipes his eyes and pours Frank a non-alcoholic O'Doul's.

"Busy night?" Bill asks.

Frank nods silently before turning to me. "You been watching the news?"

"The fire?" I ask.

"Building has links to your Russian friend, Krasnyi Lebed."

"Was he inside?"

Frank squints as if trying to get a better read on my face. I can't tell if he's amused or angry, but I'm leaning toward angry.

"There's at least six bodies and signs of a gun battle."

"Rival gang?" I ask.

"Not their style."

"Hmmm." I take a swallow of beer.

"One witness saw two women fleeing the scene." Frank glances around at the crowd. "Plus a group of very large and boisterous men."

"Hmmm." I take another swallow.

"One of the women was described as having red hair and wearing a green trenchcoat."

"Hmmm," I say for the third time and hand my empty bottle to Bill in exchange for a fresh one.

"Did you go to the gun range today?" Frank asks.

I shake my head. "Too busy."

Frank reaches into his pocket and removes a small bottle of clear liquid and a clean handkerchief. He takes my right hand and turns it palm side up.

"You mind?" he asks.

I turn my attention to my fresh beer, not wanting him to see the nervousness in my eyes.

He sprays the liquid on my palm and waits.

Nothing happens.

After a minute, he wipes off the remaining liquid with his handkerchief.

"OK," he says. "Now tell me what you were doing there."

I turn to look him in the eyes. "First tell me what that was about."

"Diphenylamine solution," he says. "If you fired a gun recently, it would turn blue. I'd hate to think that I'm helping a killer."

"You could simply *ask*."

Frank's lips twitch. "Have you killed anyone today?"

"No," I say, relieved that I can be honest. "Not today."

The street door opens again, and Roxanne bursts into the bar like Hell's slobbering hounds are on her tail. She takes one look at me and I understand why Kristy was so frightened. There's a streak of poison running deep within this one that's been festering for too long. It's in her eyes and in her blood.

My hand tightens around the beer bottle in case I need to defend myself, then she spies her sister. Her face instantly softens and with a squeal of delight, Roxanne runs into Bailey's arms and squeezes her tight. The affection appears genuine.

The wrestlers let out another mighty cheer and call for more beer as the reunited sisters weep with joy.

Frank lifts the O'Doul's to his lips.

"This better be good," he says.

———

"This isn't the place to discuss it," I tell Frank. "Feel like walking us girls home?"

"And here I thought you were planning an all-nighter."

"Me?" I say as if insulted. "Perish the thought."

I slide off my stool and walk over to Bailey and Roxanne.

"We've got an escort home," I tell them. "Best we take it."

Roxanne looks at me with a mixture of both hate and resentment, but it's fighting with something else: a gnawing need for acceptance.

"What about me?" she asks.

Bailey looks at us in confusion, unaware of what's happened in her absence.

"You're welcome too," I say. "But you need to want to be here. I'm not putting up with any more shit, I've already got enough of my own."

Roxanne nods. "I want to be here ... with Bailey."

"Good enough."

The wrestlers groan and protest as I leave the sisters to bid their goodnights. While walking away, I notice one of the men slipping a card with his phone number into Bailey's hand. Bailey blushes slightly when she catches my eye.

I smile my approval in return. A good strong protector might be exactly what she needs—especially now.

While the two women extract themselves, I step outside the bar to clear my head. The night is dark and moist. It reminds me of the disinfectant wipe that Pinch pushed into my hand while a gunman's brain matter slid down the wall.

Always the professional.

Frank said there were six bodies inside the building, and I watched Pinch kill one of them in front of my eyes. Yet I don't feel a twinge of remorse. True, they weren't nice men; in fact, at least two of them showed little compunction about trying to kill me. But have I changed so much that a human life can now be placed on a scale? Tip toward evil and your passing doesn't matter?

I pinch the skin of my forearm between finger and thumb. It hurts. No armor there, still just flesh.

The deliberate clunk of a car door makes me lift my head to glance across the street.

Krasnyi Lebed is standing on the sidewalk beside a chauffeur-driven Rolls Royce. Flanking him on either side are two men with masks of determined evil—gargoyles carved out of granite and humanized by Italian tailors. They are different from the behemoths who guard his office; these men are bred to kill rather than break bones.

Lebed doesn't say a word. Just stares. And for once I don't have a cheeky comeback. I'm honestly too scared.

The door behind me opens, and Frank exits the Dog House with Bailey and Roxanne in tow.

I don't turn around, even though I want to tell them to go back inside and bolt the door.

The Red Swan offers me the thinnest of smiles as he lifts one of his gloved hands to his throat and slowly drags his index finger across the flesh.

Frank moves to stand beside me as Lebed slowly climbs back inside his car. He doesn't even care that Frank sees him. He doesn't care at all.

THIRTY-SIX

Frank is rooted beside me in silence as the Rolls drives off. After it turns the corner and disappears from sight, he reaches into a pocket and removes a square tin of his favorite cigars.

Unwrapping two, he snips the ends off with a slim stainless-steel cutter and hands one to me. I slip it between my lips as he flicks open a Zippo lighter and touches flame to tip. He does the same with his own.

His hand is steady, but a vein throbbing in his forehead tells me that he's using the ritual to contain a burning rage.

Bailey and Roxanne watch us smoke, nobody knowing what to say—or feeling too frightened to open their mouth.

"Let's walk," Frank says, indicating the direction of my apartment.

The four of us walk.

"Lebed," says Frank after the first block, "doesn't make personal appearances. He has people for that."

"He wanted me to see his face," I say.

"He's telling you that whatever you did at that building, it's personal."

"No," I counter. "He's telling me he's afraid."

"Of?"

I nod in the direction of the two women walking with linked arms a few steps ahead of us.

"Of whatever secret their father knows."

"And he thinks you'll expose this secret?"

"He's had twenty years to make it go away and failed. So, yeah, he's scared that I'm closing in."

"Are you?" Frank asks.

I shrug. "I'll get there."

"And will this secret protect you?" He jabs his chin at the women. "And them?"

I shrug again. "Maybe."

"*Maybe* isn't good enough, Dix. This son of a bitch threatened you in front of witnesses." His voice cracks and becomes a growl as gray smoke pours from between his lips. "He threatened you in front of *me*."

"He thinks he's untouchable," I say.

"Well, he better think again."

I touch Frank's arm and give it a light squeeze.

We walk the rest of the way home in tense silence, but I know Frank isn't nearly done talking.

———

As soon as we enter the lobby, Mr. French's door swings open. He's holding an uncorked bottle of champagne and sporting an ear-splitting grin.

"Celebrating something?" I say quickly before he can speak.

His grin faltering, Mr. French reads my face and glances at Frank.

"Ah," he says in understanding. "Yes, well, I just ... just bought a rare stamp. The Bangladesh Falcon, in fact. It completes a rather intriguing collection that I've been working on for several years. I wanted to share the good news."

"That's marvelous," I gush too enthusiastically. "Maybe you can show me tomorrow? It's been a long night."

"Yes, yes, of course," agrees Mr. French. "That would be delightful. And," his eyes twinkle in Bailey's direction, "welcome back, Miss Brown."

As Mr. French beats a retreat into his apartment and closes the door, Frank looks over at me and rolls his eyes.

"I don't get it," he says. "For such an experienced liar, there are times when you just suck at it."

"That's because, deep down, I'm such an honest person."

"I know," he says. "That's why you need to stop lying to me."

"Would never cross my mind."

His lips twitch. "See. I nearly believed you that time."

———

In my apartment, Bailey and Roxanne retreat to the bedroom while I open a can of soft food for a sadly neglected Prince and fix a tall rum and ginger on ice for myself. I make the same for Frank, minus the cat food and rum.

By the time I curl on the couch with my drink, Frank has pulled the Governor out of its case and is running the cleaning snake through its barrel and chambers. The gun is already spotless, but I can tell he finds the task calming.

"So tell me," he begins, "why I have six dead bodies in a burning building that you're seen running out of?"

"It was hot," I say. "And you know I can't stand the heat."

Frank stops cleaning the gun and glares at me until I buckle.

"OK," I relent and tell him everything. Well, almost everything. I don't mention Pinch. I can't. Pinch was there because I asked him to be. He killed those men because that's what he does, and I knew that going in. I may not have planned for a bloodbath, but I sure as hell was glad to leave that building alive.

"So let me get this straight," says Frank. "You used the wrestlers to create a distraction so that you could rescue that woman in there." He points at the bedroom. "Because somehow you feel responsible for her involvement with the Russian mob."

I nod.

"That doesn't explain six dead bodies," he continues.

"No," I agree. "But I didn't kill them, and I have no idea who did."

"What about the fire?" Frank asks.

"Wasn't me. It started on the floor above where Bailey was being held."

"Strange coincidence."

"Lebed has a lot of enemies."

"And the enemy of my enemy—"

"Isn't anyone I know," I finish. "My plan was crude but simple. Create a noisy diversion to keep the guard busy—he's the one you found stuffed in the garbage can, by the way—sneak in and grab Bailey while nobody was paying attention, and run like hell." I point at the gun in Frank's hand. "That stayed at home."

Frank reloads the Governor with a 50/50 split of shotgun shells and .45s before placing it back in its case.

"Keep this close," he says, standing up. "I'll have a patrol car parked outside overnight, but we're going to need a more permanent solution soon. I suggest you find this man you're looking for before Lebed does, and use whatever secret he holds to strike a bargain. No story is worth having the Red Swan after your head, because he's one son of a bitch who always gets his way."

"Always?" I ask.

Frank bristles. "For now."

After Frank leaves, I lock the door, slip out of my clothes, and slide the Governor under my pillow on the couch. Once I settle in my makeshift bed, Prince leaps onto my chest and sticks his flat nose against mine to stare deeply into my eyes, as though he can read the jumble of my thoughts and wants to help unravel them.

I scratch his cheeks and chin; his purr is a balm for my stress and nerves.

Finally, I close my eyes.

They're not shut long before snapping open again with the nagging thought: *How did Lebed know he'd find me at the Dog House?* He wasn't parked outside when we arrived.

I glance toward the closed bedroom door where the two sisters are sleeping.

Has Roxanne made a deal? I ask myself. *My head in exchange for her sister's?*

The thought weighs on my mind as I reluctantly close my eyes again. Tiredness makes me paranoid. Then again, so does being awake.

THIRTY-SEVEN

WHEN THE PHONE RINGS before the sun makes its appearance, I immediately think of Dixie's Tips No. 1, and don't answer it.

When it rings again, I groan and convince myself that if it's really important, they'll call back.

When it rings for the third time, I pick it up and curse myself for forgetting Dixie's Tips No. 2—*again.*

"Say your name," says the caller when I place the receiver to my ear.

"Dixie," I say. "With two *g*'s, but the second one is silent. What's yours?"

"You already know."

It's Pinch. He sounds irritable, which, in the short amount of time I've known him, is unusual.

"You OK?" I ask.

"I'm golden, but the Red Swan wants your head."

"He must know that's not a smart move," I say. "He threatened me in front of a cop. If anything happens—"

"He's angry right now. Not thinking. Watch your ass till he cools down, OK?"

"Yeah." Shit. "Thanks."

Pinch hangs up and I drop the phone on the coffee table. Prince Marmalade, stretched across my feet, opens one eye in a manner that asks if I'm quite done causing a disturbance so early in the morning. We both drift back to sleep just before the phone rings again.

"You forget something?" I ask grumpily. "Some cheerful news that a tsunami is rushing toward shore or something equally as uplifting?"

"You never just say hello, do you?" says a high-pitched, yet still gruff voice.

I groan. "Morning, boss."

"Editorial meeting at eleven, looking forward to having you in attendance."

"What time is it now?"

"Closing in on eight."

"You must eat worms for breakfast."

A slight chuckle. "Two dozen every day. See you at eleven?"

"Wouldn't miss it."

I close my eyes and drop the phone for a second time. It starts ringing before it's even landed.

"This is getting ridiculous," I say, grabbing the phone on its first bounce. "Is it Bug Dixie Day?"

"I'm sending a car over," says Frank. "Be ready in ten."

"Don't you people sleep?" I ask.

He ignores me. "The fire marshal has issued the all-clear to enter the building. I want you to walk me through what happened before the coroner removes the bodies."

"Neat-o. Guess I won't eat breakfast first."

"Cereal is fine, but I would avoid anything fried."

"Ha, ha," I groan. "No wonder you're dating a coroner. Nobody else finds you funny."

"You've got nine minutes," says Frank. "Brush your teeth."

I hang up and look down at Prince. "Put the coffee on while I have a shower, will you?"

Prince's ears twitch, but he doesn't even bother to open his eyes. As I walk to the shower, I know there's not going to be any coffee waiting when I get out.

Men and cats. Bloody useless.

———

Detective Russell Shaw knocks on my front door and shows an inappropriate lack of disappointment at finding me mostly dressed and ready to go. I was sure he would be picturing me clutching a daringly short damp towel to my bosom and flustered at having been caught *au naturel* in my empty—well, mostly empty—apartment.

Poor kid must lack imagination.

I leave a note for Bailey and Roxanne and lock the door behind me.

In the car, Shaw studies me with X-ray eyes. But instead of trying to see beneath my clothes, I can tell he's trying to see beneath my skin.

"What?" I ask. "Never seen a naturally beautiful woman at the crack of dawn before?"

He tries not to grin and mostly succeeds. "No, just curious."

"About?"

"This. Me escorting you to a fresh crime scene—again."

"So?"

"I haven't been allowed inside yet," he says. "We only received the all-clear ten minutes ago, but Frank wants you there with us."

"So?" I repeat, which I can tell gets on his nerves.

"You're not a forensic specialist, you're not even a cop. And to make it worse, you're a *reporter*."

I decide not to repeat myself again in case the pressure causes his ears to pop off like a plastic Mr. Potato Head I had as a kid. "And your point is?"

"You shouldn't be allowed anywhere near the scene. At least not until we've finished our investigation."

"So, you're saying Frank's lost his marbles?"

Shaw's lips fumble with uncertainty. "I'm not saying anything against the sergeant. It's just unusual is all."

"Hmmm. You know what I find odd?"

"What?"

"That you haven't asked me out."

"What!" His cheeks blush. His level of discomfort somehow makes me more relaxed.

"It's obvious that you're attracted to me."

"I-I've never shown—"

"You're young, but that's OK. I like showing new dogs old tricks."

Completely flustered, Shaw can't seem to find his tongue for the entire rest of the journey. Pity. I could have shown him what to use it for.

Frank meets us at the car and escorts me past the police barrier and into the building's lobby, where a large makeshift tent has been erected both to block my curious media brethren and as a forensic lock.

On one table inside the tent, somebody has stacked a neat pile of fresh body bags. Resting beside them are two plastic snow shovels whose purpose I really don't want to guess at. On another table, someone has kindly arranged a box of assorted doughnuts and a large stay-warm container of coffee from a nearby cafe.

I'm heading for the coffee when Frank cuts me off.

"Put these on." He hands me a sterile package containing a blue paper suit, complete with a hood.

"Are we playing doctor?" I quip. "'Cause I think Shaw would make a great nurse."

Frank snorts while Shaw blushes again as the three of us pull the baggy paper suits over our street clothes. After we're dressed, Frank hands us paper booties and disposable latex gloves.

"Don't wander," Frank warns. "The fire marshal has mapped a safe route, but the structural integrity has been compromised, so stay behind me at all times."

"And what about the coffee?" I ask hopefully.

"Later."

Reluctantly, I leave the coffee and tantalizing thoughts of deep-fried dough behind to follow Frank out of the tent. The three of us walk into a soggy mess of soaked and charred debris that's been swept down the stairs from the upper floors by the fire hoses.

"Watch out for needles and glass," says Frank.

"Charming," I fire back. "Did the local knitting guild have a rave?"

Shaw snickers behind me, but I don't reward him with one of my come-hither smiles. I'm starting to get worried about what we may find on the floors above—and how I'll explain myself.

On the first landing, we stop in front of the dead man Pinch shot through the eye. The fire never reached this far, but the water certainly did. The man is ghostly pale and slumped forward to expose the gaping wound in the back of his head. Water pools in the hollow of his skull along with what's left of his brain matter. Behind him, the wall is streaked with long fingers of dirt, erasing the telltale splatter of his violent demise.

That could have been me, I tell myself to stop from being sickened by the sight, *if Pinch hadn't been watching my back.*

Frank pins a tiny red flag into the wall where a ragged hole the size of my fist punctures the plaster.

"He was shot," explains Frank. "The bullet expanded inside his skull and punched out the back of his head." He indicates the red flag and turns to point up the stairs. "By the angle, we know the shooter stood above him." He turns to me. "Know him?"

"He wasn't here when I ran out," I say, betraying no emotion. "I would've noticed."

Frank points at the man's hand, still holding a gun. "He was expecting trouble." To Shaw, he adds, "Check if that was fired, or if he was beaten to the draw."

The young detective instantly squats down to slip an evidence bag over the gun without disturbing the corpse. From past crime scenes, I know he'll retrieve the weapon after the police photographer has recorded the scene.

When Frank starts up the stairs again, Shaw turns to me and hisses, "You were here?"

"No, she wasn't," Frank answers before I can open my mouth.

"God didn't give him those big ears for nothing," I say, glad to find my dark bravado hasn't deserted me completely.

———

The second floor is uneventful, although Frank shares that somebody scrambled to salvage what they could from the rooms before the water and fire ruined the contents.

"A neighborhood crack operation," he explains. "The rooms on the first floor are strictly low-rent hangouts for low-rent customers. So long as you're buying, smoking, and injecting poison in your veins, there's a spot on one of the couches for you. Spend enough and you can graduate to the redneck VIP lounge with massaging La-Z-Boys and crack hos with scabby knees."

Frank glances over at me to gauge my reaction, but I've been a reporter too long to be shocked by the sad reality of the streets. I say, "So having this place burn to the ground wasn't necessarily any great loss?"

Frank shrugs. "They'll relocate and start again."

He continues, "The rooms on this floor were used to cook cocaine into crack. A simple DIY process without all the toxic hassles of meth, although someone was trying to be inventive." He shakes his head. "The fire department found vials of blue, orange, and red rock. There's even a rigged-up dumbwaiter between the floors, so the den mother didn't need to climb the stairs to supply her customers."

"What does Narcotics say?" Shaw asks.

"Barely on their radar," says Frank. "Most serious junkies consider crack a starter drug. It gives you a boost but wears off too soon. May as well snort a can of Red Bull. The colored rocks are bothersome though. Lebed may have been using this place to tar-get younger users."

"How young?" I ask.

Frank sighs. "They're using powdered Kool-Aid to give it a fruity smell, so I'm guessing elementary schools."

"Bastards!"

"That just becoming clear?" When I flash him a dirty look instead of a reply, Frank asks, "Nobody tried to stop you on these floors? Either going up or coming down?"

I shake my head. "No one."

Shaw glares at me.

"If I had been here," I add quickly.

"That's unusual," says Frank. "Normally, the cook house would have a couple of armed guards outside to dissuade the first-floor customers from climbing the stairs."

I shrug. "Coffee break?"

Frank doesn't smile and judging by the intensity of his stare, Shaw looks like he's about to burst a few blood vessels in his eyes.

———

On the third floor, we enter the room where Bailey was being held. Frank moves carefully around the dark stain that streaks the hall-way, and I find myself holding my breath.

When we enter the living room, I exhale loudly in relief.

There's no body.

Frank points to another dark stain on the floor and follows it back into the hallway with his finger. "Somebody was seriously in-jured here," he says. "Must have dragged himself out."

"Maybe when he saw Bailey wasn't here," I suggest. "He came looking for her because of the fire upstairs, but we were already gone."

I point to the overturned chair in front of the blank television set. "She was tied there."

"Bailey was here, too?" Shaw squawks. "The woman in your apartment with the junkie sister?"

"Of course not," I answer.

Shaw looks at Frank in frustration, but Frank gives him nothing.

"Let's go up," Frank says.

———

The fourth floor is the most disturbing by far. Open and spacious, the giant loft looks like a gut-shot dragon coughed up a cancerous lung and spewed it from one end to the other. Every square inch is charcoal black and reeking of burnt wood, paint, gunpowder, and human meat.

Fortunately, most of the windows are broken, allowing for a breeze to soften the cloying taste, but the breach has also allowed the city's famous early morning mist to drift inside and crawl across the ceiling, making the space chokingly claustrophobic.

Jesus, Pinch, I think, *was all this really necessary?*

Frank points to a charred body that's curled nearest the door.

"He's not nearly as cooked as the rest," he says. "Must have arrived to the party late."

I glance at the body and notice his right foot is twisted at an impossible angle, as though a hollow-point bullet has shattered the bones. Fire may have burned away the rest of his hair and licked at his face, but I'd know this guy anywhere.

I turn away to hide a shudder and swallow a lump of bile that is threatening to climb up my throat.

"It's too dangerous to walk around up here," says Frank, "but this is where the bulk of the gun play happened."

He lowers himself to his haunches for a different perspective and points at several human-shaped black lumps scattered around the debris. "Not sure what they were up to in here, but these men were taken by surprise by someone who knew how to handle themselves."

He points to scorch marks and bullet holes that only he can see; it's all black soot and water damage to me.

"He tossed an incendiary into that far corner to split the group apart and then took them down one at a time. He used the smoke and fire to his advantage—definitely a professional. The only anomaly is the guy by the door."

My attacker. The one I shot and left in the hands of the Good Samaritan.

"If that guy had gone downstairs instead of up, he might still be alive."

"And we might have some answers," adds Shaw.

Frank ignores him and looks at me. "This mean anything to you?"

I shake my head. "Not a thing."

Despite what Frank said, I can be a damn good liar.

"This didn't have anything to do with drugs," Frank says. "The pushers and cooks downstairs were purely collateral damage. This was something else. Something personal."

"The Red Swan has no shortage of enemies," I add.

Shaw looks at both of us and grits his teeth. I can tell he's dying to ask Frank what the hell I'm doing here and how I know anything about the Red Swan's involvement, but to his professional credit, he keeps his mouth shut.

Unfortunately, that also drops him off my list of desirable bed partners.

I only like yes men when they say yes to *me*.

THIRTY-EIGHT

"Do you need a ride home?" Frank asks as he escorts me down to the lobby.

"Thanks, but I have to get to the office. I'll take a cab."

Before reentering the tent, Frank takes hold of my arm and squeezes it lightly to make sure he has my full attention.

"Be careful, OK?" he says. "When I finish here, I'm planning to have a talk with Lebed, let him know I'm watching."

"Think he'll listen?" I ask.

Frank's mouth tightens with residual anger. "I'll make sure."

After discarding my paper outfit and booties, I exit the building and head in the opposite direction from the bored media scrum awaiting any scrap of news to feed their chirpy breakfast-TV hosts. An enterprising coffee truck provides a convenient distraction as the skeleton crew of cameramen and wannabe broadcasters is lined up for plastic-wrapped pastries and double-doubles with extra double.

I'm not paying attention as I dart past the mouth of the alley, and a leathery palm snakes from the darkness to close over my mouth, instantly muffling my startled scream.

Dragged into the depths, I'm both terrified and pissed. My terror is obvious, but my anger is a white-hot poker as I realize that despite repeated warnings from Frank and Pinch, I've still been too cavalier.

"It's OK," a hoarse voice whispers. "I'm not going to hurt you."

I recognize the voice. It belongs to my Good Samaritan.

I bite down on his gloved finger, attempting to pierce the bone.

He yelps and releases me.

"Shit! Didn't you hear me? I'm no—"

I drop to my haunches and sweep my foot in a wide arc, clipping his ankles and lifting his feet off the ground.

With another curse, he crunches onto his back on the rancid alley floor, and I'm on top of him. By the time his eyes stop rolling, I have my knife out of my boot and against his throat.

"Don't ever do that again!" I hiss.

"OK, OK." He holds up his hands. "I surrender."

"What the hell are you playing at?"

"You wanted to talk."

"You scared me to death! I thought you were Lebed."

"S-s-sorry," he says. "I ... I'm not too good around outsiders anymore."

I climb off his chest and hold out my hand to help him up. He accepts but grips my forearm rather than my hand, forcing me to do the same. He's awkward rising and I have to put some muscle into it to bring him to his feet.

"Let's walk," he says, wiping at his dirty coat and moving deeper into the alley. "I don't like to stay in one place too long."

"Why?"

"Same reason you're scared."

"The Red Swan?"

He nods.

"Is that why you killed that gunman last night even though I asked you not to? I just saw his body."

"If I'd let him live, he would've come after both of us." The Samaritan's eyes glisten with a feral intensity. "I know these animals—you don't. Not yet. They don't just hurt people because Lebed tells them to. They enjoy it." His voice rises in anger. "It gets them fucking hard. If Lebed does grab you, you better be prepared to kill, because he won't hesitate to do a hell of a lot worse."

I stop walking and ask, "What did he do to you?"

"I was a journalist, too," he says. "Not in the spotlight like you. Just on the desk, but still..." He carefully removes one of his gloves and displays the blackened stumps where his fingers used to be. "This," he says, "was for writing a cutline that Lebed didn't like."

"I heard about that," I say. "From Victor Hendrickson."

"Yeah," the Samaritan sighs. "Red Swan paid him a visit, too."

"But that was twenty years ago," I say. "Why are you still hanging around in Lebed's territory?"

The Samaritan starts walking again. "I've been avoiding him for a long time," he says, "but a friend asked me to be his eyes."

"His eyes?" I ask.

"Things are changing," he explains. "My friend can't stay in the shadows any longer, but he needed me to look out for..." He hesitates.

"That's why I was outside the tea house when that Russian pig attacked you. I thought that maybe—"

"Maybe I was someone else," I finish.

He nods sheepishly.

"Who?" I ask, already sensing the answer.

"His daughter," says the Samaritan. "My friend's daughter."

"Joseph Brown's daughter," I say. "Bailey Brown."

The Samaritan nods. "She was never supposed to come back here, to get involved again. Now everything is changing."

"For better or worse?" I ask.

"That remains to be seen."

———

We continue to walk, sticking to the shadows and alleys, scaring the occasional rat and suspicious cat. My Samaritan knows most of the disheveled castaways and junkies who are rising to scrounge breakfast from a bottle, needle, or street kitchen, and he nods to them as we pass.

"How long have you been living on the streets?" I ask.

"I don't." He smiles. "These are my work clothes. After Lebed's men butchered my hands, I went a little crazy. Booze, pills ... lots and lots of pills. Thought about joining the thousands who've swan dived off the Golden Gate, but I was saved by a smile."

"A smile?" I ask.

"She's a redhead, like you, sent from heaven itself. She convinced me I still had value, and we started a street mission together. Then her father died and we used the inheritance to buy a piece of land outside the city. We're building a community there for those who don't have a community. Families who've fallen on hard times, you know? You'd be shocked how many car windows I knock on to find a family inside with nowhere else to live. This whole country is built on a foundation of broken promises, and we've forgotten that we'll be judged not on how we treat our wealthiest citizens but on how we treat our poorest."

"And Joe Brown is with you?" I ask.

"I call him Radar." My Samaritan chuckles. "You know, from that TV show *M*A*S*H*? If you need something, anything, Radar will find it. I don't know how he does it." He winks. "And I don't pry too closely either. Some things are best kept a mystery."

"But your mission is religious?" I ask.

"There but for the grace of God," says my Samaritan.

"And yet you killed that man last night."

He stops walking and turns to meet my gaze. "I did kill him," he says matter-of-factly. "I didn't know I was still holding onto that much anger, but when his throat was in my hands, not even the devil could have pried my fingers loose." He breaks off eye contact. "Obviously that's a metaphor; I haven't had actual fingers for a very long time."

"And what about Joe?" I ask. "Why did he leave his daughters at the mercy of Lebed?"

He starts walking again. "You'll need to ask him."

"I'd like to. So would his daughters. They're both safe by the way, no thanks to him. Can you arrange a meeting?"

"He's coming to town."

"When?"

"Tonight."

"Will he meet with us?"

My Samaritan points to the mouth of an alley where a stand of cabs is lined up waiting for passengers.

"We'll be in touch," he says.

"You better be," I snap back. "It's time everyone got some answers."

THIRTY-NINE

BEFORE CLIMBING INTO THE taxi, I try to calculate if I have enough time to rush back to the apartment and let Bailey and Roxanne know their father is definitely alive before my eleven o'clock meeting at the office.

It would be the generous thing to do, but my grumbling stomach argues that if I head toward the office now, I'll still have time to get something to eat before the meeting starts.

Bailey and Roxanne have waited twenty years for this news, my coffee-deprived brain argues, *what's another two hours?* Selfishness, mental fatigue, and caffeine-withdrawal win.

The taxi drops me at Mario's Deli, where my nose and salivary glands lead me inside.

Mario beams when he sees me. "Dixie, you so skinny and pale. I have a wonderful breakfast special this morning to put color back in your cheeks: local sage sausage, organic egg, and melted Gruyère with just a dab of my special spicy ketchup. I serve it on a fresh, butter-kissed bun kneaded and baked with my own hands."

"Does it come with coffee?" I ask.

Mario beams wider. "Take a seat."

Eddie, on the other hand, doesn't appear quite as thrilled.

"You want me to sit elsewhere?" I ask.

The Wolf glances once at the partially open door behind him and the looming shadow contained within before shrugging and indicating that I'm welcome.

As soon as I slide into the booth, Mario brings over a large mug of piping hot coffee with a small container of cream on the side, just the way I like it. I savor the aroma for a moment before adding a splash of cream and taking a large swallow. Every nerve ending in my body sighs with relief. *Is this how Roxanne feels when she shoots up?* I wonder.

"Rough night?" Eddie asks.

"What have you heard?" I ask back.

"Enough that I wasn't expecting to see your face again."

"Ever?"

"Red Swan is pissed."

"Then he shouldn't kidnap my friends," I snap.

Eddie's lips twitch. "I woulda placed odds that there was no way you were getting that gal out of there alive. Where'd you get the fire-power?"

I shrug. "That was coincidence."

"Coincidence?" Eddie actually laughs. "Man, you have a set of balls on you that makes me feel like a eunuch."

Mario delivers my breakfast sandwich with a side of seasoned chunky hashbrowns and a fresh top-up of coffee.

"She a growing girl," he says to Eddie.

"Yeah," Eddie snorts. "Her ball sack gets any bigger and she won't be able to fit through the goddamn door. I'm surprised she's not wearing clown pants."

I take a bite of my sandwich and almost collapse into a puddle of writhing ecstasy. "Mario," I say in all seriousness despite the golden egg yolk running down my chin, "will you marry me?"

Mario winks at Eddie. "Three's a crowd, Dix, but I'll consider it." He laughs as he returns behind the counter.

I take another bite. It's just as good as the first, which makes me think polyandry might not be so bad.

"So are we still cool?" I ask Eddie.

"For now. Lebed is taking this personal, but he hasn't issued a contract on you yet. At least not that I've heard."

"A contract?" I sputter, spraying food. "Seriously?"

Eddie shrugs. "That's how these things are done. But you've got certain friends that Lebed doesn't want to rile up. Still, I'd be careful crossing the street—accidents do happen."

"You running a book on me?" I ask.

Eddie nearly grins. "You're not that famous, Dix. Nobody really cares."

"Flatterer." I take another bite of sandwich.

"It is what it is," says Eddie.

————

Walking into the *NOW* newsroom, people turn and stare, which makes me wonder if I've forgotten to wipe the yolk and sausage grease off my chin. I make a sharp right and duck into the morgue.

"Hey, sweetie," says Lulu as I enter. "You get those blueprints I left for you last night?"

"I did, thanks, came in handy." I swivel the desk mirror on Lulu's desk toward me and study my face. All clean.

"Problem?" Lulu asks. "You try to pluck your eyebrows with pliers again?"

I jab my thumb over my shoulder in the direction of the newsroom. "Everyone was looking at me."

Lulu smiles.

"Oh, honey. You work the strangest hours of anyone here. Some of those young folk probably think you're a myth. Plus this new publisher has started cracking the whip in some weird ways." She stands up to lean over the counter and look me up and down. "On the other hand, you didn't hear about the new dress code, did you?"

I shake my head.

"Issued this week," she explains, "along with a ban on chewing gum in the office and smoking in public view where it might reflect badly on the paper. The memos will be in your mail slot."

I look down at myself. "Am I not dressed OK?"

Lulu sighs. "Jeans are banned."

"Seriously?"

"He wants everyone looking more professional."

"Do we get a wardrobe allowance?"

"Nope. Dress better; same pay. That's why everyone was staring."

"'Cause I know how to rock a pair of jeans?"

"Because you're breaking the rules."

"Crap."

"Crap indeed, sweetie. Crap indeed."

When I re-enter the newsroom, everyone is making his or her way to the editorial boardroom. I join the end of the line. Mary Jane Clooney—dressed in her usual look-at-me-I-have-boobs, far-too-young-for-her-age sluttire—spots me and flashes a bright smile. The twinkle in her eye is the same as that reflected in a Roman general's when a Christian is fed to the lions.

I shuffle to stand at the back of the boardroom as Stoogan makes a few introductory words before passing the floor over to Kenji Kobayashi, our publisher. Oddly, I find that if I passed him in the hallway on the way to the bathroom, I wouldn't have actually recognized him.

Publishers by nature rarely descend to their newsrooms. It's the editors' job to organize the daily rabble, miscreants, and talent pool, reporting to the inner sanctum only when summoned. I also hear that since Ken took over, editors need to remove their shoes before entering his office. This rumor, mostly perpetuated by me, has yet to be proven.

But so long as they don't mess with the copy, I rarely pay much attention to that side of the newspaper game. Unfortunately, the layers of protection between a reporter and his or her publisher have been crumbling at the same rate as the economy. And when the curtain is finally pulled back, they always appear so much smaller in person.

The publisher opens his mouth, and the heart of every journalist breaks just a little more. Each word is about finance, cutbacks, economic woes, percentages of ads versus editorial space, doing more with less, rising insurance costs, elimination of profit sharing…blah, blah, depressing blah…until he tries to rally the troops at the end by telling them the new dress code will boost spirits by showing the city that we're professional and committed and…

I stop listening as my bullshit meter gets clogged by too much effluent.

At the end of the speech, I attempt to be one of the first to escape the room but am stopped in my tracks by Stoogan calling my name. And despite my burning desire to flee, he's still the best boss I've ever had; if I'm loyal to anyone, it's to him.

With a brave smile, I turn and push through the departing crowd to the front of the room. The closer I get, the more likely it appears that Stoogan is planning to introduce me to the publisher. And by the look on Mr. Kobayashi's face, it also appears likely that he's disappointed in my choice of clothing, which admittedly does smell a bit like damp smoke, burnt flesh, and fermented garbage—but just a bit.

"Dixie," says Stoogan as I finally break through the final line of cowardly, departing souls. "I don't believe you've actually met our new publisher, Kenji Kobayashi, before."

I hold out my hand. "Haven't had the pleasure."

The man studies my hand for a second, making me wait before reaching out and giving it a light squeeze. If he uses that hand to masturbate, it's no wonder he looks so grumpy.

"Dixie is working diligently on our cover feature for this week," explains Stoogan.

"The Father's Day piece?" Kobayashi asks.

I nod. "It's turning into quite the story."

"Uplifting?" he asks.

"Definitely. Father missing for twenty years. Tearful reunion with two daughters, which should happen tonight. The works."

He looks me up and down. "You didn't get the memo about the new dress code?"

I don't spit in his eye, which, I think, is very mature. "Just heard about it."

"Why is that?" he asks.

"Dixie doesn't keep regular office hours," Stoogan interrupts.

"Why not?"

"She's a roving reporter," Stoogan adds. "We find it works better for everyone when she's on the street. She brings us the stories that everyone talks about."

"I find lack of regular hours makes people lazy," says Kobayashi.

"I disagree," says Stoogan before I can open my mouth. "The best stories don't fall into our laps. We need to go out and find them."

"That sounds messy," says Kobayashi.

"It can be," I say before Stoogan cuts me off with a stern look.

"And that's why it's not for everyone," he adds in a firmer tone. "I run a diverse newsroom to make sure we cover all our bases. Sometimes Dixie is our scout and at other times a pinch hitter. Our award nominations year in and year out attest to that."

Kobayashi scans me from toes to hairline, and I think I notice his nose twitch—and not in a cute *Bewitched* way. "Read the memo," he says, and then leaves the room.

"What a prick," I say when he's out of earshot.

Stoogan winces and shakes his head. To change the subject, he asks, "What's that smell?"

"Not you, I hope. You were great. Very forceful."

"I'm serious," he says and sniffs the air. "Is it you?"

"I was in a burned-out building this morning."

"The one we're reporting on?"

"Probably."

"The one that none of my reporters can get inside of to find out what the hell happened?"

"Likely."

Stoogan nods. "Underwood, the rookie, thought he spotted you this morning and phoned it in. He wanted to know how you gained access."

"I hope you told him I stole the secret to invisibility by sleeping with Criss Angel in Vegas."

"Since he actually saw you, I don't think he would have bought that."

"Nice fantasy, though."

Stoogan rolls his eyes. "Help him flesh out the story with what you know before you leave. Let the publisher see you're a team player."

"But I'm not," I say.

"Pretend."

FORTY

Standing on the sidewalk in front of *NOW*, I wish I had one of Frank's cigars. The thoughts running around in my brain are chaotic and unfocused, like bees that have broken formation and lost their way. A smoky distraction is needed to settle everything down, but I may need something a little stronger than tobacco.

I sense the car approaching and look up, expecting it to be the taxi I ordered.

It isn't.

The vintage Cadillac is all nose and sharp angles with tinted windows and a custom-lacquered matte blackness that seems to repel light. A voice in my head tells me to run, but my stubborn feet refuse to obey.

The Cadillac crawls closer and the rear window rolls down to expose one of the two men that I saw standing beside Lebed outside the Dog House last night. His face is a slab of chiseled stone, flat and gray, and his dark eyes repel the light as effectively as the car.

Prickly sweat breaks out along my hairline and my feet grow roots, but another part of my brain, the storyteller, wonders what kind of pain is needed to so effectively extinguish the light in someone's eyes.

The killer lifts a black-gloved hand, cocks his thumb, and points the barrel of his index finger at me. As a kid, I loved this game; as an adult, it nearly makes me piss myself.

I lock eyes in defiance and decide the only thing I can do is exactly what I would have done when I was six. I lift both hands and cock my own thumbs. Double trouble.

A gunshot cracks, splintering the air and stopping my heart.

But I'm not the victim.

The killer in the car howls as his severed finger spurts blood like a broken hose. Before he retreats from the window, I see a flicker of light return to his eyes—it's dark blue and pulsing with ice-cold hatred.

The Cadillac accelerates and vanishes.

I uncock my thumbs and look around. On a nearby rooftop, a dark shadow rises from a prone position. It's not a tall shadow, and he nods at me before swinging a rifle over his shoulder and retreating from sight.

If you're going to have a guardian angel, I tell myself, *it helps if he's a damn good shot.*

When my feet decide to start moving again, I cross to the middle of the road and nudge my toe at a small, black tube laying in a fresh splash of blood. The tube's outer casing is stitched calf hide, while its interior is oozing human flesh and bone—the killer's pretend barrel, his trigger finger.

So much for the Red Swan sending a message; Pinch's reply is easier to read: *Fuck you!*

The blare of a car horn brings me back to the present. It's my taxi.

I kick the gloved finger into the gutter and climb into the cab. I don't begin to shake until after we turn the corner.

———

King William of Orange winks at me from his usual perch on Mrs. Pennell's window ledge as I climb out of the cab. His furry face makes me long to curl up on the couch and cuddle my Prince, to shut off my brain for a while and give my body time to recover from the shock.

But if I wanted that life, I should have gone for a boob job and found myself a shallow millionaire—there are certainly plenty of them around, or so Mary Jane tells me.

In the lobby, Mr. French's door is the first to open. This time, he's not holding Champagne.

"Miss Flynn," he says. "I have been watching the news. Did we...did we—"

"That wasn't you," I assure him. "We were there to rescue Bailey. That's all."

"But the fire, the shooting—"

"Coincidence," I say, repeating the lie and starting to believe it. "The building belongs to a nasty man with a lot of enemies. We were lucky to get Bailey out in time."

"So we did good?" he asks.

I smile, cross the short distance between us, and envelop him in a surprise hug. I'm not a very physical person, and the embrace is awkward for both of us, since my need for comfort makes it more something I'm taking rather than giving.

Plus there's the vast height difference.

"We did great," I say, assuring myself as much as him.

When I release the poor man, Mr. French's effervescent smile is back where it belongs.

"I never doubted it for a moment," he says. "I was just telling Baccarat that there had to be an explanation. We are so pleased that Miss Brown is safe."

"I'll let her know."

"Yes, yes, please do."

———

When I arrive at the top of the stairs, Kristy and Sam are waiting on the landing.

"We've been watching the news," says Sam. Her arms are wrapped tight across her chest, a shield of muscle, flesh, and bone.

"Are you okay?" asks Kristy. Her chest is unguarded, open and exposed.

"I'm fine. Thanks."

"You don't look it," says Kristy.

"When do I ever?"

"Guns again?" Sam snaps. The lines around her mouth are so tight they look like broken stitches.

"Coincidence," I say. "I went to rescue Bailey, nothing more. I didn't start the fire."

Sam's eyes blaze white-hot. "Trouble has a nasty way of following you around, Dix."

"Maybe," I say, "but so does hope." I point at my apartment door and flash a glimmer of gnashed teeth. "Those women in there lost their father twenty years ago. Roxanne was stolen away and made into an addict and whore, and Bailey is so full of unanswered questions she's practically bursting out of her own skin. So, yeah, I caused some trouble. I pulled them both from the clutches of a monster and that has repercussions, but tonight I'm also bringing them together with a man neither of them knew was still alive. Tonight, Roxanne will meet her father for the first time, and maybe—just maybe—that will bring some healing. You know me better than this, Sam. I may be a bitch at times, but I don't do it selfishly."

"Sam wasn't—"

"Yeah, she was, Kristy," I interrupt. "And I can't blame her for being frustrated, but I also can't change who I am. If I could do my job without bringing it home with me, I would. I'm not egotistical enough to think I'm changing the world, but if I can make a difference in someone's life every now and again, then that's what I'll do. Yes, I love you both; no, I don't want to see any harm come to either of you, and I'm sorry if I cause you worry and stress and sleepless nights, but, well, that's part of the price for having me as a friend."

There's an awkward pause where the air feels thick and hot before Sam says, "Feel better?"

"Not really," I admit.

Sam moves forward to wrap me in my second awkward hug of the day.

She whispers in my ear, "We love you, too, Dix, but work harder to keep the trouble off our doorstep."

"I'll try," I say quietly.

Kristy joins in for a three-way cuddle before we break apart and head into our respective apartments.

———

Closing the door behind me, I see Bailey and Roxanne look over from the couch where they've been drinking coffee and playing with the cat. Showered, dressed, and alert, they look more like sisters than ever before.

"Hey, Dix," says Bailey. "You OK? It sounded like an argument out there."

"I'm fine. Kristy and Sam saw the news and were worried that's all."

"I couldn't find your TV," says Roxanne.

"I use the laptop if there's something I'm interested in."

"That's weird. Everyone has a TV."

I smile. "I prefer to read."

Roxanne looks at me as though I've just declared that I would rather practice satanic witchcraft than peer into the lives of our new breed of reality stars: pregnant teenagers, child beauty queens, foul-mouthed illiterates, and gossipy sex fiends with IQs slightly smaller than their bust size.

"I wanted to watch the news," she says.

"There's a radio in the bedroom."

Roxanne glares at me again as if I've just made the stupidest suggestion that she's ever heard.

Instead of explaining myself, I say, "But I have news for you. Your father is alive."

"What!" Bailey gasps. "How do you know?"

"I met with someone today who claims to be a friend of his. He's been watching out for you two."

"Well, he's not very good at it," gripes Roxanne.

"Where is he?" asks Bailey, ignoring her sister.

"He's living on some kind of communal farm outside the city. Seems he never went far."

Roxanne fixes me in a hard stare. "Told you I saw him."

I nod. "You did."

"But he never—" Roxanne stops talking and wipes a sudden pool of tears from her eyes. She's also chewing the inside of her mouth, and I can see her teeth turning pink from the blood. "He never once... Never spoke. Never called out. Never tried to grab my hand and pull me away." Tears stream down her cheeks now; a hurt and broken child. "He could have *done* something. Anything. At least let me know he wanted me." Her voice breaks. "Nobody ever wanted me, except for what they could take." Her eyes lock onto mine again, but they're so misted that I'm not sure she even sees me. "Didn't he see that? Didn't he want to take me away?"

"You can ask him," I say.

Bailey gasps again. "When?"

"Tonight. He's coming into the city. His friend is going to call me with the details of when and where."

"He's been around all this time," says Roxanne, her voice distant but edged in broken glass. "And he waits until some reporter brings us together for a fucking story before showing his face."

"I'm sure it's not—" Bailey starts.

"What the fuck do you know?" Roxanne hisses. "You abandoned me, too. You both left me in that dive to be fucked and used by strangers until I became this." She tears at her skin, her nails scratching lines on her arms. "There is no little girl left inside for a father to find. There is no baby sister to play dolls or dress up in mom's clothes. There's only this..." She rips at her dress and her hair. "A whore and a monster and a waste of fucking skin."

Bailey wraps her arms around her sister, trapping her arms and squeezing her tight. She makes cooing noises and motherly clucks, rocking back and forth to bring calm to the chaos.

Feeling like a third wheel, I leave the apartment and head downstairs.

I knock on Mr. French's door, and when he opens it, I ask, "You don't happen to have any cigars, do you?"

FORTY-ONE

Although he prefers his pipes and exotic hand-rubbed blends of richly flavored tobacco, Mr. French keeps an exquisite cherry wood humidor packed with an assortment of cigars for guests.

He beams at my request as though I've paid him the highest of compliments, which makes me feel a little less like a mooch. He leads me excitedly through his apartment to show me his collection. When I tell him I want to sit on the front stoop and just let my mind melt for a while, he hums and haws before producing a thick Cuaba Pirámides.

"This one is from 2008." He smiles with delight when I frown, as this allows him to figuratively slip into his retired professor's robes and impart some wisdom. "Like fine wine, cigars are a natural product that benefit from aging in the right environment. The years have been kind to this one, bringing out notes of chocolate, cinnamon, and a pinch of nutmeg that weren't evident when it was first rolled."

"Aren't Cuban cigars illegal?" I ask.

"Most of the best things are."

He snips the tapered end for me before handing it over with a thin stick of cedar and a heavy silver lighter that resembles the jowled face of a British Bulldog.

"You light the cedar first," he explains. "And use its flame to light the cigar. Makes those first puffs much smoother, plus the ritual is all part of the fun."

"Will you join me?" I ask.

"I would be delighted, Miss Flynn, but I am afraid I must decline. I have a Skype call lined up with a fellow philatelist who has unearthed an unusual find that I am anxious to see."

"Stamps wait for no man. Perfectly understandable," I say.

Mr. French beams again. "Enjoy the cigar."

———

Sitting on the front steps, I follow Mr. French's cedar-stick ritual until the cigar is lit. The draw is smooth and fills my mouth with velvet smoke.

"You shouldn't expose yourself like this," says Pinch, appearing on the sidewalk below me. "You're making yourself a target."

I release the smoke from between my lips with a heavy sigh. "I think you may have scared them off for a bit," I say. "That was a hell of a shot."

"I was aiming for the window."

"Bullshit."

Pinch grins and moves to sit beside me on the steps. "I didn't know you smoked," he says.

"I don't," I reply. "Except for when I do."

"Ah. Spoken like a woman."

"That's me."

"You don't have another do you?"

"We can share."

I pat the space beside me, take another deep pull, and hand him the cigar. He doesn't hesitate to place it between his lips.

Exhaling, he hands it back and says, "Nice."

"Mmmm," I agree.

We sit and smoke for a while, sharing the cigar in silence like a pocketful of secret kisses doled out one by one.

"The Red Swan has a fierce temper," Pinch says.

"Shhh. I'm trying to relax."

"We need a plan to get him off your back."

"Already have one."

"Oh?"

"Joe Brown has information that Lebed doesn't want made public," I explain. "Swannie's been searching for him for twenty years."

"How does that help you?"

"I found him. We're meeting tonight." Smoke rises from my mouth to dance upon a salty breeze. I can taste wood, spice, leather, and earth. "If Joe shares that information, I can use it to protect all of us."

"Do you think he will?"

"I rescued both his daughters. The guy owes me."

Pinch plucks the cigar from between my lips and raises it to his own. "Not just a pretty face," he says.

FORTY-TWO

RETURNING TO THE APARTMENT, the atmosphere has a vein of electricity running through it. It's not enough to burn or make my don't-give-a-damn hair stand on end, but its presence prickles the skin and creates uneasy goosebumps.

"You girls hungry?" I ask.

"I could eat," says Bailey.

"Roxanne?" I ask. "What do you feel like?"

"You don't have much," she answers. "I already looked."

I laugh, which breaks the tension and allows both sisters to share a smile.

"I'm not much of a cook, granted, but I think I have all the ingredients for a giant plate of cheesy nachos."

"Dinner of champions," says Bailey, smiling.

"Wanna help?" I ask. "Roxanne can open the beers and you can chop."

From the fridge, I pull out two bell peppers—one red, one yellow—a block of aged white cheddar, a chunk of blue cheese that looks a little under the weather, two wrinkled jalapeños, and a jar of pickled banana peppers. From the freezer, I retrieve two spicy Chorizo sausages that I vaguely remember cooking sometime recently.

While the oven warms, I defrost the sausages in the microwave and open a bag of tortilla chips.

Roxanne hands everyone a bottle of Anchor Steam and we clink glass as if we're just three fun-loving girls planning a night in without all of life's excess baggage weighing us down.

I layer the chips in a large pan, shred and crumble the cheese, and add the chopped bell peppers. Bailey discovers a small can of black olives in the cupboard and excitedly adds them to the mix. We make two layers, adding sliced sausage, jalapeños, and banana peppers to both.

With some more rummaging, I unearth half a jar of salsa that's only a little crusty around the edge, and a container of sour cream. Unfortunately, the sour cream has expired; the nose test tells me it's not worth the risk.

After sliding the nachos into the oven to melt, I open my second beer and collapse onto the couch. Prince Marmalade immediately rises from his spot on the other cushion and strolls over to curl on my lap. Aw. Despite all the womanly attention lately, he still loves me best. I scratch his ears and feel his purr rumble through me like a massage for my soul.

Bailey keeps an eye on the baking nachos and brings them over to the coffee table when the cheese is bubbling and the sausage is warmed through.

The three of us eat with our fingers and sip our beers.

I wish we could laugh and talk about boys, but the night ahead weighs heavily on us all. Instead, we talk about little except how the blue cheese complements the jalapeño and what a pity it is that the sour cream was expired.

When the phone rings, we all jump—even Prince.

Wiping my hands and mouth on a paper towel, I head back to the kitchen and pick up the phone.

"Dixie here," I say.

"Do you know my voice?" asks my Good Samaritan.

"I do, but you never told me your name."

"I'm sure you could find it if you wanted."

"True, but I'd rather hear it from you."

"Tim Collins, but my friends call me Stubs."

"Nice friends."

He chuckles. "Shows they're comfortable enough around me to joke. It took me years to get there myself."

"Is Joe Brown in town?"

Bailey makes a noise, and I turn to see both women sitting on the edge of their seats, eyes locked on my lips as though they need to see the words being formed.

"He's here."

"When can we meet?"

"Ten tonight."

"Where?"

"There's an auto wreckers off Rankin Street below 280. Do you know it?"

"I can find it."

"It's owned by a friend. The front gate will be unlocked. If Lebed's men are following or you decide to involve the cops, we won't be there."

"I understand the risks. Let Joe know his daughters are anxious to see him."

There's a pause before Tim says, "I've never seen him so nervous. He looks terrified, but in a good way, you know?"

"He shouldn't get his hopes too high," I say. "These girls have been hurt. Healing will take time."

"Yeah." My Samaritan sighs.

I hang up and look over at the sisters. "We meet at ten," I say.

In unison, the sisters exhale and recline back in their seats.

"Anyone else need a fresh beer?" I ask, my hands shaking with nervous energy as I reach into the fridge.

————

When I call Mo's Cabs, Mo coughs in my ear.

"How do you keep customers when you sound like a plague farm?" I ask.

"A *sexy* plague farm," he corrects in his guttural Bronx accent. "I've been told that I drive women crazy."

"But I don't think your wife meant that in a good way."

Mo laughs and coughs in my ear again. "What can I do you for, Dix?"

"I need to get somewhere tonight, but I need to make sure that I'm not followed."

"See, that's why I love you. It's never just 'Take me to the liquor store and wait while I spend my pension check on dirty mags, cheap booze, and those tasty little peanuts coated in crushed potato chips.'"

"That's awfully specific, Mo, but you're right, I don't usually ask for that. At least not when sober."

"So where do you need to end up and when?"

I'm about to tell him when a stab of doubt makes my neck ache. Last night, Lebed showed up outside the Dog House directly after Roxanne was told that Bailey and I were there. And despite the lies I've been telling all day, I'm not a big fan of coincidence.

"Hold on a sec."

Turning to Bailey and Roxanne, who are nursing their beers on the couch, I say, "You should pick out some of my clothes to wear. It'll be cold tonight. Dress in layers."

I wait until both women are in my bedroom and out of earshot before I return to Mo and quietly give him the address.

"Keep this on a need-to-know basis," I add. "Only the last driver should have the final destination."

Mo chuckles. "Man, you sound like a character out of one of those early Ken Follett novels. *Eye of the Needle*, something like that?"

"I'm not quite a spy yet, but the stakes could be just as high tonight," I say. "There are some pretty nasty people who want to put a bullet in the man I'm meant to meet. I'd really prefer it if that didn't happen."

Mo stops chuckling. "Well, I won't tell the driver that. He'll want danger pay."

"Do you have drivers you can trust?"

"Not many, but enough. Plus, nobody knows this city's slippery entrails like ol' Mo. We'll shake any tail you got."

"These guys could be good," I warn.

"I'll be better."

FORTY-THREE

I SLIDE LILY OVER an oiled whetstone to bring her edge back to razor sharpness before guiding her polished pearl hilt into the moleskin sheath sewn inside my boot. I next check the rechargeable batteries on my compact camera and digital voice recorder. Fully charged. I drop them both into a pocket of my green trenchcoat.

Still feeling underdressed and apprehensive, I pace the room before crossing to the couch and extracting the blue case nestled underneath.

Bailey and Roxanne are in the bedroom, out of sight and busy getting dressed, when I open the case and study the Governor. My current license is only valid for transporting an unloaded firearm from home to the range and back. Getting caught with a loaded gun on my person is a federal offense that even Frank would have difficulty squashing.

After a moment of hesitation, I double-check the safety and slip the gun into the small of my back, hidden beneath the trenchcoat.

I'd rather face Frank's wrath than have Red Swan's men chop off my fingers—or worse.

When the sisters are ready, we head downstairs and climb into the waiting taxi.

After the first block, I ask, "Are we being followed?"

The driver, a bulbous-nosed man with one disturbingly lazy eye, snaps his gums. "Two cars. Both black. Best y'all hold onto something."

Bailey squeals as the driver suddenly accelerates through a red light to the blare of a half-dozen car horns. The horns continue to protest as I glance behind and see a lone black car snaking through the same intersection in hot pursuit.

Our driver whips the car to the left and down an alley before taking a sharp right into a second, narrower alley that I didn't know was there until we're inside it. Metal trash cans tumble into the air in our wake and several late-night rummagers are forced to leap behind dumpsters to keep from being mowed down.

"Dixie!" Bailey screams. "Tell him to—"

All three of our heads bonk the roof in unison as the taxi exits the alley like a Mexican jumping bean on steroids to bump and lurch across the next main road. Another blare of a horn makes us clutch our chests to keep our hearts in place as the car's shocks screech indignantly and try to climb through the floor.

We careen into the mouth of a third alley and I lose all sense of direction as the driver takes increasingly sharper lefts and rights with barely a kiss of brake.

Bailey, Roxanne, and I are bruised from shoulder to elbow from smashing against each other, but Big Nose Lazy Eye is enjoying himself. What few teeth he has are exposed and glistening with manic glee.

After a few more twisted miles, he pulls in front of a twenty-four-hour convenience store and tells us to get out, walk through the store, and exit into the alley where another taxi is waiting.

We do as we're told, mostly to get away from his suicide run, but we immediately have more regrets about the gassy and greasy meal we consumed earlier as this driver proves just as reckless as the first.

"Are we still being followed?" I ask, while holding onto the door handle for dear life.

The driver, who sports an impressive Seventies-era Burt Reynolds moustache, grins. "Not seen hide nor hair, ma'am."

The road whizzes by until finally, with a screech of tire, he pulls to the curb behind a third taxi. As soon as we scramble out, Moustache pulls an illegal U-turn and races back in the direction we've just come.

Climbing into the third cab, the plump and balding driver turns to us and says, "You three look a little green."

I grimace. "What do you put in their coffee, Mo? Red Bull? Smack? Hand sanitizer?"

Mo guffaws. "Freddie spent a few years as a stunt driver in Hollywood until he was run out of town for test driving more than a director's Porsche, and Bearl picked up several blue-ribbon trophies in the smash-'em-up derbies back home. He's very proud of those ribbons."

"It shows," I groan. "And what about you? Didn't know you still drove."

"Only on special occasions. Now be a pal and try not to throw up on my seats."

Mo chuckles at his own joke as he puts the car in gear and pulls into the trickling flow of traffic.

"We'll take it slow from here," he continues. "Just to make sure we've shaken everyone before heading to the wreckers."

"Wreckers?" Roxanne asks.

"The meeting spot," I explain. "Your father is a cautious man."

Roxanne snorts. "That's one word for him."

———

Mo drops us in front of the auto wreckers with two minutes to spare.

"If anyone was following, I'da spotted them," he says. "This part of town is dead at night, so they picked a good spot to be alone."

"Thanks for everything," I say. "And don't go telling Frank, OK? I've got this under control."

Mo frowns. "You be careful."

"When am I not?"

Mo snickers. "You don't want me to answer that."

I grin back. "Yeah, maybe not."

I slap the roof of the car and watch Mo drive off before turning to the wreckers' yard. Taking up a whole city block, the yard is surrounded by a twelve-foot-high fence made impenetrable with ugly sheets of corrugated iron, scrap wood, and double-looped stainless-steel link. Obviously, the owner isn't going for curb appeal.

Roxanne and Bailey study the large double-wide gates that are chained in the middle and topped with razor wire.

"It looks like a prison," says Bailey.

"Except," I point up at the sharp wire that is angled out toward us, "this fence is designed to keep people out, not in. The price of scrap metal has been skyrocketing in this recession. People are stealing it everywhere, from spools of hydro and phone cable to whole railway tracks and church roofs."

Roxanne pulls at the chained gate and it slides open just enough to allow us to squeeze through.

"I hope they don't have dogs," she says with a shudder. "They can be vicious bastards, especially if they smell fear." She glances at her sister. "If there's dogs, don't run. Wait until they get close and kick them in the face as hard as you can. Don't stop kicking until they run away or stop moving, OK?"

Bailey gasps. "Jesus, Roxanne. I don't—"

"Trust me," says Roxanne. "A dog trained by an asshole is deadlier than any gun."

Inside the compound, my first thought is that I should have packed a flashlight. Perilous piles of crushed and windowless cars loom over stacks of half-dismantled fridges, freezers, and stoves, while indiscriminate mounds of shredded aluminum, iron, and copper make the yard one giant hazard area.

Everything looks so precarious that one of my dad's roof-raising sneezing fits during pollen season could bring everything down on top of our heads. And, unfortunately, I inherited the trait.

"Where do we go?" asks Bailey.

I point straight ahead to where a dim light glows in the distance. "There's probably an office or something back there."

As we walk and our eyes adjust to the clammy gloom, I fine-tune my focus to the deeper shadows, one hand behind my back and underneath my trenchcoat. I feel eyes upon us but don't see any movement.

The path we follow is the reverse of *The Wizard of Oz*—gleaming, orange-yellow metal surrounds us, while the road is pockmarked gray gravel and muck.

After a series of blind turns, we enter a dark pool of space that occupies roughly the center of the yard. On the opposite shore, in no better shape than the scrap it watches over, a construction trailer rests on stacked cinder blocks. Beneath the trailer, three sets of hungry eyes stare back at us.

"They must know we're here," I say to the sisters. "No point risking a twisted ankle or tetanus shot until they turn on some goddamn lights."

The three of us stand on the periphery of the frigid lake of darkness and wait.

Nothing happens.

Roxanne scratches at her arms and nervously kicks the ground. Every now and again she looks up as if expecting a UFO to beam her out, but none show.

"Should we call out?" Bailey asks.

"If you like," I say, "but there's no need. We're already surrounded."

"We are?"

"There are three men standing to your right, another two on the left, and two behind us."

"Really!"

I raise my voice, addressing the open space. "Are you done playing? You already know we haven't been followed."

Halogen security lights begin to click on around the circle, forcing the darkness to retreat into the deeper recesses of the crumbling, metal cliffs.

When the lights reach their full brightness, the door to the trailer opens and three men step out. One of them is Tim, my Good Samaritan; another has an elongated face that's scared of a good wash and a razor. He's dressed in greasy blue coveralls with an indecipherable name tag on the breast, which makes me guess he's the friend who runs the yard; and the third is a man I've only ever seen in a fuzzy photograph: Joseph Brown.

Bailey glances over at me, her eyes already flooding with tears.

"It's really him," she whispers with awe. "You actually found him."

I want to say something cocky or profound, but the air is so thick with a confusing mixture of emotion that I find all I can do is nod. The men surrounding us are nervous; I feel them shifting from foot to foot and hear their fingers crunching into their palms... crunching and releasing like the muscle memory of an addled boxer.

When the three men reach the center of the illuminated circle, Bailey can't hold herself back any longer and rushes headlong into the light. Twenty years of wondering washed away in twenty steps.

As Bailey runs, Roxanne slides back toward me.

"That's him, huh?" she says in a low voice.

"Not what you were expecting?"

"I don't know what I expected. He kept changing in my mind depending on where I was and what was being done to me. I made up so many stories about him, told myself so many fucking lies. The truth is never as clear as what you hope for, is it?"

"Truth can suck," I agree.

"Yeah, and dreams ain't much better."

We enter the light together and by the time we reach the middle, Bailey has wrapped herself around her father's neck and dissolved into a blubbering mess.

Joe Brown, on the other hand, stopped being a father at least two decades earlier and he looks embarrassed and confused by the attention.

When Bailey finally composes herself enough to release her grip, she steps back from the man she's spent her whole life searching for and wipes her eyes. Her mouth shifts between happy and sad as she reaches out for her sister and announces, "Dad. This is your other daughter. Roxanne." Her eyes glisten with pride, desperate for praise.

Joe studies his youngest daughter for a moment before awkwardly holding out his hand to shake.

"It's nice to finally meet—"

The rest of his words are splattered across the ground as Roxanne punches him smack in the mouth. She would have landed a few more blows, too, if the bearded behemoth in the blue coveralls hadn't stepped forward to pin her arms to her side.

"Nice to meet me?" Roxanne screams. "Where have you been, you son of a bitch? Call yourself a man? I don't see any men here, not a fucking one of you."

"Roxanne!" Bailey yells. "This is our dad."

Roxanne spits and hisses. "Maybe he was a father to you once, though I doubt it. All he ever meant to me was the hump 'n' bump that got our mother pregnant—and for the life of me I wish he hadn't. I would rather have been a dribble on his leg than given this shitty fucking life."

Joe spits out a mouthful of blood and wipes his lips. His hands are shaking.

"I-I understand how you feel—"

"You don't understand *shit*," interrupts Roxanne. "You've been living on a farm—"

"Not always," says Joe. "You can't begin to comprehend how difficult it's been. I've been trapped."

Roxanne shakes herself loose from the man holding her and flashes him a warning that says if he tries to grab her again, she'll remove his testicles with her teeth. The man believes her.

"You don't know anything about being trapped," Roxanne snarls. "Trapped is when your whore of a mother is selling her kid because she's too used up to please any man. Trapped is sucking off a retiree when you're six years old because it's all you've ever been told you're worth. The only thing *you* were trapped in was your own cowardly skin."

"That's not—"

"What?" Roxanne spits. "Fair? Don't even try to go down that road. You're a worthless piece of shit, and as far as I'm concerned, no father of mine."

"Roxanne?" Bailey bursts into tears again. "We've been searching for so long."

"You have," says Roxanne. "He's always been dead to me."

Roxanne storms away to stand with her back to us, peering into the darkness, scratching her arms and battling with her thoughts.

Bailey reaches out to touch her father's sleeve.

"I-I still want you in my life," she says. "I know you must have had your reasons for leaving us."

"It had something to do with the funeral of Alimzhan Izmaylovsky, right?" I say, taking a step forward.

Joe looks at me and narrows his eyes; his crow's-feet are canyons filled with coal dust and years of worry. "You're the reporter," he says.

"I'm also the woman who rescued both your daughters from the clutches of Krasnyi Lebed. I need to know what the Red Swan doesn't want made public."

"Why?"

"I need the insurance. Lebed is after my head now, too. All of our heads."

"Dixie," Bailey interrupts, "maybe now isn't the—"

"It's the only time," I say. "Once he leaves here, he won't be coming back. Am I right?"

Joe nods reluctantly. "It's too dangerous for me here, but," he turns to Bailey, "you could come with me." He glances over at Roxanne and raises his voice. "Both of you. You can work at the farm. Tim and Eileen have places for you. We can be a family again."

Roxanne snorts without turning around.

Bailey sniffles, but the tears stop flowing. "I have a life here," she says. "It's broken and needs work, but I think I can pull it back together. Can't you still visit or have us visit you?"

"He can't take the risk," I say coldly. "Lebed put a large price on his head." I turn to Roxanne. "How much is the bounty, Roxanne?"

Roxanne flicks her head toward me, her eyes cold and darker than the night. She doesn't deny knowing. "A hundred thousand."

"For information or his head?" I ask.

Roxanne turns away from me again without answering.

Joe releases a world-weary sigh, but he's not yet defeated. "If I tell you my story, will it bring Lebed down?"

"I won't know until I hear it."

"But you'll publish it?"

"I'll do my damnedest."

Joe looks over at the other two men and nods. "Let's talk," he says.

———

Inside the aluminum trailer, the six of us find a spot to sit or lean. A portable electric heater takes the chill off the night air, but it also enhances the pungent musk of wet dog and workmen's feet kept too long in waterproof, steel-toed boots.

"You have dogs," says Roxanne, wrinkling her nose as she rests her shoulder against one of the trailer's few windows.

The bearded man nods. "Three, but they're muzzled for now." He stomps his foot and is rewarded with a sharp, short keening. "They live under the trailer."

"Are they vicious?" asks Bailey, who settles on one end of a seedy-looking couch that appears to have been color-matched to vomit.

The beard grins. "Only if I tell them to be."

"And what if you're not here?" asks Roxanne.

The large man shrugs. "Then they'd likely tear you apart and bury the evidence before I got back."

Roxanne catches Bailey's eye. "Told you."

I settle into a wooden office chair opposite Joe Brown, who has settled half-cheek on the desk. My Samaritan has selected to stand by the door.

"So, Krasnyi Lebed comes to your apartment while Bailey is sleeping," I begin, getting Joe's attention. "Bailey told me her version of the night. She was pretending to be asleep and remembers you and Lebed being in her room. Lebed was inquiring if she was for sale."

Joe glances over at his daughter and his eyes are red with pent-up tears.

"What did Lebed want you to do?" I ask.

Joe takes a deep breath and I hear a rattle in his chest, like someone who's been holding the truth inside for far too long.

"It was one last job," he says. "A big payoff and then I was out for good."

"You had a choice?" I ask.

He shakes his head. "You're told you do, but when he went in Bailey's room, I knew he wouldn't accept any other answer."

"And what did you have to do?" I press.

"The boss, Mr. Izmaylovsky, and I were uncommon friends," says Joe. "He'd call me at odd hours to go to his place and play checkers. He preferred checkers and dominoes over chess or cards... I think he just liked having someone to talk to who wasn't part of the family, you know? It was never about work or politics. Actually, he loved to hear celebrity gossip from the tabloids. Hollywood scandal always made him laugh. And when he was tired, he'd have his driver slip me a hundred-dollar bill and drop me back home."

"And Lebed was jealous?" I ask. "Of your bond?"

Joe shakes his head again. "Not jealous, but nervous that maybe Mr. Izmaylovsky was spilling secrets or confidences that weren't for an outsider's ears."

"But he wasn't?"

"Never. Not once. But it didn't matter; Lebed didn't believe me."

"So Lebed told you to kill the boss," I say.

Joe's eyes go wide in surprise before he nods. "He gave me the poison to slip into the old man's drink and promised me a quarter-million payday." He glances over at his daughters. "I thought we could all disappear. Your mom, me, all of us. Live like royalty in San Diego or Seattle or Texas, even—anywhere but here."

"But he double-crossed you," I press.

Joe nods again. "He sent two goons to finish me off. I may be stupid, but I'm not naïve. When I saw they didn't bring the cash, I ran … I've been running ever since."

"So why is he scared of you?" I ask. "You can't have any evidence."

"Just the poison," he says. "I kept the vial. Mr. Izmaylovsky's death was ruled as natural causes, which allowed the Red Swan to assume the throne. But if the old guard back in Russia knew it was an assassination, they'd demand Lebed's head on a platter. Respect and honor is *huge* with these monsters, they don't want anyone getting the idea that it's okay to bump off their elders."

"So why have you never come forward?" I ask.

"Because it would mean my head, too. And Lebed's men wouldn't stop at me. They practice scorched-earth revenge, I had no choice but to hide."

Roxanne exhales sharply and says, "Death isn't the worst thing that can happen, *father*. Did you ever see our mother at the end? Riddled with disease and crawling on her knees for another hit. Did you ever hear my screams, or Bailey's? If your head could have stopped that, then I wish to God you'd served it up."

"It wouldn't have been just me," Joe protests. "That's what I'm—"

"But you're the only one who got away," argues Roxanne. "Your scars are barely skin deep compared to ours."

The dam behind Joe's eyes finally cracks and a lone tear trickles down his cheek. "I missed you all so much. I just … just didn't know how to help."

Roxanne snorts and glares out the window while Bailey crosses the room to give her father a hug.

"Is it okay if I take a picture?" I ask, knowing my timing sucks but wanting it over with. "For the paper."

Joe frowns and Bailey sniffles.

"It gives added weight to the story," I explain. "We need the photos to make the cover and get everybody reading."

Reluctantly, Joe nods.

"Can you join them?" I ask Roxanne. "Please."

With a world-weary sigh, Roxanne peels herself away from the window and walks to the desk, where she sits with her back to her father and her arms folded tight across her chest. She practically sneers at the camera.

I quickly snap off a couple of frames before any of them change their mind.

"So what now?" I ask, dropping the camera back in my pocket.

"I need to get back," says Joe. "My skin is crawling being this close to it all again." He turns to his daughters. "I wish you'd think about joining me."

"Not gonna happen," says Roxanne. "My life may be shit, but it's the only one I know."

"It doesn't have to be," says Bailey. "You could live with me. We could rebuild." She looks over at me. "If the Red Swan will let us?"

"I think we can make a bargain with him," I say. "He leaves us all alone and I don't mention the assassination of his boss."

Joe's eyes go wide. "But you promised."

I shake my head and show my teeth. "I promised your daughters first. If Lebed doesn't want to play ball, I'll publish everything and send it directly to Moscow. But I want to get back to my normal life, and your girls want to make a new one."

"You bitch," he hisses. "You tricked me."

"No," I snap back. "I'm just being the parent you never were and putting the lives of your daughters first."

Joe rocks back but then springs forward again and bares his own teeth. "I want that camera," he growls. "If you're not bringing Lebed down, you can't use my photo."

"Not gonna happen," I say. "The camera's mine. Let's go girls. We've outstayed our welcome."

As I step forward, my Samaritan bars the door and holds out one of his gloved hands in a gimme-gimme gesture.

I peer up into his face.

"You know I'm not giving it to you," I say. "And you should also know that you're not taking it. Don't even try."

I feel the bearded man moving in behind me. I snake my hand beneath my trenchcoat to the small of my back and spin, my arm whipping out at top speed.

The Governor collides with the side of his skull in a bone-crunching crack that makes his eyes roll and his knees buckle. Roxanne laughs as the bearded man topples sideways to the floor with blood spurting from his head. Before the Samaritan can react, I've spun back so that he finds himself staring down the abyss of the Governor's barrel.

"I've loaded this with .410 shotgun shells," I tell him. "Your skull will explode like a fucking watermelon. Now stand aside."

As a former journalist, he's intelligent enough to hold up his hands and retreat away from the door.

Keeping my gun trained on him, I glance over at the two sisters. "You coming?"

Roxanne grins as she steps onto and over the groaning form of the yard owner to join me at the door. Bailey hesitates only slightly, gazing into her father's eyes before kissing him gently on the cheek and sliding off the desk.

Together, we exit the trailer.

FORTY-FOUR

Outside, we feel most vulnerable within the circle of light. The looming cliffs around us take on the shapes of frozen monsters, as though a futuristic battle took place in a bygone age, and the air tastes of copper.

"Are they just going to let us walk out of here?" Roxanne whispers.

"What choice do they have?" I counter.

A voice yells from the trailer behind us: "Wait!" Joe cries. "Please. Just one minute."

I stop and the three of us turn.

Joe descends from the trailer alone, his hands raised to show they're empty, and walks out to meet us. "This plan of yours," he says when he reaches us. "What makes you think Lebed will believe you?"

I remove the digital tape recorder from my pocket and hold it up for him to see.

"I recorded everything. Your confession makes a compelling story and the only thing Lebed can do is deny it, but by that time the damage is done. There are already people within his own organization who don't trust him. This would give them the nudge they need to stage a coup of their own."

"How do you know that?" Joe asks.

"One of them tried to shoot me," I say. "But I shot him instead."

Joe pales. "Will you tell Lebed about the farm? Tim and Eileen shouldn't suffer after all the work they've done."

My eyes soften. "As far as I'm concerned, I have no idea where you go after you leave here. Tim saved my life, more than once. His secret will never leave my lips."

Joe sighs with relief. "OK. I'll have to trust you." He opens his arms to his girls. "One last hug?"

Roxanne doesn't move, but Bailey breaks ranks in the same instant that a supersonic crack renders the air.

I feel a sharp heat passing above me, so close that wisps of loose hair snap and curl. But the bullet isn't meant for me.

Joe's left eye implodes and is forced out the back of his skull. There's no need for a second shot. Joe is dead before he hits the ground.

I spin around as Bailey screams and Roxanne drops to her knees in shock. The watchers from the shadows are rushing toward us, but not one of them is carrying a gun.

I peer deeper, rending the shadows apart, searching for movement in a broken landscape of sharp angles and dented curves. Near the fence, I see the shape of a man with a rifle over his shoulder. He isn't tall and his silhouette is far too familiar.

"No!" I cry out. "No, no, no!"

I take off running, heading for the fence, desperate to have my own eyes proved wrong.

The silhouette turns, freezes in place for a second, and then vanishes.

"Wait!" I scream. "You fucking wait!"

I take the corner at blind speed, several yards from the front gate, and run into an iron bar that nearly removes my head from my shoulders.

With an anguished cry, my feet fly into the air and my back thumps to the ground, knocking the air from my lungs.

"Son of a bitch," I wheeze airlessly.

Attempting to scramble back to my feet, I discover the iron bar is actually attached to an iron man.

"I have been looking for you," says a thick Russian accent.

Glaring down at me is a stone-faced killer with a bandaged right hand where a bullet recently took his trigger finger.

"Shit! Is Lebed here?" I ask.

The killer moves his massive, stone-like skull. "We come to collect the man's head. You are a bonus."

I try to sit up, but the killer leans forward and knocks me back down with the intensity of his stare.

"Look, I'm sorry about your finger. Maybe it backfired."

The killer growls. "You cost me my profession and you make joke?"

"Maybe you're lucky," I say. "You guys don't actually have a retirement plan, do you? Now you can spend your days fishing or drowning puppies for orphans or something."

"I want to know who shot me."

"He told me he actually missed. He was aiming for the window."

"Bullshit."

"That's what I said."

"His name?"

"Even though I'm super pissed at him right now, it ain't gonna happen."

"Then I hurt you."

"Let's face it," I say. "You were planning to hurt me anyway."

The killer grins. "That is true."

"Bring it, nine fingers."

With a snarl, the killer reaches down with his good hand to grab my hair, but he isn't expecting me to fight dirty. I use his own momentum to jerk forward and slam my forehead into his groin, which loosens his grip. I loosen it the rest of the way by slicing his wrist open with Lily.

As he reels back in shock at the slippery depth of the cut, I clamber to my knees and give him one last warning. "Back away now or I finish it."

"I eat little girls like you for breakfast."

"No," I answer. "Not like me."

When he reaches for me again, I stab the knife into his thigh just beneath the groin and slice upward. Blood drains from his face and gushes over my hand. He freezes in place, sensing the seriousness of the wound. His bleeding left hand thumps onto my chest, but there's no power left in it to push me away.

My voice is cold and edged in steel. "I'm told you can survive this if you don't remove the knife ... but it's my knife."

I pull Lily free and watch the killer drop to his knees, a pool of warm, thick blood widening around him.

"Put pressure on it and call for your friend. Maybe you'll get lucky."

A scream shatters the darkness behind me.

Bailey.

It's followed by a banshee's howl.

Roxanne.

I glance once at the gate where my assassin's silhouette vanished and turn back toward the light.

———

When I reach the circle of light, Bailey and Roxanne are clutching each other tight. Roxanne's face is cut and turning purple where something hard and sharp has cracked her cheekbone and eye socket, while Bailey appears to have aged a hundred years.

The second Russian killer is kneeling beside Joe's body and holding the sisters at gunpoint. None of the other watchers have stuck around, not even my Samaritan.

"You!" the Russian calls when he sees me approach. "Give me his head and I leave."

Bailey and Roxanne stare at me in horror, but it's not until I walk farther into the light that I realize why. My clothes are spattered in fresh blood, and while it's not exactly Carrie at the prom, it's a lot.

"It's OK," I assure them, "it's not mine." I point at the second killer. "I ran into his partner."

The Russian turns his gun on me in confusion.

"Serge?" he asks.

"If you get him help, he may live, but you'll have to be damn quick. He's bleeding out."

The killer glances down at Joe's corpse.

"Don't worry," I add. "I'll take a photo. Lebed will get all the proof of death he needs."

"Are you bullshitting me?" he asks.

"Hey, you're the one with the gun and the dying friend. I'm doing you a favor."

"I should kill you all."

"That's one way." I stab my thumb at Bailey and wrinkle my nose. "But start with her."

As Bailey gasps in shock, the killer's eyes flicker toward her; in that instant I have the Governor in my hand and the hammer cocked.

"I tried to play this nice," I say. "But know that I will shoot you unless you leave."

"I am faster."

I don't blink. "Maybe."

The killer studies my eyes for a moment and says, "Pity you are not Russian."

"Yeah?" I sneer. "Pity you're not handsome."

He laughs and slides his gun into a shoulder holster beneath his jacket before rising to his feet and disappearing back into the shadows.

When he's gone, I shove the Governor into my waistband and cross to the two sisters.

"You guys OK?"

Bailey moans. "He was going to cut off dad's head. He actually had a knife and he ... he—"

"It's okay," I say soothingly. "He's gone now."

"But how did they know we were here?" Bailey asks. "We were so careful." She looks over at her father's corpse. "All this time searching and now...now he's really gone."

Roxanne fixes me with a weary, one-eyed glare, but I can't meet it. This time, I know she isn't the one to blame.

FORTY-FIVE

"PLEASE," SAYS MR. FRENCH. "Indulge me."

I accept the cigars and the large snifter of brandy with gratitude before heading out to the front steps. It's late, very late, but Mr. French's light was still on and I was too amped up to sleep. He also loaned me a soft fleece blanket to wrap around my shoulders, which makes me feel like a young girl again, camping out under the stars.

I take a sip of brandy and snip the end off the six-and-a-half-inch, caramel-skinned Cohiba. It lights with just a few puffs and tastes of white sand, blue sea, rich soil, and a simpler time.

The brandy is smooth, rich, and luxurious, like something you just know you can't really afford.

"Are you celebrating?" asks a voice in the darkness.

"No," I answer and hold up an unlit cigar. "I'm waiting for you."

Pinch climbs the stairs to sit beside me. "We could just share," he suggests.

"No," I answer. "Not this time."

With a shrug, Pinch accepts the cigar, snips off the end, and lights it. "Did you bring me a brandy, too?" he asks.

I shake my head. "That's my indulgence."

"Ahh."

We sit in silence, smoking our cigars, until I ask, "Why did you do it?"

"Lebed made me an offer."

"A hundred grand?"

He takes a deep puff and exhales. "Your life."

I bristle. "I had that under control."

He takes another puff. "You didn't."

"I did," I protest. "I had Joe's confession on tape. Lebed hired him to kill Alimzhan Izmaylovsky."

"Lebed knows what Joe would say, and he's already rounding up everyone he thinks would take action against him. His lawyers are also ready to march into your offices if you even try to mention his name. It'll never make print."

"My editor would never—"

"Lebed would buy the paper if he had to. Everything is for sale. Your editor would either toe the line or be replaced. As would you."

"Son of a bitch."

He smirks. "That's being too kind."

"So if he has it all worked out, why kill Joe?"

"Unfinished business."

"And the sisters?"

"They're part of the deal. He'll leave them alone."

"So you're my white knight, is that it?"

"I wouldn't go that far."

Pinch goes to flick his ash, but I touch his hand to stop him.

"The ash helps to reduce the temperature of the burning tobacco," I tell him. "It creates an air-block, cooling the smoke and slowing the burn. It improves the taste."

Pinch smiles. "Mr. French tell you that?"

I try to resist but end up smiling back. "He did. He's very wise, is Mr. French."

We smoke some more until I ask, "How did you know where to find us?"

"Trade secret."

"You couldn't have tailed us," I say. "Nobody could. I didn't even know where we were half the time." I blow a cloud of smoke and watch it change shapes. "You knew the address, didn't you?"

"If I had known the address, I would have been there before you, waiting."

"Then how?"

Pinch sighs. "You're too predictable, Dix."

I bristle again. "How?"

"People like you, and you like it when people do."

"So?"

"When you told me you were meeting Joe, I knew you would use Mo's Cabs to get there."

"So?" I ask again, still not getting a clear picture.

"All of Mo's cabs are LoJacked. All I needed was the carrier frequency and I could follow all his cabs on my laptop. Two cars driving like maniacs and a drop-off at the scrap yard couldn't have been more obvious."

"So I led you right to him." My cigar grows bitter in my mouth, but I suspect it's not the tobacco. "After twenty years in hiding, I get him killed for the sake of a Father's Day story."

"That's one way to look at it," says Pinch.

"And what's another?"

"You saved two lives. I don't know what Roxanne will do, but at least she has the option now to put her past behind her and try for a normal life. As for Bailey, it may take a few days for the guilt to pass, but I expect she'll start sleeping through the night for the first time in her life."

"But Joe Brown still didn't deserve to die."

"He was a paid killer," says Pinch.

"So are you."

"And my day will come. Just not today."

I take a sip of brandy and hand the glass to Pinch. "And thanks to you," I say, "I guess I get to wake up tomorrow, too."

"I'll drink to that," he says. "One more day."

I take the glass back and accept his toast.

"One more day."

ABOUT THE AUTHOR

M.C. Grant is the secret identity of international thriller writer Grant McKenzie. (Oops, there goes that secret.) Born in Scotland, living in Canada, and writing fast-paced fiction, Grant likes to wear a kilt and toque with his six-guns. Often compared to Harlan Coben and Linwood Barclay, Grant has three internationally published thrillers to his name—*Switch*, *No Cry for Help*, and *K.A.R.M.A.*—that have earned him an avalanche of positive reviews and loyal readership around the globe. As a journalist, he has won numerous awards across Canada and the United States, including one in 2012 from the Association of Alternative Newsmedia—the same organization that Dixie's fictitious *San Francisco NOW* belongs to. You can find him online at: http://grantmckenzie.net.

ACKNOWLEDGMENTS

Being a writer is never a solitary endeavour, since there are so many voices (foreign and domestic) in my head when spinning a tale. However, once imagination has birthed the story, it takes real rather than fictitious humans to bring the story into the readers' hands. And to this end, I couldn't ask for a more enthusiastic and generous team than I have found at Midnight Ink. Every person involved in the creation of Dixie's adventures is so very, very important to its success, and if you, dear readers, are picking this up in a bookstore or online, then the team has done its job.

Word of mouth is also so very important to a writer that I value all the support that bookstores and all their fabulous employees have shown to my work.

Lastly, without my brilliant, supportive, and kind readers, writing would not hold the joy that it does. I write to be read, and nothing brings me more delight than to hear from a reader who has enjoyed one of my books and recommended me to their friends. I cannot thank you enough.

www.MIDNIGHTINKBOOKS.COM

From the gritty streets of New York City to sacred tombs in the Middle East, it's always midnight somewhere. Join us online at any hour for fresh new voices in mystery fiction.

At midnightinkbooks.com you'll also find our author blog, new and upcoming books, events, book club questions, excerpts, mystery resources, and more.

MIDNIGHT INK

MIDNIGHT INK ORDERING INFORMATION

Order Online:
- Visit our website www.midnightinkbooks.com, select your books, and order them on our secure server.

Order by Phone:
- Call toll-free within the U.S. and Canada at 1-888-NITE-INK (1-888-648-3465)
- We accept VISA, MasterCard, and American Express

Order by Mail:

Send the full price of your order (MN residents add 6.5% sales tax) in U.S. funds, plus postage & handling to:

> Midnight Ink
> 2143 Wooddale Drive
> Woodbury, MN 55125-2989

Postage & Handling:

Standard (U.S. & Canada). If your order is:
> $24.99 and under, add $4.00
> $25.00 and over, FREE STANDARD SHIPPING

AK, HI, PR: $16.00 for one book plus $2.00 for each additional book.

International Orders (airmail only):
> $16.00 for one book plus $3.00 for each additional book

Orders are processed within 12 business days. Please allow for normal shipping time.
Postage and handling rates subject to change.